LOVING MOTHERS

BOOKS BY MIRANDA SMITH

Some Days Are Dark

What I Know

The One Before

Not My Mother

His Loving Wife

The Killer's Family

The Family Home

The School Trip

The Weekend Away

The Writer

LOVING MOTHERS

MIRANDA SMITH

bookouture

Published by Bookouture in 2024

An imprint of Storyfire Ltd.
Carmelite House
50 Victoria Embankment
London EC4Y 0DZ

www.bookouture.com

Storyfire Ltd's authorised representative in the EEA is Hachette Ireland
8 Castlecourt Centre
Castleknock Road
Castleknock
Dublin 15 D15 YF6A
Ireland

ISBN: 978-1-83525-966-5
eBook ISBN: 978-1-83525-965-8

To anyone who thinks you deserved it.
You didn't.

ONE

Halloween Night

Darkness came early this time of year.

The houses lining the sidewalks of Hickory Hills were empty, but the windows glowed with soft yellow light, like jack-o'-lanterns come to life. Every so often, a crisp breeze cut through, rustling fallen leaves on the ground. In the distance, the scent of a burning campfire peppered the air.

It was the perfect night for a Halloween party.

People filled the streets, most of them dressed in costume. Vampires and witches and monsters and villains. Beneath the detailed makeup and elaborate ensembles, each person wore another mask, the role they were accustomed to wearing every day, not just on Halloween.

There was Mary Holden, the Queen Bee of the neighborhood. She stood tall with her shoulders back, offering a slight smile to everyone that passed, while at the same time peering at them with judgement. Her goal had always been to appear better than the rest of them, and she had succeeded.

Donna Bledsoe, the Vixen, had squeezed into a tight black costume, her eyes roaming the crowd for another conquest. Life hadn't always been easy since the divorce, but it certainly wasn't boring. Her eyes lingered on a shaggy-haired bartender more than a decade younger than her.

The Fitness Fanatic of the group, Naomi Davis, had packed her young daughters off to spend the night with grandparents. It gave her a pang to see them leave, but at the same time, part of her was thankful for the release. She was still struggling to find herself again in the wake of having children, and a night surrounded by friends, all of whom she felt had life figured out, was exactly what she needed.

The Trophy Wife, Janet Parks, shimmied down the sidewalk, her husband trailing behind her. Tonight, like every night of her life, felt like a movie where she was the star. She delighted in the drinks and the celebration and the revelry. Most importantly, she celebrated the fact she had no real responsibilities, and tried desperately not to think about a time when that might change.

Watching them all from across the street, was the Spinster, Annette Friss. She hadn't been young or vibrant in some time, and the other women in the neighborhood looked at her with pity. Likewise, she stared at them with confusion, wondering how women who lived on the same street could be so different.

The last woman to walk past was Stella Moore, the Newcomer. She'd moved to Hickory Hills in hopes of the one thing we all want out of life sometimes: a fresh start.

All of them had different roles to play. In all likelihood, they'd taken turns playing each other's parts at some point or another.

In between the drinking and gossiping and dancing, a whole other narrative was unfurling, and by the end of the night, all their roles would be overturned, all their secrets exposed.

Three teenagers stepped away from the lively gathering. They wandered into the nearby forest, away from the watchful eyes of their parents.

What happened next would forever destroy the charming façade of Hickory Hills.

TWO

MARY

Who has the audacity to call someone before nine o'clock in the morning?

That is Mary's first thought.

The call doesn't wake her. She's been up since six, hauling boxes out of the attic. November 1st means the beginning of Christmas decorations in the Holden house and, as sad as she is to see the ceramic vampires and velvet pumpkins go, she is eager to see them replaced with sequined presents and garlands of fairy lights. Her enthusiasm is interrupted by the early morning call. The lack of etiquette. Most people have the decency to wait until after ten to start pestering neighbors.

Unless it's an emergency, she thinks.

"Have you seen Shelby?" It is Shelby's mother on the line. Donna Bledsoe, two doors down. Her tone is irritated, a bit breathy.

"Not since last night," Mary says.

"So she didn't stay at your house?"

"No," she says. "Did she say she would?"

Mary's sixteen-year-old daughter Grace has been best friends with Shelby since they were in pre-school. So inseparable, people often wondered if they were sisters or cousins. The two even favored one another, although Mary thought Grace possessed a natural beauty that other girls, including Shelby, lacked.

"No, but she's not here and I just figured..." Donna answers the question, then pauses. Her breathing gets heavier. "The girls are always together."

"Calm down," Mary says, as though soothing an overwound pet. "I'm sure everything is fine."

But Donna doesn't sound fine. Not in the slightest. She sounds like a woman whose life is crumbling at her very feet, and hearing her utter anguish unsettles Mary, reminds her of that uncomfortable feeling you get when you see someone with cancer. Their pain, their disease, isn't contagious, but doesn't it feel better to be away from it?

"I'll text Grace and see if she's at school," Mary says. "Even better, I'll message Ken. He can pull her attendance."

One of Mary's many great decisions in life was marrying Ken Holden, the current vice principal of Hickory Hills High School. When he first accepted the job, she thought it would be convenient to have summers off, but now that she is the mother of a teenager, she appreciates having the extra set of eyes on Grace at all times. It helped that he came from a wealthy family, too. They'd never be able to afford their lifestyle on his measly salary alone.

"You'll let me know once you hear back?" Donna says, still sounding desperate.

"Sure. Don't worry yourself to death. Drink some coffee." She makes her voice chipper. "Still coming over for lunch?"

"That's the plan."

Donna's voice is far away, as though she can't think of anything beyond what the next minute might bring.

"It's fine, Donna," Mary says. "It always is."

Her neighbor mumbles something incoherent before hanging up.

Mary's palms are covered in glitter from the miniature trees she's been unpacking. She wipes them on her leggings, making an even bigger mess, and glances out the circular window in the attic. She sighs.

Poor Donna. Poor any woman unfortunate enough to have a teenage daughter. It's a wonder any of them survive it. Most people can handle a needy baby or a curious toddler, even a talkative child, a headstrong adult. But a teenager? It must be a biological necessity for adolescents to force boundaries, test limits, push their parents to the brink of insanity.

Of course, Mary is luckier than most. Grace hasn't given her that hard a time, just the odd squabble here and there. Sometimes Mary thinks she should write a parenting book in her free time, something that could help those struggling. Lord knows the parents of Grace's peers haven't had it as easy, Donna included. Then Mary remembers her obligations—President of the Hickory Hills Home Owners' Association, secretary of the high school's PTA, lead soprano in the First Baptist Choir, sole decorator of the Holden family Christmas—and figures her plate is full enough. She's already given back plenty.

Still, there is something in the chill of Donna's voice that sends a shiver down her spine. It's not like the girls to not come home, but last night was hectic. Halloween, and she'd been busy manning the neighborhood party and overseeing the Trick-or-Treat Parade, traditions started more than a decade ago, by her, when she'd decided the local children needed something wholesome and spectacular to mark the season. Over the years, the shindig has been quite the spell for the adults, too. It's one of her favorite nights of the year, and she can't bear to think something might have happened...

She pulls out her phone, before she gets busy and forgets to text Grace:

Is Shelby at school?

While she's waiting for a response, she grips the plastic handles of the storage bins marked Holiday and starts carrying them down the stairs. For years, Ken would do the heavy lifting, while she did all the decorating, but due to his knee replacement last spring she didn't want to bother him. That, and she didn't want to wait until the weekend when he'd have time. That would waste days of sparkle and splendor and holiday cheer.

She's made three separate trips from the attic to the living room when she realizes Grace hasn't texted her back, so she makes good on the second part of her promise and calls Ken. He answers on the second ring.

"Morning, lovely."

"Is it a good one?"

"Rather slow, considering. I figure half the student body is sleeping off a hangover. Funny how October thirty-first results in double the office referrals, and on November first those same ruffians are absent due to *sickness*."

She smiles. Ken always makes her smile. Then she remembers why she's calling. "Speaking of, can you check if Shelby is at school today?"

"Bledsoe? Grace's Shelby?"

"Yes. Donna called and said she didn't come home last night. She sounded worried."

"Give me just a second," he says, voice strained, and she can picture him now in his office. Boring laminate desk provided by the school, decorated and organized by her. Heavy black picture frames holding carefully selected photos: Ken, Mary and Grace on last summer's cruise; Ken, Mary and Grace at a Christmas tree farm; Ken, Mary and Grace posing at their front door before the fall homecoming dance. Always the three of them. Her whole world, small and big all at once.

"Nope," Ken says. "Says here she's absent."

"That's odd," she says. "Even if she skipped out on going home, I figured she'd be at school."

"What did Grace say?"

"She hasn't gotten back to me." That worries her. Mary knows Grace has her phone on her at all times. She rolls her shoulders and shakes the hair falling across her forehead. "Nothing to worry about, I'm sure. I'll let Donna know. She'll probably turn up soon."

"Hope so," Ken says. "I'll ask Grace about it at lunch."

"Good plan," she says. "Have a nice day."

"You too," he says. "Don't exhaust yourself decorating."

Mary smiles again. Her husband knows her so well.

A half hour later, she has hauled all the boxes from the attic to the main floor, organizing them in order of what goes where. Red and green decorations in the dining room. Red and gold in the living room. All the miniatures that go in the kitchen are silver and white to match the marble countertops. And then there are the bedroom trees—

Her pocket vibrates with a reply from Grace. She'd almost forgotten she was waiting for one. The clipped message reads:

Idk. Why?

Mary rolls her eyes. She already knows Shelby is absent, thanks to Ken, but she doesn't understand why Grace, all teenagers really, must be so short. Don't they realize that communication skills are some of the most important to master?

Her mother called me, and she's worried. She said she hasn't been home since last night. Do you know where she is?

Why would i?

Another eye roll. Mary hates texting. This annoying back and forth could be resolved in a matter of seconds if they were on the phone, but she never calls her daughter during school hours, for fear that Grace receiving a demerit for using her cell would reflect poorly on Ken.

She's your best friend.

Not anymore.

This response stops Mary. She holds the phone out, staring at the screen, as though a mistake has been made somewhere. Grace and Shelby have always been thick as thieves. Wouldn't she know if they'd had some sort of falling out?

Since when?

Not rn. Talk later.

Mary sits in silence for several seconds, long enough for the screen to turn black from inactivity. Their conversation, as stilted as it was, unsettles her. Grace, Shelby, Donna and Mary —they'd all been together last night at the Halloween party, along with the rest of the Hickory Hills subdivision, but now everyone is acting out of character, and she doesn't know why.

If Shelby's mother doesn't know where she is, and her best friend doesn't either, where could she be?

And why is her daughter claiming they aren't friends at all?

THREE

STELLA

Last night really did it, I believe.

Finally, I'm one of the women of the neighborhood, not an uninteresting newcomer. Lord knows, it's taken long enough. We moved into 657 Hickory Hills a few months ago, and it still feels like I'm trying to keep up with all the changes.

Hudson's new school, which comes with a whole array of procedures and PTA responsibilities.

The neighborhood and its HOA requirement, the who's-who around the block.

Getting the home office set up and learning the kinks of the Internet provider.

For weeks, I've wondered if moving here was the best thing for Hudson and me, but after last night, I'm starting to feel like I belong.

"Shit!" Hudson swears in the passenger seat, digging in his backpack.

"Language," I warn, keeping a careful eye on the car ahead of me. We're in the morning drop-off lane for his high school. One of the first lessons I learned is it's best to arrive early.

Hudson closes his bag and leans against the headrest, his hand against his brow.

"I forgot my binder at the house."

"Do you need something?"

"Obviously, Mom. They wouldn't require us to have one if we didn't need it."

"I know, it's just it's the night after Halloween," I say. "Surely, you don't have any assignments due."

I look over at him, in awe at how much he's grown in what feels like a short amount of time. Even though it's just the two of us now, it seems we don't get to connect as much as I'd like. I reach my hand over, brushing the hair away from his forehead, and stop.

"Hudson, what's that by your eye?"

He raises his shoulder and shoos me away. "It's nothing."

"It looks like a bruise." In the rush of getting out of the house, I didn't notice. Didn't pause long enough to really look at him.

"I tripped at the party," he says, fanning his hair back into place just the way he likes it. "Super embarrassing. I hope no one else notices."

At the mention of the party, my mind returns to last night. My buffalo chicken dip had been a huge hit, although I think some of the neighbors preferred the cookies and cream mousse. My grandmother's recipe, that one. I'd spent days going through what I should bring, cross-checking it with the sign-up sheet on the neighborhood website. I wanted to make the right impression. Not too cheap, not trying too hard.

"I hate the hours at this new school," he says. It's been quite the adjustment moving from six periods a day to block scheduling. "I can't get in a routine."

"Give it some time," I tell him. "It's only been a few months. In January, you'll have brand new courses."

"I wish I could have stayed at my old school," he says. "Then we wouldn't have had to move to this stupid house."

I don't say anything, mainly because we both know that was never possible. There were multiple reasons we couldn't stay where we were, but I'm not going to ruin his day by going down the list. My eyes flicker toward him, landing on the bruise, before I refocus on the traffic.

"Fall break is coming up soon."

"Not like we're going anywhere," he says with full disdain.

A vacation isn't in the budget right now. Between closing costs on the house, the price of furniture, the lapse in pay I've had between quitting one job and starting another, it's just not in the cards. Hudson knows all these things, but being the typical angsty teenager, it's easier for him to think about everything we don't have rather than what we do.

New house. New beginnings. Safety.

I'm grateful for the opportunity for us to start over. Together.

"This line takes forever," he says, putting his feet on the dash. "I can't wait to get my license."

"Almost there."

Both at the front of the line and the benchmark for his license. Even though Hudson turned sixteen last month, he has a few more weeks before the required time limit for his learner's permit is met. After that, he'll be able to drive legally, and my only problem will be financing a car. He's already made it clear he does not want this one.

"There's got to be something you like about this place," I say. "You seemed to be enjoying yourself last night at the party."

It hadn't only been a success for me, but for Hudson, too. He spent most of the night following the neighborhood girls around. Not in a creepy way. It just so happens there's more girls his age nearby than boys. Thinking back, that might have been the highlight of my night, watching as he blended in with his peers so smoothly. It's not always been easy for Hudson to make friends.

Finally, it's my turn to pull up to the orange cylinder at the drop-off port. Hudson's door is open before I even put the car in park.

"Have a good day, hon," I say, low enough so that no one standing along the curb can hear.

"Love you, Mom," he says, slamming the door.

There he is. The little boy still alive inside that teenage body. I watch him walk into the school. Baggy shirt and jeans. Shoulders slumped. Hair hiding half his face. He wears the role of a moody adolescent well, but every now and then, I'm gifted with glimpses of the sweet boy he still is, the kind young man I hope he'll be, and that's enough to convince me all the recent changes are for the best.

I drive away from the school, thankful to not have to pause the car every few minutes. A sense of freedom falls over me. The entire day is mine, until four o'clock that is, when he arrives back home. I've been letting him make the twenty-minute trek home in the afternoons; there isn't that mad rush to get anywhere then.

As I'm nearing the gated entry to our subdivision, a passing car grabs my attention. Tapping the brakes, I look in my rearview, watching until the vehicle disappears from my sight.

It is a dark car. Tinted windows. Government tags. Almost identical to another car from my past. Driving ahead, I roll down my window, pressing the gate code into the lock pad with unusual force. That car couldn't have been the same one. Still, it's unsettling how something as simple as a familiar car provokes such a frightened reaction.

I pull forward, watching as the gates close behind me, freedom and safety falling over me once again.

FOUR

MARY

Mary has not even started on the kitchen decorations when she receives another call from Donna, her voice more frantic than before. When Mary explains neither Ken nor Grace has heard from Shelby, Donna lets out a desperate cry, a painful sound that makes Mary's stomach drop.

"She still hasn't come home," Donna begins. "Did you talk to Grace? To Ken?"

"Ken said she's not at school," Mary says, although she figures Donna already knows that. As frantic as she is, she's likely already called the school herself. Mary has no intention of telling her the details of her daughter's texts. "Grace hasn't heard from her either."

"Something about this isn't right," Donna continues. It's unclear whether she's speaking to Mary or to herself. "No one knows where she is! No one has even spoken to her in the past twelve hours. Do you think I should call the police?"

Mary pauses. *Should Donna call the police?* It's unlike her to not have an immediate answer. Twelve hours seems like a short amount of time and an eternity all at once when considering a teenager, a child. If she couldn't find Grace, wouldn't she have reached out to the police already? Or would it be too soon? Too embarrassing if she turned up a few hours later, hungover and unharmed?

"It couldn't hurt," Mary says, at last. "At least there would be people looking for her."

Another strange sound escapes Donna's throat, which makes Mary worry more. Strange images flash through her mind. People in bright vests traipsing through ravines. Flashlights and hiking sticks and lace-up boots. Flyers with a young girl's face. All images stolen from one too many made-for-TV movies, of course, and while part of her wonders if she is being dramatic, another part of her shivers with unease.

Mary realizes her friend still hasn't said anything. Soft, muffled sobs fill the distance between the phone lines.

"Donna, call the police," she says, as authoritative and calm as she would be instructing a stranger who needed directions. "I'll be over soon, and I'll bring the others."

"Thank you," Donna says, sounding grateful to be told what to do.

"Everything is going to be okay," Mary says, hanging up the phone with absolute confidence.

Mary is used to taking charge in a crisis. It's a role she took on at a young age, after her mother died and her father developed a drinking habit. Suddenly, she was the one in charge of not only herself, but also her younger brother. A hardness formed in her, melded with her very being, like a suit of armor. And now, whenever needed, Mary relishes taking the lead, being there for those that are lost.

One of the many lessons she's learned throughout her life is that there is strength in numbers. Her first stop is the house across the street. Naomi Davis opens the door wearing a Lululemon ensemble, a fresh flush to her cheeks from her morning Pilates session.

"It's a little early for lunch, isn't it?" Naomi says, patting her dewy skin with a towel.

Mary explains the situation that's unfolding, that Shelby Bledsoe has run away, and that Donna needs them. Within minutes, the two women are heading down the sidewalk to gather another soldier.

Janet Parks opens the door a full minute after they first knock. She's clothed in a Lilly Pulitzer dress, modest jewelry across her neck and on her earlobes. A Stanley cup is in her right hand, and Mary would bet Grace's college fund that there's already some type of alcohol inside.

"Little early for a drink," Naomi says, eyeing the cup.

"It's a smoothie," Janet says, moving it away from the open door.

Mary and Naomi trade glances, both unconvinced. Grace's college fund is secure, she's sure of it.

"Lunch is canceled," Mary explains. "Donna needs us at her house right away."

"Is everything all right?" Janet asks, thirsty with curiosity.

No, it is not, which Mary and Naomi proceed to explain. As expected, Janet slaps a hand to her chest, mouth agape. Across the way, Mary notices Annette Friss in her front yard tending to the garden. She drops the trowel in her hands, listening. Soon, the whole neighborhood will be aware there is a crisis on their street.

As they make their way to Donna Bledsoe's, Mary glances back at her own house. It looks beautiful in this mid-morning light, orange rays backlighting the house, exposing the sheen of dew on the grass. Mary has worked so hard for this home, this life, this family, and, for a moment, she's overcome with sharp fear about how quickly it could all be taken away. She longs to be near Grace, to wrap her arms around her daughter when she returns from school, squeezing tighter than she did yesterday.

Mary has defeated scandal in the past, but never anything that affected her child. She resents the unsettling feelings rising inside her. The proximity of this whole thing is starting to annoy the hell out of her.

FIVE

STELLA

Along the drive back, I recall moments from last night.

The women were far more inviting than I expected them to be. They kept complimenting my costume—a handmade cat ensemble I'd stitched myself, using one of my grandmother's old designs. It's one of the few familial gifts I have, the ability to sew. The other women appeared to have put more money into their costumes than time. There were several Barbies walking around the party—Classic Barbie, Flight Attendant Barbie, Disco Barbie. Lots of sexy costumes, too. Sexy Nurse. Sexy Vampire. Sexy Teacher. One woman had such a detailed Ursula the Sea Witch costume, it must have cost hundreds for the fabric alone, and I'm sure she hired out the stitchwork.

Still, I blended in among the elaborate outfits, and when the other women complimented me, it seemed genuine, not in that snarky *Mean Girls* way. We're far past that, aren't we? Even now that we're mothers in our thirties and forties it's sometimes hard for me to shake the persnickety girlhood dynamic of my youth. I think most millennial moms have that nervous anxiety when confronting a new group of women, especially in a neighborhood like Hickory Hills, but that bitchy façade was absent last night.

There had been dancing and drinks, lively conversation. Miraculously, none of the neighbors asked about my husband, or lack thereof. It was all about me, where we came from, what I do to pay the bills, how Hudson likes school, he's so handsome with that head of hair!

Thinking back on the conversations from last night, I feel like I'm floating, as I pull the car into the driveway of our two-story bungalow. It's one of the smallest lots in the subdivision, but that doesn't bother me one bit. It's still in the neighborhood, which is all that counts.

I spend the rest of the morning emailing clients. For the past six months, I've worked as a freelance copy writer. Really, I've had the job much longer, but I only started making good money recently. And by good money, I mean enough to cover a mortgage, utilities, groceries, and whatever Hudson might need. There's not a lot of wiggle room in the budget beyond that, but it's okay. I love having the freedom to work on my own schedule, doing something that I enjoy.

For years, I'd wanted to work as a writer, ever since finishing my degree. I'd catch up with former classmates online and they'd tell me about the pros and cons of working for themselves, how to find reliable clients. I thought it would be the ideal job, allowing me to use my skills while still providing me enough time to give Hudson whatever he needs.

My mind returns to the bruise on his face. He says he fell, and I believe him. Rather, I *want* to believe him. Hudson has a tendency to find trouble, but things are supposed to be different here.

I go into the kitchen, making myself a fresh coffee. Since working from home, I've learned caffeine is a necessary tool to get me through the day. Once I've added some fixings, I walk outside, the midmorning air still cool and refreshing, exactly what I need to deal with the rest of the day's workload.

Across the street, I spot Annette Friss. She was at the party last night, and when she sees me, she gives me a big wave. Last week, she ignored me entirely when we crossed paths. Further proof my status in the neighborhood is climbing.

Usually, I find her working in the garden this time of morning, but today she stands by her mailbox. What used to be her mailbox, that is. The metal compartment lies on the grass, splintered wood beside it and on the street.

"Did that happen this morning?" I ask. I hadn't noticed it down when I took Hudson to school.

"Last night," she says, aggravated. "Some idiot knocked into it with their car. Second time this year."

Annette's driveway, which is lined with brightly colored flowers and lush shrubbery, does sit at an unfortunate spot; a speeding car wouldn't be able to see the mailbox in time.

"I'm sorry," I say. Trying to lighten the mood, I add, "Did you have fun at the party?"

Before she can answer, a car turning down the street captures our attention. A police car, lights flashing, although there are no loud sirens. It moves past us slowly, carrying with it an eerie sense of silence, like we're in a scene from a movie.

Even after it passes, that silence lingers.

"What do you think that's about?" I ask.

For some reason, my voice cracks. All the hairs on my body stand to attention—I've always been uncomfortable around police. Seeing them here feels like an omen of bad things to come.

Annette looks down the street. "I heard one of the neighborhood girls didn't come home last night."

"Really?"

"Shelby Bledsoe. Four doors down."

I look down the street, all the little boxes looking the same, unsure which house is hers, unsure which guest from last night never made it home.

"How tragic," I say, hurrying into the house before she can say anything else.

SIX

MARY

This certainly wasn't the lunch Mary had been expecting.

Usually, she and the other homemakers in Hickory Hills convene after a large community gathering to trade stories and gossip, but today's luncheon has taken a somber turn.

Mary is now sitting in Donna Bledsoe's living room, watching as her friend speaks to a uniformed police officer about her missing daughter. Janet and Naomi sit across from her, unable to tear their eyes away.

"When was the last time you spoke to Shelby?" The officer sitting beside Donna appears young and laid-back, but at least it is a woman. Women are better at dealing with these sorts of things, Mary thinks. They can read between the hysterics and drama to withdraw crucial pieces of information.

"I last spoke to her around ten o'clock," Donna says, between broken sobs. "A couple of hours before the party ended."

"And what was she doing?" the officer asks.

"She'd run off with some of the other kids from the neighborhood," she says. "I'd pushed her curfew to midnight, but I fell asleep. It's not like Shelby to not come home."

Mary shifts in her seat. That last part isn't true, now is it? Shelby's been known to break curfew. And lie. And sneak out of the house. And there was the incident last spring when—

"Were you all at this party last night?" The officer poses her question to the other women in the room.

"Yes." Naomi is the first to answer. Petite with hard shoulders, she'd appear wiry if it weren't for her perfectly coiffed blonde hair and dash of red lipstick. Before they left her house, Naomi stole five minutes to freshen up; she never leaves the house without being presentable.

"It was a neighborhood party," Janet adds. She's shiftier than Naomi. She fidgets, trying to get comfortable, appear natural. Janet never does well in stressful situations.

"Did any of you see Shelby at the party last night?"

"All the neighborhood kids were there," Mary says, her posture stiffening. "She spent most of the night running around with her usual group of friends."

Her stomach drops when she thinks about Grace's text from earlier. *Not anymore*, she said, claiming they weren't even friends. Of course, she'd never be foolish enough to mention that in a moment like this, but it still unsettles her. A conversation to be had later in the day.

"And none of you noticed anything strange last night?" the officer asks.

All the women shake their heads, except for Donna, who buries her face into the wad of tissues in her hands.

The officer turns her attention back to Donna. "I know this seems obvious, but have you tried calling her?"

She nods, fidgeting with the tissue. "Every time I call her, it goes straight to voicemail, like it's off or something. Her location won't update, either, so I have no way of tracking her."

"I'll send out an alert for our local officers to be on the lookout," the officer says. "In the meantime, reach out to anyone you think might be in contact with your daughter. It's still early. She could be sleeping off a hangover somewhere, not even aware she has caused a fuss."

"I'm sure that's all it is," Janet blurts out, desperate to help. "I mean, we were all young once, right?"

"Is there anything we can do in the meantime?" Naomi asks the officer, more serious.

"Talk to anyone from the party. See if they remember seeing her." The officer turns to Donna. "And you can give me the names of the kids she was with last night. It could be helpful."

There's a strange sensation encompassing the room. The tone straddles the line between panic and overreaction, and Mary can't stand not knowing where they might land. Grace's text messages flash through her mind again.

"I'll run over to my house and get some leftover finger sand-wiches from the party," she says, standing quickly. "No one ever thinks straight on an empty stomach."

She exits the house. The pleasant smile on her face masks the profound sense of discomfort that's come over her since she first stepped into the Bledsoe home. She can't even describe it. Not fear, per se, because a big part of her still believes there could be a simple explanation for Shelby's disappearance. More like alarm, dread.

When she steps outside, the warm afternoon sun lands on her face. She closes her eyes, takes a deep breath of fresh air, particularly appreciated after hours inside the stifling house.

"Excuse me," a voice says. "Mary Holden, right?"

Mary opens her eyes. A woman in jeans and a wrinkled T-shirt is standing by the mailbox beside the Bledsoe house, her arms folded over her chest. Her face looks familiar, and yet Mary can't place her.

"Yes?"

The woman raises a hand as though initiating a peace treaty. "I'm Stella Moore from down the street," she says. "We spoke at the party last night."

"Of course," Mary says. She can't remember anything they talked about, but at least now she knows who the woman is. "You moved into the little bungalow at the end of the street."

"That's right." The woman smiles, crossing her arms over her body again. Her eyes dart to the Bledsoe house and back to the police car at the curb. "Is everything okay?"

Great, she thinks. Just what Hickory Hills needs. Another nosy neighbor. Then, she remembers what the police officer said. It's important to get the word out, far and wide, fast and efficient.

"Actually, no. Do you know Donna?"

"We met at the party."

"Her daughter, Shelby, never came home. No one has seen her since last night."

Stella plants a flat palm against her chest. "How old is she?"

"Sixteen."

The woman relaxes. "Hopefully she'll turn up soon. Kids that age, right?"

"Right." Mary takes a step forward. "If you'll excuse me."

Stella takes a step to the left, blocking her path. "Is there anything I can do? I noticed some of the other neighbors came over. I'm more than happy to help."

Mary takes a minute to consider the offer, weighing it against Donna's fragile state. She can barely go ten seconds without bursting into tears. Perhaps having a stranger on the scene isn't the best move at the moment.

"I think things are covered." She walks past, then stops. "You could talk to your son, though."

"My son?" Stella's voice changes. Gone is the helpfulness and cheer. She sounds choked, like Donna did earlier when she first called.

"Hudson Moore is your son, yes?" Mary asks.

The woman nods. "We just moved here. Neither of us know many people in the neighborhood."

"Well, your son certainly knows Shelby," Mary says. "They're boyfriend and girlfriend, you know."

SEVEN

STELLA

A burning sensation begins in my stomach, rises, until it feels like my rib cage is on fire. Mary Holden continues to stare at me, the expression on her face difficult to read.

"What?" It's the only word I can manage.

"Hudson and Shelby are an item," she says, plainly. "They were all over each other at the party last night. Everyone in the neighborhood saw."

Now, my cheeks begin to burn. I'd seen Hudson running around with some of the other neighborhood kids, but I never saw him *all over* anyone.

Mary cocks her head to the side, reacting to my confusion. "Didn't you know?"

I've never known Hudson to have a girlfriend. He's always been too shy, too in his own head. For a moment, a flash of pride runs through me, but it's quickly snuffed out when I remember what Mary said previously. That Shelby Bledsoe is missing.

"It can't be that serious," I say, stepping away. "We've only been here a few months."

Mary shrugs. "It's a small community. Most mothers around here are invested in what the neighborhood children are doing."

She looks over her shoulder, at the Bledsoe house. "It's why we're all so worried about Shelby."

I don't respond as Mary walks past. My arms are crossed over my chest, and now my gaze falls on the house in front of me, my mind conjuring images of what might be happening beyond the door. A missing child, a worried mother, busy friends. I don't appreciate the implication that I'm not invested in my child's life. Just when I thought I was connecting with these women, Mary found a way to make me feel like an outsider again.

What bothers me more is that she's right. I had no idea Hudson had a girlfriend. Can't even remember him talking about a Shelby or anyone else at his school. All he ever does is complain about moving here, as if we had much of a choice.

And then there's the bruise. Hudson insisted he fell at the party, but what if it's something else? He could be in trouble again, and I'd never even know it.

I turn, marching back in the direction of my house. I can't very well join the other women for lunch, not when they're all championing around Donna Bledsoe and her missing daughter. In fact, I don't think I can be around any of the women right now.

I need to talk to Hudson first.

When Hudson comes through the front door, smelling of midafternoon sun and sweat from his walk home, and throws his backpack on the kitchen table, it's almost five o'clock. A solid hour after when he usually arrives home.

Normally, I wouldn't notice. Most afternoons, I'm locked into writing until dinnertime, but following my conversation with Mary, everything catches my attention. Everything relating to Hudson that is.

"Where have you been?" I ask, standing to greet him in the living room.

He's already sprawled out on the sofa, his bare feet digging into one of my throw pillows. His gaze fixed on the television screen, he answers, "School."

"I know that," I say. "I mean after. You're usually home by now."

"I went by the gardens," he says. "Ms. Friss said it's good to keep an eye on them, and I can't rely on Zane half the time."

Annette, the neighbor across the street, is in charge of the Lawn and Garden division of the neighborhood association. As soon as she saw I had a teenage son, she was swift to offer him a job. The community gardens rest at the tail end of the subdivision, beside a small walking path and a man-made pond. Everyone says it's the highlight of the community in the spring, but it requires routine maintenance, and with winter approaching, Hudson and another local boy, Zane, take turns raking leaves and other upkeep.

"I didn't think you had a shift until this weekend," I say.

"I just told you Zane is unreliable," he says. "Am I in trouble for doing my job?"

"I didn't say you were in trouble." I sit beside him on the sofa, stiffly. That zombie show he watches all the time is on, and he's already fully invested. "I only noticed you got home later than usual."

He sinks deeper into the couch, not lifting his head to give me any attention.

"Have you made friends at school?"

He shrugs his shoulders, dodging an answer.

"How about in the neighborhood?"

"Yes, I've made friends," he says. "Does that make you happy?"

"Of course it does." My spirit illuminates at the thought of it, Hudson making friends, getting along with others, belonging. Then, I remember Shelby Bledsoe, and the light dims.

"Have you met a girl named Shelby?" I ask, failing to find a better way to start.

He rises up on the couch, placing his feet on the floor. "Yeah. She lives a few doors down."

"Did you know she was missing?"

He leans back further, his torso burrowing into the backrest. "Missing?"

"Yes. Apparently, she never came home from the Halloween party."

"I mean, I didn't see her at school today," he says. "That doesn't mean she's missing."

"The police were in the neighborhood earlier. Her mother has filed a report and everything." I pause. "Did you see her at the party last night?"

"No. I mean, yes. The whole neighborhood was there."

And according to Mary Holden, the whole neighborhood saw him and Shelby being physical all night. I've racked my brain all afternoon, wondering why I never spotted them together. Shamefully, I wonder if I was too wrapped up in my own need to make friends and belong.

Hudson stares at the floor. There's something unreadable on his face. "She never came home?"

"No."

Suddenly, my face is flushed. I feel like there's something not being said. Something that should be said.

"Hudson, are you and Shelby close?"

He cuts his eyes at me, tilting his head. "What do you mean?"

"One of the other mothers in the neighborhood," I say. "She said she thought maybe the two of you were dating."

He stands. "Gosh, Mom. We're friends. That's it."

Suddenly, I'm standing, too. "It's what one of the other mothers said, not me. She said she saw you two kissing."

"That's bullshit!"

"Language," I lecture him, trying to regain control of the conversation. "You don't know anything about what happened last night? Why she didn't come home?"

"No." His phone is already in his hands, his feet trudging up the stairs.

And just like that, he's gone again, and I'm left alone, questions hammering down like the rain that's about to begin outside.

EIGHT

MARY

Despite the drama of this afternoon, Mary is determined to make dinner as normal as possible.

There haven't been any updates from either the police or Donna, and Mary promised her that she would check back this evening, but she had to get the roast in the oven. And quarter the potatoes. And chop the carrots into perfect half-moons.

She's just finished pulling apart the meat—so tender all she needed was a pair of kitchen tongs—when Ken descends the stairs, humming. He stands behind her and kisses her cheek.

"Smells delicious," he says. "As always."

"We both had a little too much to drink last night," she says, remembering the Halloween party fondly. "A starchy meal is in order."

Ken wraps his arms around her waist, the two of them swaying from side to side. She's so thankful for this, that after all their years together his eyes still sparkle when he sees her, that he still compliments her cooking, that he appears as infatuated with her now as he was two decades ago when they met.

Outside, rain is drizzling, the sun beginning to set, triggering the automatic streetlights. They've no sooner turned on than a police car drives past their window, headed in the direction of the Bledsoe house. The magic of this moment with her husband is gone. Her softened demeanor turns rigid again, and she notices him tensing, too.

"Still no word about Shelby?" Ken asks.

"Not since I last left Donna's," Mary says. The meat and vegetables are arranged in a shallow serving bowl, and she carries it to the dining table in the next room. "I promised I'd go back over after dinner."

"Go now," Ken says, following her. "I imagine Donna's a total mess. She probably needs you."

"I was there all afternoon," she says. "Besides, I want to talk to Grace. See how she's handling all this."

"I know." Ken pulls out a chair and sits, placing a linen napkin in his lap. "I checked in on her at lunch and she seemed okay. Of course, that was hours ago. It's hard not to panic when it's been this long, and they still haven't found her."

Mary sits across from her husband but doesn't even consider getting a plate of the food she's so lovingly prepared. Instead, her eyes go to the front door, waiting impatiently for Grace to return from volleyball practice.

"Did she say anything to you at lunch?" she asks. "About Shelby."

"Just that she hadn't talked to her. She didn't seem worried at all, but that's kids. I'm afraid of how she'll handle it when she hears her best friend still hasn't returned home."

"I am, too," Mary says. She pauses. "It's just..." And she can't decide if she wants to continue.

Ken stops chewing, pats his mouth with a napkin. "What is it?"

Mary exhales slowly. "When I first called Grace this morning, and asked her if she had spoken with Shelby, she seemed really dismissive about the whole thing."

"I'm surrounded by teenagers all day," Ken says. "Trust me,

when it comes to anything in life, their reaction is either total shock and awe or deep disinterest. There's very little in between."

Mary remembers that age, the swirl of emotions building inside, trying to decide how to react to the world around her. Teenagers' emotions run the gamut from muted to excited, and often come across quite baffling. But Mary knows her daughter, and she completely understands the friendship between Grace and Shelby. That's why Grace's words have been bothering her since this morning.

Mary knows there is something abnormal about Grace's response, and she feels she must share it with Ken. She takes a sip of wine.

"Grace told me she and Shelby aren't friends anymore."

"What?" Ken asks. "Since when?"

"I don't know." Mary shrugs. "That's why I thought it was so strange. Just this week, they were joined at the hip, like they always are. And I'm sure I saw them together at the party last night."

Ken thinks, his gaze moving to the window across from the dining room table, the view of which just happens to provide a glimpse of the Bledsoe house, and even though it's too far and dark to make out anything, Mary wonders what he is thinking. She realizes he's just as concerned as she is. By Grace's comment, by the timing of the remark, by all of it.

"Young girls get in fights all the time," he says. "I'm sure it's nothing."

"But Shelby is missing—"

Mary stops talking when the front door opens, the intrusion exposing the vulnerability of their conversation, making her feel like a stranger has walked in on her while she's changing, naked and defenseless.

Grace walks into the room, her large duffel bag thrown

across her body. Her hair is pulled back, but there's a fuzzy halo circling her face, the telltale signs she's just left a strenuous practice.

"Thank God," she says, dropping her bag on the floor and plopping down into the chair beside Mary. "I'm starving."

Normally, Mary would insist that Grace freshen up first. The scent of sweat and fading deodorant don't belong at the dinner table, but she bites her tongue.

"How was practice?" Ken asks, his voice level. A typical man, not giving away any of the concern he just expressed.

"Long," Grace says, reaching for the food at the center of the table ravenously. "I mastered my serve."

"That's great, sweetie," Ken says, picking up his wine.

Mary, who still hasn't touched her food, feels queasy. She's imagined having this conversation with her daughter all day, and yet she doesn't know how to start. She longs for an appropriate segue—like, was Shelby at practice?—but Shelby gave up sports her freshman year, and it wasn't common for the girls to make plans this late on a school night.

"Have you spoken to Shelby at all today?" Ken asks. Mary is so grateful he brought it up, she could kiss him.

Grace's posture turns rigid as she skewers a piece of meat. "No. I already told you."

"She still hasn't come home," Mary says, her voice gentle.

"So?"

"Grace, this is serious. I've been with Donna all afternoon. The police are involved."

"The police?" At this, Grace lifts her eyes to meet her mother's. Her expression is a mix of curiosity and fear.

"Yes. Donna has filed a missing person's report and everything. The fact that Shelby still hasn't returned home is very worrying."

Grace holds her stare a moment longer, and she sees the

softening, the disintegration from a moody teenager to the young child she once was, the child that longs for her mother's approval. Then, just as quickly, the moment is gone.

"There's no telling where she is," she says. "I certainly wouldn't know."

"Your mother said you claimed to not be friends with her," Ken says. "That's news to the both of us."

"Do I have to tell you everything about my life?" Grace counters.

"Of course not," Ken says, "but as your mother explained, the situation is quite serious."

"We're not trying to pry," Mary says. "But even if you've had some kind of falling out, Shelby was one of your closest friends. If there's something you should tell the police—"

"I'm not talking to the police." Grace stands abruptly, her meal only half finished. "Whatever Shelby has gotten herself into, it has nothing to do with me."

She pushes back her chair, turning on her heels in the direction of the staircase.

"Grace," Ken starts. "Your mother is only trying—"

"I'm taking a shower," she cuts him off, desperate to end the conversation. She rarely snaps at her father like that.

Mary and Ken are left alone at the table, not the first time they've been left speechless by the emotional outbursts of a teenage girl, and yet, this time it feels different. Darker. A hint of something worse yet to come.

When her phone begins ringing, she's grateful for the distraction, until she sees who is calling. Donna. Again.

"I got a message from Shelby!" she exclaims as soon as Mary answers the call.

"That's good, right?" The heaviness in Mary's chest lightens. "What did it say?"

"No, it's not good." She sounds even more panicked than

she did this morning. "The message said she was running away."

Mary scoffs. "My goodness, the girl can't even drive! Where on earth would she go?"

"She didn't say," she says. "The message said she needed space and to leave her alone."

"Did you track the location of her phone?" Mary asks. "Like the police officer suggested this morning?"

"I did." Donna exhales in defeat. "It's not showing anything. Whoever has her phone must have switched it off again. Something about this isn't right."

"Maybe she's just blowing off some steam." Mary tries to hide the accusation in her voice. It's no secret the relationship between Shelby and her mother has been difficult, at times. And this isn't the first time Shelby has taken off. Last spring, she skipped town with an older boy for an entire weekend. Donna had thought Shelby was visiting her father, and when she couldn't get ahold of her, she was understandably frantic. In hindsight, Mary wonders if this is Shelby's pattern. Stirring up drama when she needs a little extra attention. Of course, she won't remind Donna of this incident now, not when her friend is already sick with worry.

"If she ran away, she must have told someone where she went, right?" Mary says, trying to diffuse the tension.

"Grace doesn't know anything?"

"No." Her answer is too quick and harsh. Of course, if Shelby was going to tell anyone her plans, it would be Grace, but her daughter claims not to know anything, becomes aggressive every time Mary broaches the topic. She clears her throat. "Look, I'm just finishing up dinner. I'll come over, and we can call the police again. Give them the update."

"Well?" Across the table, Ken is watching her as she hangs up, wanting to be filled in.

"Donna said Shelby sent her a message," she tells him. "She said she was running away."

Ken inhales deeply, and when he blows out the air, his cheeks swell like a puffer fish. "That's a good thing, right? I mean, if she left on her own, she can't really be missing."

"I hope you're right," Mary says, standing, the meal before her left untouched.

NINE

DONNA

Halloween Night

Donna Bledsoe sauntered to the beverage stand for another drink.

Ever since the divorce, she loved a good party, and Halloween night was one of her favorites. As usual, she'd been Mary Holden's right-hand woman as they planned the event, picking the right decorations and designating responsibilities to their other neighbors. There was something thrilling about watching everything come together.

"Same order?" The man behind the bar was dressed like a penguin. Not a costume, rather the same boring white shirt and jacket that all the hired help from the catering company were wearing.

"Make it a double," she said, winking.

The bartender must be half her age, but that didn't temper the sexual chemistry between them. He'd caught her eye early in the afternoon when the catering crew first started setting up in the middle of the cul-de-sac. They'd flirted when she ordered her first drink. Donna loved this type of interaction with men.

Even if it didn't go anywhere, the reminder that she was still desirable, that she had the ability to seduce, was enough.

She wasn't sure how she'd end her night—with the bartender, or someone else—but she felt confident it would be a good one.

"Mom, can I have some cash?"

Her daughter's voice doused water on whatever fire was starting between her and the bartender. On a good night, Donna could pass for younger than she was, but having a teenage daughter aged her. Made her feel less like a cougar and more like a hag.

"Why do you need money?" Donna asked, trying to maintain eye contact with the bartender.

"Ms. Friss is selling baked goods to raise money for the community gardens."

"There's tons of free food around," she said. "You don't need to waste money."

"Moooom!" Shelby whined, dragging the word into multiple syllables.

If she had any cash on her, Donna would have forked it over just to get Shelby out of her hair. Why wouldn't she just take off?

"Look, run back to the house—" Donna, who'd not yet turned to face her daughter, stopped when she caught sight of her. "What are you *wearing*?"

"A devil costume," she said.

"That's not the costume you showed me."

"I changed at the last minute," she said. "I wanted to match Grace."

Donna took in the sight. Flimsy glitter fabric stretched tight across her daughter's body, topped with shiny metallic wings and a matching set of horns. The outfit made Shelby look much older than sixteen, but that wasn't what angered Donna the most. She'd considered wearing that very same outfit to tonight's party, before deciding to wear a black jumpsuit instead.

"Did you take that out of my closet?"

"You said you were going to be a vampire." Shelby shrugged her shoulders. "I didn't think you'd care."

"Double vodka martini?"

The cute bartender placed the drink in front of her, but this time his hungry gaze fell on Shelby, not Donna. Amazing how quickly Donna could do the math. He must be closer to her daughter's age than her own, and she felt embarrassed by the entire interaction. She grabbed her drink with one hand, not bothering to leave a tip, and yanked Shelby's elbow with the other.

"I do mind," Donna said, her voice low in Shelby's ear. "You're way too young to be wearing something like that."

"And you thought it would be better for you?"

Donna blushed, remembering how she felt when she'd first slipped into the red dress. She'd always been slim, so it fit fine, but the flashy material highlighted her other physical insecurities. The cellulite spidering across her thighs. The noticeable sag in her chest. Even the crow's feet around her eyes appeared more pronounced. Donna loathed these reminders of how old she really was.

And now, she looked at that same outfit on Shelby, how it accentuated her daughter in all the ways it ridiculed her. A necklace she'd never seen before complemented the ensemble, her daughter's name in a cursive font at the center of a ruby and diamond encrusted pendant. Shelby was tan and taut and effortlessly beautiful. As much as Donna wanted to react to her daughter with pride, all she could feel was envy.

"Go home, now," she said. "Take it off and put on something else."

Shelby jerked her arm away. "No. I already told you; I'm matching Grace. She's an angel."

"Of course she is," Donna said snidely, taking a swig of her drink.

Across the street, she caught sight of Grace Holden. As expected, her costume was far more demure. Hemline just above the knees, sheer sleeves stopping at the wrists. She was the epitome of innocence and perfection, just like her mother. The snake of jealousy inside her roiled again.

"I said go home and change."

"How about you just let me do what I want?" Shelby eyed her with a defiant stare, a reaction she'd no doubt inherited from her mother.

Donna couldn't stand the sight of her own once young and perfect face staring back at her.

"Fine. You want to dress like the neighborhood skank?" Donna waved one arm wide. "Be my guest."

Shelby's face crinkled into a frown, and there was hurt in her eyes. "Why do you have to be so mean?"

"Why do you have to be so difficult?" Donna took another sip of her drink.

"I'm taking off," she said, stomping away. "Have fun at your party."

Donna was relieved to see her go. She loved her daughter, but being a mother came with all sorts of complications. She'd struggled at almost every single stage. First, the colic and interrupted sleep. Then the tantrums and school politics. None of those earlier trials had prepared her for having a teenage daughter, though. Sometimes Donna wasn't sure what was more difficult, raising Shelby alone or combating her own fleeting youth.

Donna never got to experience the wild, fun years most people have in young adulthood. She'd already been a wife and a mother then. Now that the divorce was final, and the alimony covered her lifestyle, she was ready for this stage to be all about her. Was that so much to ask? Couldn't Shelby allow her to have some moments to herself?

Donna shook off the confrontation, happy to have Shelby out of her hair for the rest of the night. Her drink was halfway gone; she looked over at the bar. The possibility of something happening with the bartender was out the window, but there were plenty of men to choose from in the neighborhood, particularly on a night like this, people lost in revelry.

At the other end of the bar, she spotted a tall man wearing a Frankenstein's monster mask. She couldn't tell who it was from his gait alone, and when he peeled off his mask to take a swig of his beer, she realized she'd never seen him before.

He was cute enough, she thought. Perhaps he would do for the night.

TEN

MARY

Mary waits impatiently for the slow-drip Nespresso machine to dispense her morning coffee.

She had very little sleep last night, having spent most of the evening at Donna's poring over the message sent from Shelby's phone.

Sure, it was the first communication anyone had received from Shelby since the party, but it revealed very little. It was a two-sentence message which read:

Mom,

I need some space. Don't try to find me.

The message had caused more harm than good, Mary thought.

And then there was Donna's theory, that Shelby hadn't left it at all.

"If someone hurt her, they'd have her phone," she pointed out, in between dramatic sobs. "It doesn't confirm Shelby sent the message!"

"But she has done this type of thing before," Mary reminded her, gently.

It was impossible to ignore the incident last spring. Shelby had run away before, so it was a possibility she'd done it again. Ken agreed with her when she'd filled him in on the latest updates. Seeing how exhausted she was, he'd agreed to take Grace to school so Mary could catch up on sleep, as if her mind was able to keep still.

It wasn't just the message that was troublesome, but the impact it had on Shelby's disappearance as a whole. As promised, Mary had sat with Donna as she called the police. She waited with her for another officer to arrive at the Bledsoe house to examine the message.

The female officer who'd they'd spoken with that afternoon was gone, replaced with an older male detective in an ill-fitting suit.

"I understand your concern," he said to Donna, his voice thick with skepticism, "but if she ran away, there isn't much we can do."

"She's only sixteen!" Donna shouted, as if he needed a reminder. "Even if she did leave willingly, she could still be in danger."

"All our officers are aware—"

"They need to be more than aware!" Donna cut him off. "You should be out looking for her. Or we could set up a press conference. Get her name out there."

"We can't waste those resources if the girl has admitted to running away." The detective handed Donna's phone back to her, but she refused to take it. Mary grabbed it instead.

"A mother's instinct is very strong," she tried explaining to the detective. "If Donna believes Shelby is in danger, surely there's something you can do."

"You said she's run away before, right?"

The detective looked at Donna, but she refused to meet his

stare. It seemed like she was on the verge of saying something but couldn't find the right words.

"She wasn't trying to run away last time. She told me she was staying with her father so she could spend some time with a boy," she admitted, her voice cracking. "This is different. No one knows where she is. Things aren't always perfect between us, but she wouldn't leave me like this. I know it." Mary looked away at that point. She knew her friend was grasping at anything that would keep the police involved, but it was hard to be convincing given Shelby's history.

"If something did happen to her, we're wasting precious time," Donna said, pleading. "Please. She's my only daughter. You have to do something."

"Do you have any reason to believe someone would want to hurt your daughter?"

Donna simply shook her head, before dissolving into another mess of tears. The detective looked at Mary then.

"Reach out to anyone who might know where she is." He handed over a cheap business card. "And give us a call if there are any more updates."

He stood and left, wiping his hands clean of Shelby Bledsoe and her dramatic mother. Mary comforted her friend as best she could, her heart sinking at the realization that the situation had gotten worse. There was still no sign of Shelby, and now even fewer resources to help look for her.

"We'll do whatever we can to find her," Mary whispered to her friend.

This morning, Mary plans on making good on that promise. Moments later, Janet arrives at her front door, a stack of papers in her hand, just as she's finally drinking her coffee.

"Hot off the presses," she says, pulling out a paper from the stack so Mary can see. "And don't worry. I told everyone in town she was missing, too."

The flyer was hurriedly put together by Janet's husband

Julian this morning using Canva. It shows Shelby's most recent school picture, a description of her physical features listed below. Height. Weight. Blonde hair, blue eyes. By now, everyone in Hickory Hills is aware of the young girl's disappearance; the women plan on visiting neighboring communities to spread the word there, too.

"These are great," Mary says, stepping outside to join her on the porch. "I say we drop off a stack with each neighbor and start driving to some other subdivisions. Where's Naomi?"

"On her way over." Janet lowers her eyes. "Rick got back this morning."

"Let me guess. Trouble in paradise?"

"You know she always gets fussy when he's out of town." Janet looks across the street, as though Naomi's front door might open any minute. "She's probably checking his body for hickeys and lipstick marks as we speak."

The Davises' marriage has more ups and downs than a daytime soap opera. On the surface, everything appears heart-warming and perfect, but beneath that, the couple is still trying to bounce back from his most recent affair. It's been more than two years since the affair was exposed, but if you were to ask Naomi about it, she'd react like it happened just yesterday.

Mary tries to avoid the topic at all costs.

"I feel sorry for her, you know," Janet says, eager for an opportunity to get Mary alone. "They always seemed so happy before they had the kids."

"Children change everything. Sometimes for the good." She thumbs through the flyers, Shelby's large blue eyes staring back at her. "Sometimes for the worse."

"That's why I keep putting them off."

Mary fights herself not to snort. Janet loves naming off reasons why she's yet to get pregnant. Other people's children. Other people's marriages. The economy. It's all just filler for the real reason: Janet doesn't want them, and she's afraid if she says that out loud, people will judge her.

And they will. At least, Mary will.

What reason does she have to not be a mother? She doesn't work. Her husband makes more than enough money to fund their flashy lifestyle. Janet doesn't want to get pregnant because that would be a whole nine months when she couldn't drink, and, as of late, that seems to be Janet's favorite hobby. Even now, Mary can smell the scent of vodka and tomato juice on Janet's breath.

Really, what's wrong with her friends? They're supposed to be meeting to hand out flyers of a missing girl, but they've got to get marital disputes and their breakfast cocktail out of the way first.

"Here she comes," Janet says under her breath, stopping Mary from saying anything else.

Naomi joins them in front of the mailbox. Her cheeks are flushed, and it's hard to tell if that's because of her morning workout, or if she's been fighting with Rick.

"Are you guys ready?"

"Sure are." Mary hands over a stack of papers. "We'll start with the neighborhood, then we can spread out as needed."

"Wait up!"

Mary looks down the sidewalk to see Stella Moore approaching. She's wearing dingy workout clothes and holds several water bottles in her hands.

"Is she talking to us?" Mary asks, not taking her eyes away from her.

"Looks like it," Naomi says, snidely.

"Who invited her?"

"I did." Janet takes a step forward, like a child about to endure a scolding. "She was messaging me last night about anything she could do to help. I figured it couldn't hurt."

Mary rolls her shoulders and takes a deep breath. She's not

in the mood to entertain Stella Moore, a woman she barely knows. She's had far too little sleep, and they've already wasted enough time. They're trying to find a missing child, not host a social event. Do any of these morons understand the seriousness of the situation?

"I brought some waters. No telling how long we could be out, right?" Stella slides the bottles into her backpack, grabbing some of the flyers out of Mary's hands. "These look great. They'll really grab people's attention."

"Thanks," Mary says, sharply, turning on her heels to walk down the sidewalk. Stella Moore and her obvious eagerness annoys her, but no more than the selfishness of Naomi and Janet. All she wants is to get these flyers out there, put an end to this nuisance, so that everything can go back to normal. She thinks of Donna, likely unable to get out of bed, locked in her room crying and racking her brain for answers.

Strength in numbers, Mary reminds herself. The more people out looking for Shelby Bledsoe, the better.

ELEVEN

STELLA

When I was house hunting, the natural beauty of Hickory Hills drew me in like a warm breeze at the precipice of spring. The immaculate homes, crisp sidewalks, the manicured forest backdrop.

I never thought that I'd be roaming these streets putting up flyers of a missing girl.

I'm ashamed to admit, I felt giddy when Janet Parks invited me to help them post flyers around town. Another sign that I'm becoming part of the community, all I ever wanted for Hudson and me. After we distributed flyers to our neighbors, we moved onto other subdivisions. Outside of the gated community, there are fewer sidewalks, more space between houses. A certain layer of protection has been stripped away, and I try not to think of Shelby out here on her own.

There's four of us in our group: Janet, Naomi Davis, Mary Holden and me. A few others from the neighborhood are nearby.

"I've lived here over ten years," Naomi says, "and I don't think I've ever ventured to this side of town."

We're on a rural stretch of road between houses, posting

flyers on the sidewalk trees; the sense of isolation is over-whelming.

"Why would you?" Janet says, swatting at her arm, fending off a bug. "It's brutal out here. I can't imagine how miserable it must be in the summer heat. And there's not even a community pool."

"Given how much you work out, I'm surprised you don't come out here for hikes," Mary says to Naomi. "I've heard some of the men in the neighborhood talk about it."

"That's why they make treadmills," Naomi says.

I listen to the friends' banter, cautious to jump in. It's obvious I have two tasks at hand: find runaway Shelby Bledsoe and solidify my position as one of the Hickory Hills women.

"Is there a reason the local police aren't more involved?" I ask the women. "I figured they'd be posting flyers and orga-nizing searches, not us."

"The police have no leads at all, and now that they're convinced Shelby's a runaway, they're not even trying," Mary says. "It's the optics of being out here that's important. If we have enough flyers around town and Facebook chatter, the local news will pick up the story, regardless of whether the police are involved."

"Or maybe Shelby will hear about the fuss everyone's making over her disappearance," Naomi says, "and will decide to come home."

"Do you really think she ran away?" I ask.

"I hope she did," Janet says. "Either that or she was taken."

"What makes you think that?" I ask.

"There are only so many scenarios," Naomi says. "The least dramatic is that she took off and will return of her own accord. If that's not the case, something sinister must have happened."

"That's Donna's theory," Mary says, dodging a large mound of wound-up grass. "She's convinced that text message is a red herring. She believes someone else sent it to keep the police at bay."

"What do you think?" I ask Mary. "Your daughter is Shelby's best friend, right? You probably know her better than the rest of us."

"Shelby has been addicted to social media since she received a smartphone for her twelfth birthday. No matter how angry she was, she wouldn't cut off contact like this," Mary says, and I sense she's annoyed that she must keep breaking down these details for a newcomer. "The fact she hasn't come back by now makes me worried this could be a worst-case situation."

"So, what do you think happened? I mean, if she didn't run away," I ask.

The women are silent for several seconds. All I hear are our footsteps and the whooshing breeze. Naomi is the first to speak.

"Fine, I'll say it. We all love Donna, but she hasn't always led the best example."

Janet nods in agreement. "There's no telling what she's exposed Shelby to."

Prior to her daughter's disappearance, the few times I'd been around Donna Bledsoe she'd seemed like a completely average woman. Attractive, friendly, well-mannered. Any time I was around her she was crowded around these very women. Her friends. This same group is quick to call out her mistakes as a mother.

I find it difficult to judge Donna so harshly. Maybe it's because I know so little about her, but I understand all too well the difficulty in balancing your own problems while trying to raise a child. With a shudder, I wonder if my past has left an imprint on Hudson, even unintentionally. How would the other women look at us if they knew everything we'd been through?

"Ever since her divorce, Donna has been quite active in the dating world," Mary explains.

"That's one way of putting it," Janet says. "She makes my years in college look like a nunnery by comparison."

"Every week there's a different man in and out of the house," Naomi says. "All that time, it never occurred to her that she might be exposing her daughter to someone dangerous?"

"Who were these men?" I ask. "If you really think they could be involved, someone should turn their names over to the cops."

I'm surprised to hear these words come out of my mouth. I've always been nervous around the police. In fact, I'm not sure I would have volunteered to help distribute flyers if they were involved.

"If the police asked her to give names, it would be impossible," Mary says. "Her bedroom is like a traveling circus. There was Harley-Davidson guy."

"The guy with the long hair," Janet adds.

"Don't forget Tatted Up Timmy," Naomi says. She looks at me. "At least that's what we called him."

The women laugh in unison. A lighthearted, yet cruel sound.

"It'd be like trying to clear this area of weeds," Janet says, kicking at the ground in front of her. Sure enough, there's a bundle of weeds every few steps. An untamed wilderness. Are they suggesting Donna Bledsoe's home life could be just as dangerous?

"Donna made the mistake many women do after divorce," Mary says. "She put herself first, when she should have been looking after Shelby."

I walk several paces, putting distance between myself and the other women, but I'm hesitant to roam too far. "If one of those men did harm Shelby, I can't imagine how Donna must feel. She'll never forgive herself."

"I know it sounds like we're being harsh, but we all love Donna. Really," Mary says. "None of us think she did anything to deliberately hurt Shelby, but her negligence very well could have caused this."

A breeze rushes past, sending a shiver down my spine. Or perhaps it's something more. All of this is making me uncomfortable. Traversing unfamiliar territory. The ominous flyers. The idea of something happening to Hudson, or any child his age. Listening to the way they talk about one of their dearest *friends*.

"How's Grace holding up?" Naomi asks Mary.

She sighs. "As you can imagine, she's completely devastated. She barely slept last night she was crying so hard."

Something in the way Mary clears her throat and rolls her shoulders makes me think she's not being entirely truthful, but what reason would she have to lie? Perhaps the disappearance of her daughter's closest friend hits too close to home.

"I'm sure it's scary for her," Janet adds. "She's too young to be dealing with trauma like this."

"How about Hudson?" Mary asks me, an intense look in her eyes. "Not knowing where his girlfriend is must be worrying him to death."

"He is worried," I say cautiously, clearing my throat. "But I don't think their relationship is as serious as you make it out to be. He doesn't have a clue what could have happened to her after the Halloween party."

"Hudson said he and Shelby weren't together?" Mary asks, stopping where she stands.

"There may be some mild flirtation between them, but they're not a couple," I say, trying to keep my voice calm, cool.

"That's absolutely not true," Mary says. "I saw them with my own eyes at the party. They were all over each other."

Hearing that phrase again makes me wince. I don't want to think about my son's love life, especially because that sounds so unlike Hudson. The quiet boy who keeps to himself until pushed. Shelby is certainly a beautiful girl. It's easy to see why he, or any other boy, would be infatuated with her. But if she was his girlfriend, why wouldn't he just tell me?

And why has Mary Holden brought up this alleged tryst a second time? It's almost like she's stating it for the record, trying to make the connection between the missing girl and my son clear in everyone's minds.

"I'm not denying they've spent time together," I say, choosing my words carefully. "We've only lived here a few months. Whatever is going on between them, it can't be that serious."

"You know how young love is," Mary counters. "It's the most intense feeling in the entire world."

Of all the claims these women have put out there, that's the one I know to be true. I recall when I first started dating my ex-husband, Beau. It was a whirlwind romance that quickly led to marriage, the two of us eloping at City Hall.

About a month before our nuptials, I'd had a nightmare, one that still feels fresh and tangible after all these years. Beau and I were walking through the woods, not unlike the isolated area we're in now, but the one in the dream was deeper. As we moved beyond the trees, it became increasingly apparent we were alone. And yet, that thought was comforting, not frightening.

Back then, all I wanted was more time with him. More closeness. More, more, more.

In the dream, we reached a clearing in the woods with a weathered shed. Vibrant wildflowers in yellows and purples enclosed the building, and the sun was shining precisely on that spot. I made a comment about how this would be a beautiful place for a wedding, even though in our real life, we'd already decided to have as little fanfare as possible.

Beau walked into the shed, came out with his hands cupped together. "Stella, you have to see this."

He lowered his hands to reveal a small, black snake, and in

the next second, he threw the creature at me. I remember waking up just before the scaly skin grazed my flesh.

For weeks after I had that dream, I worried it was an omen, my subconscious' way of warning me to end things while I still had the chance.

If it weren't for young love.

The racing heartbeat I had whenever I looked into his eyes, the security I felt when he wrapped his arms around me. How we'd move together, like we were the only two people in the world.

I clung to those feelings, allowed them to override every logical, sensible fear I had. Looking back now, I wish I'd ended things the very morning I woke up from that dream. It would have spared me so much heartache. In the end, I suppose it was a premonition, representative of all the things I wanted our love to provide and, ultimately, the cold reality it gave me in return.

Love is a feeling, and feelings can't be trusted.

I just hope Mary Holden's suggestion that Hudson's feelings might have something to do with Shelby's disappearance aren't warranted.

When I look back at the women, their heads are raised in my direction, watching me. Every interaction I have with them, I realize, whether it's a late-night Halloween gathering or a midmorning outing, is an interview, their way of deciding whether I'm worthy of being in their group.

Last week, I wanted nothing more than to feel like I was home in Hickory Hills, that Hudson and I had finally found a place where we belong, but the way they threw Donna Bledsoe under the bus was ruthless. If they decided to turn against me, what would they do?

"Tell me more about Donna's men," I say, hoping to refocus the conversation away from Hudson. Or me.

It works. Mary is the first to dive in, followed by the other two, each offering stories that are equal parts intimate and embarrassing. They might be out here spreading the word about Donna's daughter, but if I were her, I'd be ashamed to call any of these women my friends.

Who knew such ugliness could hide behind such beautiful faces?

Just like that black snake hiding within the charming shed in my dream.

TWELVE

MARY

After returning from distributing flyers, Mary showers and redresses. She walks into the living room and lights a candle. Marshmallow and vanilla. One of her favorite scents.

She feels as though she needs to cleanse her spirit from all the toxicity, even though she'd be the first to admit she has had a hand in all of it. She was the first to mention Donna Bledsoe's many love interests. A bit tacky, she knows, considering everything that's happening, but a more strategic part of her brain believes these details could be relevant. It's been over twenty-four hours since Shelby was last seen, which makes the likelihood of her running off slim, even if there is some suspicious text message stating otherwise. If someone is responsible for the girl's disappearance, they could have sent the message from Shelby's phone. They must start considering who that might be, and the unfortunate truth is that Donna Bledsoe has quite a few notches in her bedpost.

Donna should have known better than to behave that way with her young daughter in the house. Parading men in and out, never once considering that she might be exposing Shelby to someone dangerous. If this disappearance is at all sinister, Mary is almost positive it will link back to one of the men in Donna's life.

We're not friends anymore. The sentence lingers in her mind, the words spoken in her daughter's voice. She must believe anyone else is involved rather than her own daughter. More than that, she must keep putting other suspects out there. Mary knows what it's like to be at the center of small-town gossip, and she's determined to protect Grace from that same treatment.

Mary settles on the sofa. She lied when she told the other women she had somewhere to be. She doesn't need to leave the house for at least an hour when she has to pick up Grace for a dentist's appointment.

She just couldn't take being around them anymore. Talking about Donna. Thinking about Shelby. Her mind needs a break from it all. She turns on the television and starts flipping through channels. Even though she's home most afternoons, she rarely watches television. Soap operas and afternoon talk shows are boring. They're too redundant, predictable.

A snippet of a Discovery Channel documentary captures her attention. The ribbon at the bottom of the screen reads: *Lions of the Serengeti.* Her thumb is on autopilot to click to the next channel, but she stops, staring at the screen.

A lioness is flat against the ground, camouflaged by the golden earth and tall grass. Several feet away, a herd of antelopes is feeding, completely unaware of the danger in their midst.

Mary is mesmerized. Animals have always fascinated her. Not the domesticated kind—the Holdens don't even have a pet —but more exotic varieties. Jungle cats and elephants and giraffes. Even scaly reptiles interest her, the kind that tend to make other housewives squeal in fright.

When she was younger, Mary wanted to be a zoologist. It's what she'd set out to study when she enrolled at college. The plan had been to get her undergraduate degree in zoology, then study a more specific field for her post-graduate degree. She'd hoped to travel to different continents, study the animals in person, like one of the broadcasters behind the camera in this very documentary.

Most people would never guess it when looking at her, taking in her ironed clothes and expensive perfume and voluminous hair. More than once, she'd considered how this Adult Mary was far different from the Mary of yesteryear, before she'd forgotten her dreams of traveling the world to conquer the jungles of suburbia.

Mary closes her eyes and tries to travel back through time, back to her youth, before she met Ken and became a mother and adopted so many of the routines her life now revolves around. She imagines another life, where she'd continued her studies, earned advanced degrees and traveled the world. Envisions a base camp settled on the plains of Africa, the sun on her face, the mix of fear and wonder in knowing so much danger and possibility lurked just around the corner.

For a moment, she's overcome with a longing to escape. To venture back in time, to be that girl again. Or, even now, to take a fraction of what she spends on her wardrobe in a month and use it as a down payment for a trip across the world.

She opens her eyes, just in time to see the lioness' bloody jaws feasting on an antelope's throat, the others in the herd prancing away in fright. She looks at her living room—crisp and white, and smelling like vanilla and marshmallow thanks to the candle in the kitchen—and she accepts she's thankful for the life she has. It's natural to imagine other possibilities, she tells herself. She's heard the other women talk about it, too. The careless mistakes they made in their youth before everything fell into place.

She looks at the picture frame resting on the coffee table,

remembers how lucky she is to have Ken and Grace, and turns off the television.

Mary calls ahead and asks Ken to sign Grace out of school early. When she pulls up to the blue metal awning at the front of the school, her daughter is sitting on a bench, staring at her phone. She must have heard the car pull up—dismissal isn't for another hour, and the only other cars in sight are parked—but Grace remains still, transfixed by the device in her hands.

Mary honks the car horn.

Grace jumps, as though stimulated with some sort of electric shock. She immediately locks eyes with her mother, then lets out a grandiose sigh.

"Why are you here early?" she asks when she gets in the passenger seat, voice filled with disdain.

"You have a dentist appointment."

"Oh."

Grace somehow manages to make Mary feel like she's constantly in the wrong, even when all she's done is schedule a routine teeth cleaning.

"I thought you'd be happy to duck out of school," Mary says, putting the car into drive. "You used to love it when I'd sign you out early."

"Fourth block is, like, the only class I actually enjoy," she says, and suddenly it's clear to Mary where she went wrong. She impeded on her daughter's social time. Ever since Grace entered high school, her popularity has been climbing. Normally, Mary acknowledges this with a great sense of pride. She's always hoped her daughter would be exactly as she is—smart, beautiful, popular.

She just never imagined the full package would come with such a streak of attitude.

Grace reaches into her backpack and plucks out an earbud

from a zippered pocket. She's about to plug it into her head when Mary says, "Don't do that."

"What?" Grace says, shoulders raised.

"It's only a twenty-minute drive," she says. "I thought we could talk to each other. I've been alone all day."

"I'm sure that's not true," Grace says. "You probably spent your entire afternoon with the housewives."

Her daughter is right, and Mary feels an edge of resentment over how predictable her life has become. And yet, not predictable. Instead of lunching at each other's houses, they posted up flyers of Shelby Bledsoe. She has a few sacred moments alone with her daughter, and she wants to use them to finish the conversation they started yesterday at the dining-room table. She read once in a parenting magazine that the car is the best location for tough conversations with teenagers—there's nowhere for them to escape.

"You know, there's still been no word from Shelby."

"So?"

Her daughter's flippant response to the entire situation angers her; it's all she can do not to snap, but she breathes deeply, trying to control herself.

"Donna had a message from Shelby saying she ran away." She watches her daughter closely. "If she were planning something, don't you think she would have told you?"

"Well, she didn't," Grace says, defiantly, pulling her feet onto the seat.

"I don't understand why you aren't more upset about this," Mary says. "I don't understand why you're claiming she's not your friend."

"She's not my friend," Grace says. "Besides, why do you want me to be upset?"

"I never want you to be upset, but you and Shelby have been inseparable since you were girls. The only person closer to her is Donna, and she's an absolute wreck. I feel like we should be doing more to help find her. Anything."

"We had a falling out." Grace props her feet onto the dash, something Mary usually warns her against, but she allows it for the sake of keeping the conversation going. "It happens."

"But when? I saw you two together at the Halloween party. Everything seemed fine then."

"That's where we got into the fight," she says. "We haven't talked since."

Grace and Shelby had a fight. The night of the Halloween party. The night she went missing or ran away. Mary's mind flashes back to yesterday, to the conversation she and the other women had with the female officer in Donna's living room. They'd each been asked questions, responded with innocent answers. This is the kind of information the police are searching for. What changed between the last time Shelby was seen and when she was reported missing? Any major events, like a falling out with her best friend?

Grace, like all teenagers really, is so blinded by her own self-ishness that it's impossible for her to see. If something bad did happen to Shelby, having a fight with her friend before it happened is suspicious. Her daughter might act like she doesn't care about her friend's whereabouts, but it would be in her best interests—in everyone's best interests—if she turned up unharmed.

"Will you tell me what the fight was about?" Mary asks, her voice buckling as she waits for a snarky rebuttal.

"It's personal," Grace says, staring at her phone. "I think you and everyone else are making a big deal out of nothing. Shelby will turn up. I'm sure of it."

"What about that new kid in town? The Hudson boy. I saw all of you at the party together," she says. "They're dating, aren't they?"

"No," Grace says, quickly.

"I could have sworn the two of you were talking about how cute he was when he moved to the neighborhood. And I saw Shelby and Hudson kissing at the Halloween party."

"That doesn't mean they're dating, Mom."

Wasn't that what Stella insisted today when they were together? Mary had been so smug, so sure. She doesn't like the idea of being in the wrong.

"When I was younger, going public with someone meant it was serious."

"These days people just want to have fun. What's wrong with that?" Grace says. "You act like you know so much. You really don't know anything."

Again, Mary is left irritated by the truth behind her daughter's words. Three days ago, she thought she *did* know everything. The ins and outs of the neighborhood. The dynamics of those around her. The details of her own daughter's life. Now, she admits, she knows very little, and what she suspects is almost too awful to think, let alone say out loud. Mary wants to find out what Grace and Shelby were arguing about so she can protect her daughter, but every time she broaches the topic, she's met with another insult.

Grace grabs the earbud again, places it in her ear, and this time, Mary doesn't stop her.

THIRTEEN

STELLA

Warm water pours over me, washing away the sludge from being outside distributing flyers. What it won't wash away is the uncomfortable feeling I had around the other women. Perhaps I was being naïve, but I'd thought moving to a different town would provide better opportunities. New places, new friends.

Today's encounter didn't feel particularly fresh or new. It was more like being transported back to my *Mean Girls* high school era, except now all the women are in their thirties and forties.

I get out of the shower, patting my skin dry with a towel before putting on a casual outfit. At some point I need to devote time to my clients, but the day is already halfway over, and the time I'd usually spend working on my freelance projects I wasted around town with the women. Now I have a slew of errands I need to run before Hudson returns home this evening.

While I'm still responsible for morning drop-off, Hudson has been walking home in the afternoons and, on the days that he is working, he goes straight to his shift at the community gardens. It's good for him to have some responsibility. His first real job, and yet another reminder that the child I've lovingly cared for is coming into his own, growing up.

As I sit in front of my vanity, speed-running through a quick makeup routine to make myself presentable, I recall my conversation with the women earlier. I don't like the way Mary Holden seems fixated on Hudson. She's twice now made it a point to mention his relationship with Shelby, which I maintain is a complete exaggeration. There's an obvious level of intent behind her words that makes me uneasy.

When I think of my son, his most outstanding attributes come to mind. His quiet, methodical personality. His dark-brown hair, clear blue eyes. He's everything I ever wanted in a son and more.

Yet, when the rest of the world looks at him, they see something else. They interpret his shyness as strangeness, his caution for premeditation. And mistakes he has made have been used unfairly against him.

At least, that's how it was at his old school. The incident with that other student snowballed out of control before anyone could stop it. Hudson never meant to hurt anyone; he simply lost control of his emotions, something that's easy to do when you're a hormonal teenager.

But other people didn't see it that way. The administration. The parents. Even when I tried talking to them, tried explaining the context behind what had happened, no one wanted to hear me out. Their minds were already made up.

I don't want the people here to start forming biased opinions about Hudson, especially as it pertains to Shelby Bledsoe. Moving here wasn't supposed to be just a fresh start for me, but for him as well, and there's so much to worry about in the present. On a general level, I'm concerned about what's happened to Shelby Bledsoe. What started as a young girl who didn't come home or ran away seems to have morphed into something darker. Her own mother believes someone sent the text message to cause confusion, and why do that unless there is something nefarious to hide? But if the worst has happened, the other women made it clear Donna Bledsoe is to blame.

I wonder, whenever something goes wrong with a child, why is it always the mother's fault?

On a more personal level, I want to get to the root of the relationship between Hudson and Shelby. It bothers me the way Mary Holden talks about them, like she has a hold over me. When he returns from the community gardens, I plan on asking him again. I'd be lying if I said I didn't get the feeling he was holding back before.

The sky is nowhere near as bright as it was earlier when we were out posting flyers. The hint of warmth is gone, too. I suddenly worry about Hudson working outside if he has gone to the gardens again. Knowing him, he didn't pack his jacket like I asked.

As I pull my car out of the driveway, I spot Annette Friss watering the flowers along her fence line. She gives a tidy wave as I pass, and I again feel that sense of belonging I so crave. I haven't felt it since the morning after the Halloween party, before I was informed that Shelby was missing.

For the next hour, my thoughts rest as I trudge through the list of errands. I pick up some groceries at the store to tide us over through the weekend, then I fill up on gas and stop at the local office supplies store to buy more toner. The past two days have been a distraction, but starting tomorrow, I must get back to work. My clients depend on me.

By the time I return to the neighborhood, it's almost time for Hudson to be home. I consider turning around and picking up a pizza at the closest takeout shop when a passing vehicle catches my eye.

I see it again. That same car that was following me Wednesday morning on my way back from taking Hudson to school. It's a dark car. Tinted windows and government tags.

My pulse picks up, watching the rearview mirror with intent.

Surely it can't be who I think it is, but what are the odds of seeing the same car twice in the same week? And yet, here it is again, following me into the Hickory Hills subdivision. I press the gas, speeding up a little too much for a neighborhood row. Behind me, the car stops, pulling into a driveway and pausing.

I let out a sigh of relief, and yet the worry remains. In the past, I let issues slide, until it was too late. Ignoring what was right in front of me became my defense mechanism. Not now. Not here. I won't be able to sleep tonight until I've cleared my mind.

Yanking the wheel, I do a U-turn in the middle of the street, driving back in the direction of the dark car. I assumed it was only pulling into a random driveway to turn around, and yet as I come closer to the house, I see the car is still idling there.

I park in the precise spot where the driveway and road meet, making it impossible for the car to back out now. If it's a stranger pulling into their driveway, I'll apologize immediately, even tell them I thought I was being followed if I must. And yet, in the time it takes to come up with that scenario, I've lost my nerve. I don't want to confront anyone. Perhaps this wasn't the same car as yesterday, and I'm being paranoid.

I'm about to switch the gear into reverse when the driver's side door opens. A tall man exits the vehicle. His face I know all too well. Light hair, blue eyes. A commanding presence that makes everyone in the vicinity take notice.

Beau. My ex-husband.

All the emotions, good and bad, I'd been feeling only moments ago fly out the window as I open my own door, going to meet him in the driveway.

"What are you doing here?" I shout as I get closer.

He feigns surprise, like he's caught off guard to see me, but knowing him, knowing how he orchestrates everything around him, I'm convinced it's an act. Beau was following me, and he was sitting in his car waiting, on the off chance I'd initiate a confrontation.

"Good afternoon, Stella." A warm smile spreads across his face.

"This is the second time I've seen this car," I say. "You're following me."

"I'm sure there's an easier explanation than that." He bends down, taking his keys from the ignition, and puts them in his pocket. His chest puffs out as he stands to full posture. "It's been a while since we talked."

"There's no reason for us to talk," I hiss. The venom in my voice comes easily now, after years of locking it inside. Beau's not my husband anymore. I'm no longer trapped under his roof, and so that fear I have learned to live with rearranges into something lethal. "You can't be following me. It's ridiculous."

"I'm not following you, Stella."

"Then why are you here? Hudson and I moved two hours away for a reason," I say. "The custody agreement says you'll get to see him at Christmas. We have no reason to talk until then."

"Nice little neighborhood you've found here," he says, twisting his head around for a good look. My gaze follows his, landing on the neighbor's garden, the pristine sidewalks, the Bledsoe house in the distance. "I wondered what was so special it had to take you away from me."

"Nothing took me away from you," I say.

Beau is talented at spinning stories, and part of the reason I couldn't stay in our original town is because of the way he tarnished my reputation. Saying I stole his child from him. Walked out on my family. Left him for another man. All misrepresentations meant to paint me in the worst light possible.

He'd never admit the real reason I left. Not to himself, let alone to anyone else.

"How's our boy?"

"Hudson is fine," I say between gritted teeth, the word *our* twisting knots inside my stomach. "He's expecting me home any minute now."

"It would be nice to see him," Beau says. "Maybe we could all meet for dinner some time."

I shake my head, trying to dismiss the nonsense spewing from his mouth. "What is this? I haven't talked to you in months. You drive all the way here to, what, intimidate me? Act like we can grab dinner as if everything is fine?"

"I already told you. I'm not following you, Stella."

He takes a step forward, and my body freezes in defense mode. My mind becomes alive with memories, memories I try to suppress, but which come back now for protection.

Beau chasing me up the stairs, me throwing a pile of laundry over my shoulder to try and slow him down.

Again, Beau chasing me as I ran to the back patio, knocking over a glass vase in the process, shards of glass sprinkling over us both.

The sound of my locked bedroom door flying open. The sound the mattress made when he jumped on top of me, wrapping his fingers around my neck.

A bird chirping in the distance acts as a life preserver, fastening me to this moment. I'm no longer in our old house. It's broad daylight. He can't hurt me here. He won't.

Don't you think I'm smart enough to leave bruises where no one will see?

The memories are alive within me, but they're still the past. The new me with the new life will always have the upper hand.

I remain standing still as Beau takes another step forward. And then another. Soon, he's past me, walking closer to the street. He stops right in front of the mailbox and opens it.

"What are you doing?" I ask him once I've found the courage to turn around.

"Checking my mail." He makes a point to study the envelopes in his hands, refusing to raise his eyes to meet me.

"What?"

"I told you. I'm not following you, Stella. This is my house," he says. "I live here now."

My blood turns uncomfortably hot, itching beneath my skin. "You're lying."

"I can assure you I'm not," he says. He pulls back his jacket, revealing a brass badge at his waist, and beside that, a gun. "Hickory Hills PD was hiring. I couldn't pass up the opportunity to be closer to my family."

The sight of his gun causes my breath to stall in my throat. Another memory comes into focus. At the old house. I'm on my knees in the spare bedroom, my hands in front of my body, a useless form of protection. He staggers in the doorway, drunk and laughing, his service weapon pointed right at me.

"Beau, you can't be here," I whisper, my strength from earlier near gone. "You can't buy a house in the same neighborhood."

"Why not? Nothing in the divorce tells me where I can and can't live." He walks toward the house—his house—making it a point to keep his distance.

"We moved here to get away from you," I say. "You can't just follow us here."

"Legally, I can. Unless you take out that restraining order you like to threaten me with," he says. "I'll give you a name of a buddy on the force, if you want to go through with it."

He knows I won't. Being married to him was traumatizing enough, and having to withstand the rumors he spread about me in the wake of our divorce was terrible, but Beau is a police officer. Trying to get anyone on the force to take my side over his is nearly impossible.

"I'm begging you," I say. "We can work something else out, but you can't live here. Not this close to Hudson and me."

"Hudson already knows," he says, his words piercing my heart with an arrow.

"What?"

"He wanted to know if he should tell you, but I told him not to worry about it. You'd find out soon enough."

I'm backing away now, tripping over my steps as I make it back to my car. If Hudson knows his father is here, why didn't he tell me? I never thought he'd go out of his way to help keep his father's secrets.

"Don't be so dramatic, Stella," Beau calls after me in a mock-soothing tone. "I think there's a lot of benefits to us being neighbors. I can keep an eye on you. Make sure my family stays safe."

I get into the car and slam the door shut.

Beau never cared about our family. He certainly never cared about my safety. And just when I thought I'd moved beyond our past, just when I thought I'd be able to start over fresh, he's back in my life.

There's no escaping him.

I manage to whip the car around and speed off before the tears begin to flow.

FOURTEEN

MARY

Mary puts the last of the dishes into the dishwasher, delighting in the mechanical hum as the machine kicks into gear. Another chore completed, one more box to check off on her to-do list.

She looks at her watch. It's almost eight o'clock. Usually, this is the time of night she begins to settle down. There's a collection of television recordings she keeps throughout the week, and she enjoys trying to catch up in the small window between now and when sleep consumes her.

But everything in her routine has changed since Shelby went missing or ran away. With each passing day, hour, minute, Shelby's absence becomes more frightening.

Mary dries her damp hands with a dishrag and walks in the direction of the downstairs den. The door is shut, which means Ken is working. Again, if this were a normal week, a normal evening, they'd be going upstairs together, bickering over which of their many shows to watch tonight. Instead, he's using this time to catch up on what he's getting behind with at work. Shelby's disappearance has thrown everything off-kilter there, too. At the dinner table, he informed her that mental health counselors were talking to the students at the school in groups, helping them process her absence, and hopefully preventing any copycat runaways. She wonders if any of the counselors talked to Grace, and what she said.

She considers knocking on the door but thinks better of it. It's pointless to disturb him, and she's already agreed to return to Donna's house later this evening.

Still, there's another reason she wants to turn to her husband. She needs his guidance when it comes to Grace. From the time he entered her life, she's always confided in him, viewed him as mentor first, and then a lover. He still doesn't understand the full extent of Mary's concern, and she knows there is no one she can blame for that but herself. She needs to be more direct with her feelings, tell him their daughter got into an argument with Shelby right before she went missing, and she fears...

Ah, she can't even bear to think the full thought. How can she bring Ken into this world of paranoia and uncertainty? It's not fair. Men have no interest in dealing with trivial teenage drama, which leaves all the heavy lifting to her. Instead of going to him for support, she needs to go to Grace for answers.

Mary climbs the steps to the second story, intent on talking with Grace before she returns to the Bledsoe house. Just as Mary is about to turn the knob to her daughter's bedroom door, she hears voices.

"That's just Ms. Sanders," Grace says, her voice light with just a hint of snark. "She's like that with everyone."

Ms. Sanders teaches Spanish at the high school, one of those salty curmudgeons who refuses to retire, thus taking out her grievances on everyone around her, students and teachers alike. Even Ken has complained about her on occasion.

"I'm telling you, she's even worse with me," says another voice. A boy. Grace has her cell phone on speaker. He continues, "I don't know what it is about that woman, but she *hates* me."

"I don't think you're the kind of guy people hate," Grace says.

Was that a hint of flirtation in her voice? Or just clumsy banter? Grace has always been beautiful and funny and smart, but she's never had any serious feelings for a guy before. When Mary was her daughter's age, she was turning heads left and right, and, if she's being honest, she wasn't even half the catch that Grace is.

And yet, her daughter has never acted that interested, instead traipsing around the neighborhood with Shelby and getting into mischief with other girls on the volleyball team. She's too sensible to get involved with romantic relationships. Mary pulls on her memories and can't think of a single time she's ever heard her daughter on the phone with a boy.

"Well, you haven't known me that long, have you," the boy replies. His voice falls flat. Again, she can't tell if Grace has fumbled, or if both participants are equally bad at carrying on a conversation. Most teenagers don't really grasp how to properly act around one another until they're much older.

It's something that was always different about her own relationship with Ken. Even in the beginning, their relationship felt elevated. Mature. Adult. She'd have conversations with him that had always felt forced with other guys she'd dated, and Ken had this magical way of making her feel like everything she said was interesting. He was infatuated with her, from the very beginning, and she found his total devotion to her intoxicating.

But not all relationships start off like hers. In a matter of months, Mary and Ken had built a foundation that took other couples years to create. It's why she's never been good at talking about relationships with her peers; the terms of her marriage are so different from all the others around her, it seems. And it's why she doesn't know what to say to Grace now. Doesn't know how to offer her advice.

Her own parents' marriage had been toxic, even before her

mother died. Mary can still remember pulling the cover over her head as a child, failing to drown out the sounds of their arguments. It was during this time Mary used to visualize a different life for herself.

She would be a wife and mother who would never make her children feel they needed to cringe in shame. She would choose a man who would love and respect her. And Ken Holden was everything her young heart had dreamt of and more. Being with him came with its sacrifices, though. Mary had been happy to move away from her alcoholic father, but that also meant cutting ties with her younger brother, and the two had never rekindled their relationship in adulthood.

She thought about her brother sometimes, wondered if he escaped their childhood unscathed, like she had. He had two teenage sons, and sometimes she wished they were closer, that Grace had cousins to make memories with and turn to for advice. Instead, her childhood had been tied to Shelby, not always the best influence, but a loyal friend nonetheless. Mary always delighted at the fact that Grace didn't get roped into boy drama the way Shelby did. Her daughter is too young to take on all that responsibility.

"Hey, any updates?" the boy asks, his voice suddenly interested again.

"No," Grace says, immediately aware of what he's talking about. "I mean, my mom said at dinner they might hand out more flyers tomorrow."

They're talking about Shelby, she realizes, and suddenly the anxiety and fear of the present comes crashing back. Mary folds forward slightly.

"That's crazy!" The boy sounds like he's watching a firework display, not talking about a missing classmate.

"I know," she says. "I mean, it's a total waste of time."

"You think so?"

"Yeah. They're not going to find Shelby."

Suddenly, Mary is holding her breath, trying to unravel her daughter's tone. Why does she believe passing out flyers is a waste of time? Does she know where Shelby really is? And if she does, what could that mean?

"I thought she would have turned up by now," the boy says. "This is getting really serious."

Again, Mary struggles to decipher whether he's talking in generalizations about the situation, or if he has some secret knowledge the rest of them don't.

"Tell me about it," Grace says. "My mom won't leave me alone."

Mary is frozen in the hallway, her head so close to the door she's afraid if she missteps, she'll go falling into the room. It's wrong for her to stand here and listen to her daughter's private conversation. She knows this. But she simply can't pull away. She's desperate to know what it is her daughter refuses to tell her.

"My mom's too afraid to talk to me," he says. "She's been acting weird ever since it happened."

"Well, you're lucky," Grace says. "Sometimes I wish my mom would just chill."

Mary's spine stiffens. *Just chill.* She's insulted.

"Maybe you should talk to her. About everything," the boy says. "It might help."

Grace scoffs, and then there is a long pause. In that silence, a hurricane of questions whirl through Mary's mind.

Why won't she talk to me?

What is she hiding?

Why does this boy—whoever he is—seem to know more about my daughter than I do?

How can I protect her if she won't let me in?

Grace, what have you done?

"My mom and I aren't close like that," Grace says, finally. "We never have been."

A piece of Mary's heart feels like it's broken off, floated into the ether like a forgotten particle lost in space. Grace is her only child. Ever since she was born, she's been Mary's entire world, and yet she doesn't feel like they're close?

"Your mom seems nice enough."

Mary immediately decides she likes this boy, is grateful to him for not jumping in on the parent bashing, and yet she's still equally hopeless, listening to Grace's true feelings.

"Sure, she comes off nice. That's her whole goal. Mary Holden, the most likable woman in town. Don't you ever get the idea that people actually hate her?"

This time, the boy says nothing, his silence answering the question.

"I mean, my mom tries talking to me about things, like she takes parenting lessons from some syndicated teen drama, but it never feels real. Authentic. It's like there's this wall between us." Grace pauses. "And I can't tell her the truth about anything as long as that's there."

Mary takes a step back, away from the door. She wishes she'd never listened in on this conversation, wishes she didn't know the truth about how her daughter felt.

And the most painful part of it all is that she knows Grace's assessment is right. Mary does place a barrier between herself and those around her, even with her own daughter. She doesn't know why she is this way. It's not so she can be *likable Mary Holden*. That part was wrong.

Mary wasn't always this way. There was a time, when she was younger, that she felt free, open, the way Grace claims to be now. Somehow, that openness didn't come with her into adulthood, and she doesn't know why. She doesn't know why there is a wall between her and everyone else. As though she's trying to protect something. Hide something.

"Well, what do I know? I've only been here a few months,"

the boy says, the comment pulling Mary back to the conversation.

"Your mom has been hanging around with my mom and the other housewives," Grace says. "Give it some time. You'll see what I mean."

Barely lived here.

Your mom has been hanging around.

Mary suddenly realizes that the boy on the other end of this phone conversation—this horrible conversation which has eviscerated her confidence as a mother and brought up the unknown details of their neighbor's disappearance—is Hudson Moore.

Grace is having a flirtatious, late-night phone call with Shelby's boyfriend.

FIFTEEN

ANNETTE

Halloween Night

Halloween had always been Annette Friss' least favorite holiday.

She didn't appreciate the macabre, the obnoxiously drunk adults, the vandalism and mayhem. As she aged, however, she found she quite liked trick or treaters. Several came through the neighborhood, even ones that lived across town. Word was out that the *rich people* lived in Hickory Hills, so children came in the dozens for high-end candy.

For years, Annette sat on her front porch and handed out treats, delighting in the various costumes, from the adorable to the creative. When Mary Holden decided to start the party tradition, her plans changed. Instead, she used the night as an opportunity to raise money for the community gardens.

Mary Holden didn't like that. A neighborhood party was an opportunity to celebrate together, not panhandle, or so she said. Of course, Mary didn't mind one bit increasing the HOA fees around the time of a big neighborhood event. How else would they fund it? Surely not with her grubby hands.

All her neighbors, Annette had learned, were tight with their cash. Surprising, since more than half of them had paid well over market value for the houses they called home. Annette had bought her two-bedroom bungalow decades ago, back when the price for a modest home wasn't outrageous. It always amazed her that in a neighborhood full of professionals—doctors and lawyers and dentists and professors—none of them wanted to contribute to the greater good.

Whether the other housewives liked it or not, they couldn't stop her from setting up her small booth of baked goods. Sure, people were giving out candy by the handfuls, but Annette spent days preparing cookies and brownies and chess bars, and, much to Mary Holden's disappointment, she always made a decent profit considering.

"Trick or treat!"

Two little girls stood before the booth, treat bags held out in front of them. One was dressed like a ballerina, the other a princess.

"Beautiful costumes," Annette said, handing over candy.

The girls squealed in amusement, then the princess noticed the booth. "Ooh, brownies!"

Annette didn't believe they were neighborhood kids, and looking around, she didn't see any parents nearby. She decided to waive the fee and handed one over. The girls danced off into the night.

It was these little moments that had taught her to love the holiday. As much as she was reluctant to admit it, there was something charming about a community gathering. Most of her neighbors ignored her half the time, especially on a night like this, but she could still enjoy her interactions with the children, and, of course, the people watching.

In the center of the cul-de-sac sat the bar booth. Most of the adults had moseyed over, allowing their children to wander off. Annette watched as the mighty foursome—Mary, Donna,

Naomi and Janet—worked the crowd, except this time, there was a fifth person in their midst. Her new neighbor, Stella Moore.

Since they moved in a few months back, Annette's interactions with Stella had been scarce. She was grateful for Hudson, though, who'd done an excellent job managing the landscaping around the community gardens. Watching Stella interact with the other women, she felt a sting of apprehension, like watching a car before it rams into another.

Sure, the people in Hickory Hills ignored her, but their own secrets and misdeeds were on full display to the entire neighborhood, Annette included. She knew all about Janet's drinking problem. On more than one occasion, people had seen her pulling into the driveway drunk as a skunk, and she was certain that Janet was the person who ran over her mailbox a few months back, although she could never prove it. Rumor was that was the reason she hadn't had kids yet; she couldn't put down the bottle long enough to conceive.

Then there was that nasty business with Naomi and her husband's affair. Annette at least had more pity for her. She'd still been recovering from their last baby when it started—the secretary of all people. And in typical scandal fashion, everyone in town knew about it before Naomi. When she did find out, everyone in town knew that, too. There was a whole big spectacle of Naomi throwing his clothes and tech out on the front yard. Of course, she just as quickly took him back, which was where Annette's sympathy stopped. Men would continue their bad behavior for as long as they were allowed to get away with it. She'd have had more respect for the woman if she'd stood her ground.

Then, of course, there was Mary Holden. Annette wasn't sure about the skeletons in her closet; just knowing the woman was horrendous enough. The typical woman who skated by on looks and privilege alone, constantly looking down on those around her. Over the years, Annette had watched as Mary befriended neighbor after neighbor, only to run over them when it suited her. Sometimes she wondered how Ken, who seemed like a genuinely nice guy, could stand her. How the husbands could stand any of them.

And now here was Stella Moore, cozying up to them like all the rest. Annette was sure Stella had her own secrets, too—everyone does—but she worried the woman would be yet another casualty of the housewives of Hickory Hills.

"Hey, Miss Friss!" Hudson Moore and Grace Holden stood in front of the baked goods booth. "Can we get some cookies?"

"Aren't you getting your fill from all the free candy?" she asked.

"Everyone on the block knows you have the best homemade cookies," Grace said. "I told Hudson he had to try them."

"That's very kind of you," Annette said, plucking two Ziplock baggies and handing them over.

Hudson gave her a five and said, "Keep the change."

"That's very kind of you," she said.

"It all goes back to the gardens, right?" Hudson asked.

"It does indeed." Annette added the money to the small pile she'd collected through the night. "I hope you guys are having fun."

"This is a blast," Hudson said, enthusiastically. "My old neighborhood never did this sort of thing."

"Well, I'm happy you're here now," she said. "Don't the two of you get into any trouble."

Grace smiled wide and added, "Thanks for the cookies, Ms. Friss."

Annette watched them walk away, a dreamy smile on her face. Sweet kids, she thought, even Grace Holden.

Annette only hoped their parents wouldn't ruin them.

SIXTEEN

MARY

Mary barely slept last night.

Even though her body was riddled with exhaustion, her mind refused to quiet.

She thought about how distraught Donna had been, practically drugging herself into rest.

And, more than anything, she thought about the conversation she'd overheard between Grace and Hudson.

Ever since Shelby went missing, Mary has been trying to downplay Grace's role in all of it, but now it's too complicated for her to ignore.

Grace admitted that she got into a fight with Shelby the night of the Halloween party, the last time she was seen, and now she's having conversations with Hudson, the new kid in town whom Mary knows was romantically linked to Shelby.

When Mary asked Grace about Hudson and Shelby's relationship, her daughter said they weren't together, and yet Mary is certain just last week she knew otherwise. She'd heard the girls talking about the cute new boy in town. She'd seen Shelby walking across the street with Hudson, hand in hand. She'd watched them kiss at the Halloween party. Mary was so confi-

dent of her intel that she even threw the information in Stella
Moore's face, insinuating she might not know her son as well as
she thought she did.

The irony is that, even with all these crucial pieces of information that Mary does know and understand, there's a whole
other collection of mysteries, and her daughter is at the center of
all of them. It never used to be this way. Mary has orchestrated
her entire life with absolute intention, and Shelby's disappearance, for the first time in a long time, has forced her back into
the realm of the unknown. Mary must regain control of this
situation before it wreaks any more havoc.

She rushes to get dressed, wincing when she sees the purple
bags under her eyes and dry patches of skin on her forehead.
Usually, she spends a good hour getting ready before the start of
her day, but now there is no time. The only way to get these
thoughts out of her head is to confront Grace, and she only has
the small drive between their home and Hickory Hills High
School to get that done.

Ken left earlier, which means Grace and Mary are the only
ones in the kitchen. Normally, Mary gets up and prepares some
kind of breakfast, but there's no time this morning, and she's
pleased with her daughter's self-sufficiency when she sees a
bowl of instant oatmeal sitting on the counter.

"You're up late," Grace says to her, drinking the last of her
orange juice.

"I didn't sleep well," Mary says, grabbing the keys and her
wallet, not wasting time with small talk in the kitchen.

"Mom, are you okay?" Grace asks, her eyes locked on her
mother's un-made-up face. "You look different."

"There's a lot going on," she says brusquely, heading in the
direction of the front door.

Mary wants to get Grace in the car as quickly as possible,
find out why she was on the phone late at night with Hudson
Moore.

There's a wall between us.

For now, Mary tries to compartmentalize. There will be time to patch up their damaged relationship later; now she's concerned with protecting her daughter.

As soon as they pull out of the driveway, Mary starts.

"I heard you on the phone last night."

In the passenger seat, Grace jerks her head up, a mix of surprise and annoyance on her face. "What?"

"When I came back from Donna's, you were on the phone with Hudson Moore."

"So?"

"Why are you talking to him? With everything that's going on, boys should be the last thing on your mind."

"We're only friends, Mom. He just moved to the neighborhood. He goes to my school." She looks down at the phone in her lap. "What's the big deal?"

"The big deal is that your best friend is missing!" Mary narrowly avoids running a stop sign. She slams on the brakes and they both lurch forward. "I tried asking you about him before. You said that he wasn't dating Shelby, but I know that's not true. I saw them together, holding hands. Since then, you've admitted to getting in a fight with Shelby, right before she went missing, and now you're talking on the phone with her boyfriend."

"They're not dating," Grace says. "You know how Shelby is with boys. She flirts with everyone. It doesn't mean they all belong to her."

Mary winces at the way that last comment came out. It sounds like Grace is jealous of Shelby, like maybe she wants Hudson for herself.

"Is Hudson the reason you were fighting with Shelby?"

"No!"

"Then tell me what's going on. All of it. Because the more I dig into things, the more it looks to me like you're at the center of all this. Are you and Hudson the reason Shelby ran away?"

"Trust me. Shelby's little escapade has nothing to do with me."

"What does that even mean?" Mary slams on her brakes again, jerking her left blinker on. They're getting closer to the school, and this conversation isn't going anywhere. "It's been more than two days. Aren't you afraid something bad happened to her?"

"Whatever happened to her she brought on herself," Grace says, bending down to grab her backpack. "This whole town is acting as though Shelby is some kind of victim. They're acting like something happened to her. It's only a matter of time until she turns up, and when she does, you'll all see how much you overreacted."

The car is in the drop-off line at the front of the school, but she's half tempted to put the car in reverse and take her daughter back home, lock her in her room until she starts talking. Grace has never been one to speak in riddles, and yet it's as though it's the only language she knows when it comes to this topic. All she wants is for her daughter to be direct, to tell her the truth.

I can't tell her the truth about anything.

"It appears to me that you and Shelby had a fight the night of the party. Maybe about Hudson." She pauses. "I need to know if something happened after that. I need to know if you did something."

Grace moves to face her mother, her back flat against the passenger door. "Are you serious, Mom? I can't believe you'd even ask me that."

"Better I ask you these questions than the police."

Grace flattens her lips together, exhaling through her nose. In one quick movement, she opens the passenger door and climbs out of the car.

"Don't get out," Mary shouts. "You have to wait until we're at the front."

"I'm not listening to this anymore," Grace says, slamming the door.

Mary's vehicle is sandwiched between other cars in the line, and there are still several people ahead of her. She's unable to make an escape, unable to stop her daughter from leaving. All she can do is shout after her: "Grace! Grace!"

But her daughter ignores her, stomping through the grass and landscaping trying to get to the school, leaving her mother behind.

It feels like all the hot air has been let out of the car, and now Mary sits alone, fuming at her utter lack of control over this situation. When she gets to the front of the line, the traffic coordinator in neon green waves for a student to exit the car, but there is no student to let out. Just Mary, frustrated and annoyed.

She pulls the car through, but instead of turning back onto the main road to drive home, she cuts right, finding a space in the guest parking lot. Her thoughts are too jumbled for her to drive. She can't get over this secretive being her daughter has become in the past week, and she can't help thinking Hudson Moore is to blame for all of it.

Boys always have a way of changing the way women think. Grace's hormones might make her think she's ready for mature relationships, but emotionally, she isn't. That's why so many young girls find themselves in troubling situations at this age. It could be the very reason Shelby Bledsoe decided to take off. Mary always hoped Grace would wait a little bit longer to start dating, give her body and mind more time to mature. She doesn't yet understand how one quick move, one hard choice, can snowball into something much worse, take over your entire life.

What would Ken think if he knew his teenage daughter was caught up in the love triangle that inspired Shelby Bledsoe to run away? Worse, what if Shelby returns and tells everyone that the reason she left is because she felt betrayed by her best friend and her boyfriend? Mary raised Grace to be above such behaviors. Now, she fears, when Shelby comes back it could tarnish Grace's reputation in their tight-knit community. It would be embarrassing for her, too. And Ken. He's sacrificed so much to give them the life they have. Mary simply refuses to let such childish behavior ruin the life they've worked so hard to build.

Grabbing her purse, she weaves in and out of the groups of students on their way to class, following them inside the building. She keeps her head down, hoping none of the adults will recognize her and try to strike up a conversation. She does this until she reaches Ken's office.

He's sitting behind his desk, scrolling on his computer, when Mary bursts through the door.

"Well, this is a pleasant surprise," he says.

"I'm worried about Grace." She plops down into a chair across from his desk, desperate to avoid pleasantries and get down to business. "I'm afraid she's getting wrapped up in this whole Shelby mess."

Ken pushes back, rolling his chair away from his desk. "What do you mean?"

Mary's breath quickens, her heart racing like she's in a marathon with herself. "I overheard her on the phone last night with Hudson Moore. The new kid in town?"

"Yes, I've seen him around school. I talked to his mother at the Halloween party."

"Hudson was dating Shelby," she says, pausing for added emphasis, "and now he's talking with Grace."

"Have you asked her what they're talking about?"

Ken appears inquisitive, but not overly concerned. Men never have any urgency when it comes to these sorts of things. Can't possibly imagine their darling little girls growing up to do something distasteful.

"Of course I have, but she's keeping quiet." She clenches her fists in frustration. "You know how young girls are when it comes to boys. They can't think straight. I'm afraid Grace and Shelby might have gotten into some fight over Hudson, and that's why Shelby ran away."

"You don't look well, Mary." He reaches his hand across the table, although there's too much distance for them to touch. "You've been with Donna around the clock, and I think it's taking a toll on you."

Mary remains focused. "I want you to do some digging. Look into why Hudson left his last school."

"I really shouldn't abuse my power—"

"This is about our daughter! If Hudson Moore is involved with Shelby's disappearance, the last thing we need is him pulling Grace into the middle of it."

Ken gets to his feet, walking around the desk to stand behind Mary. He wraps his arms around her, calming her into submission. She rarely raises her voice, especially in public. The outburst must finally make him understand how desperate she is, how worried. He bends down and kisses the top of her head. "I'll look into it. I promise. Now, please go home and rest."

Even though her body and mind need it, Mary knows that won't happen. Right now, all that matters is finding someone else to blame for Shelby Bledsoe's disappearance.

SEVENTEEN

STELLA

After my confrontation with Beau, I locked myself in the bedroom for the rest of the night.

Hudson was already upstairs by the time I got home. In the kitchen, I saw he'd reheated some leftover spaghetti from earlier in the week. Knowing he was safe and fed was all I needed to avoid him the rest of the night. It wasn't purely for selfish reasons. I didn't want him to see me cry.

This practice of hiding my emotions from Hudson is well rehearsed. When Beau and I were together, it was an everyday ritual. As our marriage became more toxic, I made it my mission for Hudson to never see us argue, to never let him know about the heartache I was living with every day.

My relationship with Beau wasn't always cruel. The darker aspects of our marriage developed subtly. First, with complaints about certain bathing suits I'd bought. Comments like, "That's not the type of thing a man wants his wife to wear."

I remember laughing when I first heard him say that. Surely, he was joking. My Beau never criticized what I was wearing, never discussed women in terms of what was allowable and what was not. The stern look on his face told me he was serious, and that small phrase stayed with me a long time, repeated in my head whenever I got dressed for work, or ready to go meet friends.

What few friends I had, that is. That was the second phase. He started being critical of the friends I'd had my entire life, impeding my ability to make additional ones. Not long after we'd married, and I followed him six hours away from our hometown for his first job with a police department, I got a job at a pizza place. After a few shifts, some of the people there invited us out for drinks. He agreed without pressing, and just like now, I was overcome with the newness of possibilities.

A marriage, a home, a job, and hopefully, friends.

But when we joined them at the restaurant, he sat across from my co-workers staring them down. When they tried to ask questions, he gave brief answers, and certainly wasn't striking up any conversations on his own. He just sat there with a disinterested, dare I say disgusted, pout. Even now, I think it was the most miserable I'd seen a person in public. Ever. It would have been better if he hadn't come, but it's almost like he wanted to ruin that outing for me, wanted to stop me from building relationships outside of the one that already consumed my life.

When we returned to our apartment that night, he made comments about how my co-workers were "losers" with "no potential."

Needless to say, they didn't invite me out again.

And yet, all those were small incidents, nothing but little spats. At least, that's what I thought when they were happening. Looking back, I know they were the tremors before the earthquake. The events that pushed me away from him, that gave me glimpses into his true nature.

What came after was much, much worse.

I squint my eyes closed, pushing away the memories. There isn't a place for them here. I was supposed to leave them back in our old house, but they've followed me, like demented spirits that won't rest.

Thankfully, most of our arguments happened at night, after he'd started drinking and long after Hudson went to bed. It's difficult to recall all the mornings I'd wake up after only a couple hours of sleep, my eyes still swollen from the tears, and I'd soldier through preparing breakfast as though nothing had happened. I did that for our son.

Last night, when I locked myself in my bedroom and spent hours crying into my pillow, I did that for him, too. Protecting his emotional well-being has always been my priority, far more important than guarding my own, but now I wonder if I didn't do him a disservice. He never knew the extent of his father's cruelty because I shielded it from him, which makes it difficult for him to understand why I'm adamant about starting over now.

It might be why he felt he couldn't tell me Beau moved right down the street.

At least now, we have a few moments before both our days start when I can talk to him. I wait until we've both fastened our seat belts before I start the conversation.

"Why didn't you tell me your dad had moved to the neighborhood?"

Hudson jerks his eyes away from his phone, staring at me. "I thought he'd tell you."

"He did. Sort of," I say, looking ahead at the closed garage door in front of my car. "I wish I could have heard it from you."

"I didn't know he was moving here. I mean, when we talked, he'd talk about selling the old house, but he never mentioned moving to Hickory Hills."

"You've been talking to him on the phone?"

He lowers his head, sinking into himself. "Yeah."

I didn't know that. Or perhaps, I didn't want to know. Again, Hudson only sees the abbreviated, skewed versions that come from both of us. It's natural for him to still want a relationship with his father, especially when he's unclear what drove us apart in the first place.

"So, how did you find out?"

"He texted me one day last week and asked if I wanted to see his new house. When I said sure, I figured he'd send me a picture or something. He told me to look outside, and he was standing in the driveway."

"Where was I?"

"At the store, I think. You were getting stuff ready for the Halloween party."

Knowing Beau, he probably waited for the exact moment I left to coax our son out of the house.

"You had no idea?"

"No. He got a job here and everything. We walked down the street, and he showed me the place. It's nice. A little smaller than ours. There's a second bedroom for my stuff."

"I think all your stuff fits in our house just fine." The bitter words slip out of my mouth before I can stop them. "Sorry."

"It's not like I plan on living with him," Hudson says, turning his attention back to his phone. I wonder, is he really this bored with the conversation? Or is the device a defense mechanism for him? "Maybe things will be different with you living in separate houses, even if it is just down the street."

And yet distance is exactly what I wanted, at least until Hudson graduated. Once he decided on a college, I could move even further away, finally be rid of Beau altogether.

As we drive past Beau's house, I realize, with a shudder, that dream is becoming more and more unbelievable.

"I also want to talk about Shelby," I say, forcing a redirect in the conversation. Hudson seems to tense up in his seat.

"What about her?"

"You know I visited the surrounding neighborhoods with the other women yesterday," I say.

"Did you find anything?" His eyes raise for only a half-second, watching my reaction.

"No, but someone brought up your relationship with Shelby again," I say. "They seem convinced you two were together."

"I already told you. It wasn't that serious."

"Maybe that's your perception, Hudson. But if Shelby were around, what would she say? What would other people think? If there's more to your relationship than you're telling me, you need to speak up."

"We were talking for a while," he says after a pause.

"Talking?"

"You know, like when you're starting to date someone but not actually dating."

"Okay." The idiosyncrasies of teenage romance seem a lifetime ago. "Were you two *talking* or dating the night of the Halloween party."

"I thought we were," he says. "Whatever we had going on ended that night."

My stomach drops. It's not good that their relationship, if you can even call it that, came to an end the same night she went missing. "What happened the night of the party?"

"We just decided to end things."

"And you can't tell me a reason."

Silence fills the car. When I glance over, Hudson isn't even looking at his phone. He's staring straight ahead at the road. Thinking.

"She wasn't who I thought she was," he says at last. "I'm sorry she's missing, but I have no idea about any of that."

"I'm afraid other people won't see it that way," I say. "The other women are already talking about you guys dating. If she doesn't turn up, the police will get more involved. They might start asking you questions."

"That's fine," he says. "I'll answer them."

"What about your face?" I ask. "You got that bruise the night of the Halloween party. Don't you think that looks suspicious?"

"I don't want to talk about that."

I tighten my grip around the steering wheel. We're getting closer to the school, and he's being just as deceptive as he was the night after the party.

"You need to think about how everything looks. People say you were dating her. You broke up the night of the party. The next morning, Shelby was reported missing, and you have a black eye. It doesn't look good, Hudson," I say. "If they connect all this to what happened at your last school—"

"Are you ever going to let me live that down?" He cuts me off, turning to face me directly. "It sounds like *you're* the only person accusing me of anything. You're supposed to be on my side."

"I am!" I shout, struggling to control my voice. "That's why I'm trying to talk to you now. Get your story straight. If our neighbors say—"

"Why is it as soon as we move here all you care about is what other people think?"

That question stops me, and I stammer for a response. "I don't care what people think. I'm only trying to defend you."

"Then just believe me when I tell you I didn't do anything," he says. "And don't bring up what happened at the last school again."

We've reached the section of the drop-off line where he has to get out. He didn't jump out early this time, but the tone of our conversation is just as contentious, maybe even more so.

"You have to talk to me, Hudson," I say. "I'm the only person that can help you."

"That's not true. Dad's here now, remember?"

Quickly, he opens the car door and exits, leaving me wounded by his words.

Beau has infiltrated our lives, which is a whole other mine-field I have to manage. But right now I can't worry about him. I must reserve all my thoughts and energy for Hudson. No matter what he says, he's coming off as a prime suspect in the Shelby Bledsoe disappearance. If I can see that, it's only a matter of time before other people put it together, too.

And I still don't believe everything he's telling me.

EIGHTEEN

MARY

Mary slams the door, leaning against the frame, eyes scrunched tight, trying to catch her breath.

She's having a panic attack, or something like it. She's never really had one before, but this is what she imagines it's like. Heart racing. Sweat sprouting all over her body, building along her hairline. It feels like she's locked on a rollercoaster, at the precipice of falling, and there's nothing she can do to stop it. Unlike an actual coaster, there's no promised safety, nothing strapping her in. The sensation of impending doom is unavoidable. Her conversations with Ken and Grace did nothing to stop it.

When she opens her eyes, the sight of her festive entryway enrages her. She's tempted to rush through the house, breaking the jolly nutcrackers one by one. But she doesn't do that. Of course she won't. The worst thing she can do in a state of panic is react. She must regain control, come up with a plan. That's the only way to get herself—Grace—out of this mess.

Darting her eyes to the left, she catches sight of the refrigerator, and a brilliant idea hits her. Wine.

Mary never drinks this early in the day. That's a vice she

leaves for Janet and the other desperate housewives in their neighborhood, but she believes given her situation, just this once, it might be the answer to her problems.

As she pours, several wasted splashes end up on the counter, but she doesn't care. What's left in the glass, she gulps furiously, waiting impatiently for the liquid to calm her, cure her. Just as quickly, she pours a second glass, and by the time she finishes that, a glorious numbness has spread throughout her body, warming her limbs and slowing her heartbeat.

Think, she tells herself. You must be smart.

Waiting is the hardest part. She hopes Ken will find something on Hudson Moore; seeing as he was Shelby's boyfriend, he's the most likely suspect anyway. Even if he did something to harm her, the fact he's been talking to Grace, Shelby's best friend, poses a threat. Still, having her daughter pinned as the motive for a crime is better than having her called a suspect. Scandal may present tough waters, but nothing that can't be navigated, and Mary considers herself a skilled sailor.

Alone in the kitchen, she laughs. Her thoughts are getting a little loose, thanks to the wine, and yet she's already able to think more clearly than she was five minutes ago. She's at least able to see a way out.

Carrying the wine bottle and empty glass, she goes into the living room and sits. Her phone is on silent mode, and she plans to keep it that way until Grace gets out of school. Lord knows, she's devoted enough time to Donna over the past few days, and right now, she needs this time to herself. She won't feel guilty about it.

She turns on the television, the screen displaying the same channel from yesterday. There's another animal documentary, this time about bears. They've never fascinated her as much as the jungle cats. Their build isn't as lithe and sleek, but they're equally ferocious predators. Mindlessly, she follows along with the episode, and again, she begins to laugh. Isn't it bizarre that even now, after almost twenty years in suburbia, there's something about the natural world that gets her heart racing? In a good way, not like before. Watching these animals comforts Mary, in the same morbid way some of her other friends will fall asleep to true crime documentaries.

For the second time this week, she thinks back to what her life was like before all this. Before Shelby Bledsoe went missing and she started to question everything around her. Then her mind drifts further, to before she was a mother, before she was a wife, before she met Ken.

She closes her eyes, the wine in her system lulling her to sleep while visions of sororities and safaris dance in her head, two experiences that never got to be hers. And yet, just the idea they might happen had been enough for her then; when you're young, you can get by with so little. Then, her visions change, those same scenarios, but this time it's Grace she imagines. Pledging a sorority. Traveling the world. Falling in love with a boy who will love and respect her.

She jolts awake, having only nodded off for a few minutes. The empty wineglass is still clutched in her hands. The television again grabs her attention, the announcer describing how bears prepare for hibernation. Perhaps this is why she likes animals, she thinks. They're far easier to understand than humans. Every action is clear and justified. Gathering food, protecting their young.

Claiming their territory.

Her mind drifts again to the conversation she overheard last night. Mary understands the desires of young girls, no matter how much her daughter tries to protest. Grace is smitten with Hudson Moore, and she fears that if she claimed him as her territory, Shelby was in the way.

Thinking now only fans the flames of her returning panic. She stands quickly, needing some kind of action to distract her as she waits for Ken to call. In an instant, she has returned the wine to the kitchen, and is climbing the stairs to the second story. Her daughter's closed bedroom door beckons her. As surprising as it may seem, Mary has never snooped in her daughter's room before. There have always been enough ways to keep tabs on her that she never felt she needed to cross this boundary.

But now, what option does she have?

Grace is hiding something from her, that much she's sure of, and she's not going to move past this situation until she knows how big a secret it is. She hopes it's only a schoolgirl crush, and nothing worse. Nothing violent. A quick flash of wild animals protecting their territory flashes through her mind, then she pushes through the door.

For a teenager, the room is actually quite neat. Her bed is made, a lone stuffed animal that's survived from childhood sits at the center of the bed. Mary starts in all the obvious places, opening dresser drawers and rummaging through the neatly folded clothes inside. Each time she moves onto another area of the room, her heart leaps with joy. Maybe there's nothing to find here. Maybe the only secrets are held within her daughter's heart, and, in time, if she works toward breaking down that damned wall, she can find them out.

Mary lifts the mattress, finds nothing. She checks inside pillowcases before falling to her knees, looking under the bed. There's far more clutter here, but nothing suspicious. Nothing related to Hudson Moore or Shelby Bledsoe. Nothing at all to make Mary think her daughter might be hiding something.

Finally, she moves to the closet. Everything is neatly organized, from the clothes on the rod to the shoes on the rack. Maybe some of Mary's better qualities are rubbing off on her daughter after all. Her suitcases are stacked neatly on the floor, and when she goes to move them, she hears something shifting inside the smallest one.

In that instant, Mary's stomach sinks. Already, she seems to know that she's found what she's looking for, a discovery she'd hoped never existed at all. She unzips the suitcase. Inside is a wad of clothes. They're not folded neatly, like all the others in her room, and there's a stench that reminds her of the laundry hamper.

She unravels the bundle, inspecting each item closely. Some dirty uniforms from last season's volleyball team. Some more workout clothes, that look either too small or misshapen from overuse.

And then she sees the angel costume.

Holding it in front of her, she remembers Grace wearing it only a few nights ago. The white fabric, the short hem.

The only difference is that there's now a rust-colored stain covering the front of the dress. Mary stares at the stain in horror. She brings the fabric to her face, inhales that unmistakable metal scent.

Her daughter's Halloween costume, the outfit she wore the night Shelby Bledsoe disappeared, is covered in blood.

NINETEEN

STELLA

One of the benefits to having moved recently is that it doesn't take me long to search through Hudson's things. My attempts to talk with him directly have been ignored, so I have no other choice.

Most of his belongings are still in boxes, despite me having asked him repeatedly to unpack. His clothes are sorted in drawers and his closet, but all his other stuff, personal mementoes and keepsakes, are still loaded up. I wonder if this isn't some kind of silent rebellion. If he doesn't unpack, he won't have to accept that we live here now.

Going through with the move was the hardest part. I should have left Beau a long time ago, but that's always easier said than done. Ending a toxic relationship isn't just about escaping the bad parts; there's plenty of good elements being left behind, too.

Beau wasn't always bad.

Before we were married, I thought he was perfect for me. And even in those early years, he did things to make me smile, uplift me and reassure me that the life we'd built was the right one.

When the bad behavior started, it snowballed until it was its own beast. His controlling nature wasn't alarming at first, more like little glimpses into what he would become, but of course I didn't see it that way then.

I think the tide started to turn after I first called him out, decided to be vocal instead of ignoring how he acted. We'd been married a few years at this point, and I'd learned to ignore his sharp comments, his dominating jealousy. I told myself they were proof of how much I meant to him.

We had a shared computer. I was logging into my email when I saw that his was still up, and there was an unread message on the screen. I made the mistake of clicking on it and unearthed an entire conversation he'd been having with another woman. The messages went back months. It was a flirtatious exchange. Nothing had happened between them yet, but they were making plans on meeting in person.

Hudson might characterize it as *talking*.

It was a huge betrayal, especially considering the context of our marriage at that point. We'd married young, and I'd left our hometown, all my friends and family, to follow him, to build this life together. He made comments about my clothes, comments about the people I worked with, and the way men looked at me in public, as though I was forever tied to him. And yet he was speaking so casually with a random girl?

When I confronted him about it, we had our first big fight. He screamed at me for invading his privacy, blowing things out of proportion. Shamefully, I let him break me down in that argument, a pattern that would continue for years to come. I reasoned with myself that it was only a conversation with a girl from miles away. It was only talking. Nothing had happened, and he'd promised me, afterwards, that nothing ever would.

I believed him.

But it was only a few months later I found pictures from a night out. Beau and several of his police department friends at a club, women all over them. All of the guys were young, and only about half of them were married, so when I confronted him about those, and another argument ensued, he insisted it was harmless fun. And yet I could only imagine his reaction if I'd partaken in that kind of fun.

The worst was when we were confronted by a woman in public.

It had been an enjoyable day up till that point. The two of us had taken our bikes and gone riding in the park. A girl came up to him, called him by name. He reacted to her immediately, smiling big. He didn't shy away when she initiated a hug. I waited for him to introduce me, but they carried on a conversation like I didn't even exist.

I stood there, stunned and silent, until she walked away.

"Who was that?" I finally got the nerve to ask him.

He ignored me, walking his bike in the direction of our car. I struggled to keep up, wondering not only what had just happened, but why he seemed so angry with me. When we got to our car, he jerked my bike out of my hands and loaded it up. Why were we suddenly leaving?

"Beau, will you tell me what's wrong?"

"I know what you're doing!" he shouted. "Some girl talks to me, and I'll never hear the end of it."

"I only asked who she was," I said. "I don't understand why you didn't introduce me."

"See, you're already doing it! Starting a fight!"

His voice was loud, capturing the attention of everyone around us. I can still remember the looks other people in the parking lot gave me. Some were annoyed, nosy and wondering what I'd done wrong. Another woman making a mistake. Some looked at me with pity.

It was such a confusing moment, and one that seemed to underline a pattern. Beau talking to girls behind my back, making plans to meet. Beau partying with girls and taking pictures. Beau having relationships with other women who clearly had no idea who I was, or about our marriage.

The realization that Beau was not the husband I thought he was started to set in. Those worries and fears stayed with me, making a home inside my chest. I started to envision a different life for myself, one with a person who loved and respected me, didn't feel the need to lie to me.

And then I found out I was pregnant with Hudson.

The past sixteen years have flown by quickly, and so much has come and gone in that time.

Now, I sit on my son's messy bed, convinced he's hiding something from me, and yet I've searched his entire room and have not been able to find it. I've tried my best to be a positive influence in Hudson's life, but I worry it's not enough to counteract his father's more aggressive traits. Could he be as manipulative and deceptive as Beau? Could he be as violent?

My phone rings, providing a welcome distraction. The name on the screen reads Annette Friss.

"Stella, sorry to call," she says when I answer the phone.

"No bother at all," I say, curious if there have been any developments with Shelby's disappearance.

"I was wanting to get ahold of Hudson, actually, but I know he's at school," she says. "Zane was supposed to oversee the gardens this week but he's out with the flu, and I was wondering if Hudson could pick up a shift this afternoon. The plants won't make it to the weekend without some water."

"I can tell him when he gets home," I say. "Even though I'm sure Hudson was there earlier this week."

"Really?" Annette sounds surprised. "Zane's mother called me in a tizzy, apologizing because no one had been all week. Maybe she was confused?"

"Maybe." A strange feeling settles in my stomach.

"Either way, it would have been nice to have the head's up sooner. No one can help getting sick, but I could have at least put a plan in place. Kids these days have no work ethic," Annette says. "And all the parents do is coddle them."

"I'll make sure he goes there after school," I say. "Go ahead and send me his schedule for the week. I'll post it on the refrigerator, so he won't forget."

"I knew you were good people," Annette says, pleased, and ends the conversation.

Still sitting on Hudson's bed, I try to recall everything that's happened in the past week. I'm certain Hudson said he went by the community gardens, but according to Annette, that's not true. Why would Hudson lie about that?

On top of everything else I worry he's lying about.

The thought comes to me, maybe he was honest about going to the gardens. Perhaps he went there for a reason other than work. There's nothing in his room tying him to Shelby's disappearance; maybe there's something there. It's the only other place—other than his father's house, I think with a wince—where he could conceal something.

Five minutes later, I'm making my way along the cement path that snakes through the neighborhood, leading to the community garden. I can only imagine how beautiful it must be in the spring, when the flowers and plants are in full bloom, but right now everything is holding onto the last remnants of life, desperate for sun. The grass is just long enough to stand one more mow before winter arrives.

Down a small embankment rests a man-made pond, a small walking bridge stretching from one side to the other. Green and purple monkey grass line the perimeter, and again, I consider what a beauty it must be in the spring. Ever since we moved in, Annette has talked about how much time and effort she gives to this place but she has to rely on younger members of the community to keep it in shape.

Back to the left, hidden in the dying shade of several trees, is a small equipment shed. This is where Hudson and Zane store their maintenance supplies. Staring at it now, it suddenly seems ominous. Could Hudson's secrets be hiding within?

I pull back the metal door but see only wooden shelves filled with tools and gardening material. I sift through the items, searching for anything that seems out of place, something Hudson might have come here to hide. Ten minutes pass without finding anything before my conscience sets in. What am I doing? Am I so paranoid my son is hiding something from me that I've gone this far out of my way to find it?

Quickly, I close the shed, wiping my grimy hands on my shirt. I should be happy I haven't found anything. Maybe Hudson is telling me the truth after all.

As I walk back up the hill leading to the neighborhood, I look across at the small pond once more. Sunlight falls across the surface, turning the dark waters green and translucent. That's when I see it. A dark mass just below the water. It makes me pause, staring at the strange discoloration, my mind struggling to figure out what it might be.

A twisted feeling of uncertainty takes over me, and I run back to the shed, retrieving a rake. I cast out the stick as far as I can without falling in, trying to untangle whatever is below the waters. It only takes a few swipes to dislodge what's stuck. A large mass rises to the surface, a sickly gray color. Long tangled hair fanning out across the water's surface.

My entire body seizes with horror. I jump back, tripping over the rake, landing hard on the damp soil beside the water. Then I'm running, away from the gardens, away from the pond, toward anyone, screaming for help.

I've just found Shelby Bledsoe.

TWENTY

JANET

Halloween Night

Janet Parks started planning her Halloween costume months ago. The concept was traditional enough—Barbie—but she wanted her version to stand out. She'd scoured the internet for the perfect dress. Hot pink, sequined, strapless. A coordinating purse, shaped like a tube of lipstick, dangled from her wrist. Her hair and makeup were expertly styled, a routine put in place after watching countless YouTube tutorials.

She was in the bathroom, having escaped the party for a quick break, admiring her appearance in the mirror.

Someone knocked on the outside of the door. "Janet?"

She opened the door wide, hoping her husband, Julian, might compliment her outfit. He hadn't earlier when she first emerged from the bedroom.

"Your friends were asking for you," he said, without as much as raising his head.

"Was it Mary?" Janet asked quickly. "Does she need help with something?"

"I don't know," he said. "They said something about pictures."

"Oh." She readjusted the strap of her platform heel and walked past him, into the kitchen. "We have all night for that."

Hands in his pockets, Julian followed her into the kitchen. He only looked at her when he saw her stretching to reach the cupboard above the fridge. "What are you doing?"

"I told the girls we'd share some champagne. It's one of the bottles we got last summer, remember?"

"There's an open bar in the middle of the cul-de-sac," he said. "Why do you need to bring your own?"

"I wanted to bring something high-end," she said. Janet loved to name-drop labels and brands. She was in her materialistic era and was okay with that. Julian made a hefty salary, enough to support her entirely, and she liked flashing his generosity in her friends' faces.

"Just take it easy tonight, okay?"

Janet turned around slowly, the bottle meeting the granite countertop with a clack. "It's a holiday."

"I know," he said, "but we've talked about this. You need to slow down a little."

Janet hated these conversations. She hated that look on his face when he tried to tell her what to do. *Slow down. Take it easy.* Like she was some pet he had to control. Sure, he was the sole provider, but she contributed in other ways. She didn't need him telling her what to do.

"The doctor said abstaining from alcohol could help with fertility, remember?"

"Are we really going to do this right now?"

She grabbed the neck of the bottle with one hand and tried to walk past him, but he grabbed her forearm gently. "Janet, please. I want you to have fun but please control yourself."

Janet snatched her arm away. "I'm always in control."

Outside, the October air was clean and crisp. She breathed

it in. She was tired of having the same conversation with Julian over and over again. He wanted a baby, had been wanting a baby, but she wasn't ready. Every time he saw a drink in her hand, he'd bring up how drinking less alcohol could improve their chances of conceiving. Little did he know, Janet was sneaking her birth control pills every morning, and more alcohol when he was away from her just to drown out the sound of his voice inside her head.

Janet walked past several houses on her way to the cul-de-sac. Each home was decorated in its own spooky way. Children ran through the streets, treat bags in hand. The high-pitched squeals made her want to scream. Sure, some of the costumes were cute, but she wasn't ready to be one of the frumpy mothers following their sugar-high children from house to house. She wanted it to be about her a little bit longer.

"There she is," Naomi said when she approached. She was talking to their newest neighbor. Stella something. "I told you, Janet's costumes always hit it out of the park."

Stella turned to look at her, eyeing Janet's costume from her toes to the tops of her teased hair. "You look fabulous."

"Thanks. So do you," she said, even though she thought Stella's costume was as boring as they come. It was important for Janet to be the fashionable one in the group. The one with the best body and the richest husband.

"All right, ladies," Mary said, walking over with a phone in hand. "Let's gather for pictures."

"Just a sec." Janet shuffled in her heels to the bar, ordering a quick shot. She wanted to down it before Julian caught up to her. When he did arrive at the booth, he wrapped his arms around her sequined waist, delighting in the presence of his beautiful wife. They were always careful not to air their dirty laundry in public.

As the night raged on, there were more drinks and photos and drinks and dancing and drinks. Janet's head was spinning, but in the good way she loved. It was like she was able to control the ride she was on within her own body, and she liked having that power.

Besides, it wasn't as if she was the only person that was drunk. Most of the women were at least tipsy. Donna Bledsoe had spent half the night with some stranger in a monster mask, and Stella's voice was getting louder with each conversation she started with a different neighbor.

"Do me a favor, babe," Janet said, her sticky lips pressed close to her husband's cheek. "Run back to the house and get my smokes."

"You're out," he said.

"No, I'm not. I had some this morning. Come on, you know I only smoke when I drink."

"You always drink." His voice was low, so those around them couldn't hear, and he locked eyes with her. "I threw them out. You don't need them if we're trying to get pregnant."

Janet pulled away from him. "Are you serious?"

"Yes. You're having enough fun. Just try to learn your limits."

Janet looked around the cul-de-sac. Everyone was busy in their own conversations, their own worlds. They didn't notice her rising rage.

"I don't need you deciding what's bad for me." She stomped off in the direction of the house, determined to find the cigarettes herself. Julian must have been talking a big game, nothing more. She couldn't imagine he'd throw away her things.

And yet, when she opened the desk drawer and saw they were gone, her blood boiled. She marched into the kitchen, grabbing her car keys from the hook by the front door. If he thought he could stop her from getting her way, he was wrong. She'd simply have to buy them herself.

She pulled out of the driveway quickly before Julian or any of the other neighbors spotted her. Once on the street, it was an annoying stop-and-go of traffic, cars idling in the road to let out trick or treaters. Janet avoided eye contact when she drove past Annette Friss and her baked goods stand. She looked away again when she passed Grace Holden and Shelby Bledsoe; the last thing she needed was for them to tell their moms they'd spotted her behind the wheel.

Once she was out of the neighborhood, it was only a few minutes' drive to make it to a gas station. She bought a pack of cigarettes and a lighter. On the way out, one of her platform heels caught the edge of the door, and she stumbled.

The cashier asked if she was okay, and she flipped him off. She couldn't stand the way men leered at her. She sped on the way back to the neighborhood, exhaling cigarette smoke out the window, hoping she could make it to her garage before Julian and any of the others saw she had left.

She'd won this battle, she thought, but there were still several more to be had. He wasn't going to let the baby thing go lightly. At some point she'd have to tell him she wasn't ready, that she didn't know if she'd ever be ready. She wasn't sure if she was one of those women who was cut out to be a mother—

Something hard hit the front bumper, and Janet's car came to a screeching halt.

TWENTY-ONE

MARY

Mary ignores the first and second knocks at the door.

She's too overcome with emotion to even consider talking to another person. The moment she found that ruined Halloween costume—a bloodied angel, of all things—something inside of her broke, a part of her she didn't even know existed. Somewhere between her mind and her heart, whatever part of her being that housed the unavoidable questions we never want to fully address, the unspoken fears we want to keep locked away, had shattered into a million pieces when she found the stained fabric.

Donna must have been right all along, her own mother's instinct letting her in on the truth: Shelby never ran away. Grace must have done something awful to Shelby. Maybe she was the one who sent the text message, hoping to stall an investigation from starting up? She doesn't want it to be true, but she can't ignore the evidence in her very hands, now defiled a second time with Mary's very own tears.

When the third knock comes, Mary stands abruptly, as though she's been yanked out of one realm and transferred to the next. She marches angrily toward the kitchen, throwing

Grace's costume into a drawer, then swings open the front door.

Janet is standing on the porch, facing the road. When she turns, Mary sees her eyes are red from crying.

"You already know?" Janet asks, looking a bit star-struck.

"Know what?" Mary asks, her curiosity bursting.

"They found her," Janet manages to say, before her voice breaks. Several sobs follow, before she adds, for clarity, "Shelby is dead."

Mary's hand flies to her chest, as though the touch could somehow calm the fierce aching inside. Her knees grow weak, and she leans against the sturdy doorframe. She's overcome with the possibility she might pass out. There's only so much a person can take in one day.

"Are you sure?"

"Stella Moore found her in the community gardens," she says, looking behind her before facing Mary again. "She was in the pond."

The community gardens are the next street over, so it is impossible to see from here. All Mary can do is imagine, which is horrible enough. The police cars. Emergency vehicles. Neighbors standing around like vultures, feeding off the dead. Maybe even news crews, eventually.

"Where's Donna?" she asks.

"At home. Naomi is with her." Janet looks up, her large eyes pooling with tears. "We thought you might know what to do."

In any other situation, Mary would take their neediness as a compliment, but now? She doesn't know what she could do, what she should say. She's never experienced anything like this in her life; none of the trials and tribulations she's endured even compare to this.

The costume. Its existence confirmed some kind of violence befell Shelby, and now the rest of the neighborhood knows, too. She tightens her grip on the door.

"I'll be there right away."

Mary returns inside and takes a deep breath. She catches a glimpse of her reflection in the mirror. Her eyes are almost swollen shut from the crying. No wonder Janet had seemed concerned when she opened the door.

You already know?

Will she find it odd that her usually stoic friend was already an emotional wreck before learning about the discovery of Shelby's body? Every reaction, no matter how small, will now be scrutinized—at least in Mary's mind, if not in everyone else's.

Mary turns slowly, her eyes landing on the drawer where she's deposited Grace's stained Halloween costume. Shelby is dead. Not missing, not hurt. The worst has happened, and all that Mary knows for sure is that Grace and Shelby got into a fight on Halloween night.

She looks at herself a second time, raising two fingers to smooth the delicate skin beneath her eyes. Unfastening the claw clip in her hair, she shakes her head from side to side. She must be presentable. She must be careful. Now, if it looks like she's been crying, no one will think twice. It's a natural reaction.

She hurries upstairs, changing into different clothes, for no other reason than to give her mind and body more time to process. She must clear Grace and the bloody costume from her thoughts. Right now, she needs to focus on Donna, and gleaning as much information as she can about the crime.

Mary has been inside Donna's house hundreds of times over the years for holiday parties and lazy Sunday afternoons and weekday lunches. Yet, when she enters her friend's familiar living room, everything feels different. The life source is gone, she realizes. All children, especially someone as flamboyant as Shelby, usher in a certain level of liveliness, and having confirmation she'll never be here again, even though they've all had their suspicions for several days, makes her realize how quickly the color inside the home has been sucked away.

She drifts to the back of the house. Everyone is gathered in the sunroom, afternoon sunlight streaming in through the clear glass panes. Donna Bledsoe is in the center of the room, on her knees. The sounds coming out of her mouth are like nothing Mary has ever heard before. A spine-tingling howl. Every ounce of pain inside being projected through her screams.

Naomi and Janet are on either side of her, both rubbing her back, trying to exorcize Donna's pain to no avail. The movement reminds her of when Grace was a baby, and she'd rub her pudgy body to help soothe her after feeding.

When the women look up and see Mary has arrived, they freeze, waiting for their leader to give them the next order. And yet, Mary has no idea what to do, how to handle a situation like this. The thoughts that have been consuming her about Grace, all the plotting and scheming, wipe away, and Mary is overcome with grief and heartache for her friend.

"Donna." Mary's voice doesn't sound like her own, but she must say something to fill this dreadful silence. "I'm so sorry."

What else is there to say? A mother is never supposed to outlive her child. It disrupts the natural order of things. Shelby was all Donna had, the only thing that kept her life on a somewhat good track. Now she's gone, and no condolences can remedy that.

Donna rises unsteadily, like an animal learning to walk. This horrible situation has, in many ways, made her reborn. She'll never be the same again. Her hands reach out for Mary, and when they find her, Donna's full weight collapses into her, almost sending Mary to the ground.

"Why did this happen?" she cries. "I don't understand."

"I don't know," Mary says, weakly. Janet and Naomi stand frozen, afraid to move, watching the scene unfold.

"All I can think about was the last thing I said to her," Donna says. "If I'd been a better mother, this wouldn't have happened."

"That's not true," she says.

"Shelby was lucky to have you," Naomi chimes in.

"You are a wonderful mother," Janet adds.

It runs through Mary's mind, through all their minds, probably, that the statement might be inaccurate. They've already discussed how Donna's faults might have impacted Shelby, but no one wants to blame her. Especially now. Donna wasn't a perfect mother because she was a flawed human being, like them all. For the rest of her days, however, she'll return to this moment. She'll question whether she did enough. If she exposed Shelby to something harmful. That damned Halloween party will play in her mind repeatedly, constantly searching for a way to change the past, which it will never find.

Mary can feel a ball of emotion rising from her chest into her throat. She looks up at her friends, for once leaning on them for help. Janet and Naomi are both crying, the former so much, she must excuse herself. Useless, as usual. Leaving all the heavy lifting to Mary alone.

"You need rest," she tells Donna, trying to raise her to her feet.

"Shelby!" she cries. "I need Shelby!"

"Shelby wouldn't want to see you like this," she says. "She loved you."

That, Mary believes with complete certainty. All children love their parents. Even if they're flawed, even if they're downright horrible people. Even if there's an impenetrable wall between them, love is always there.

Donna nods slowly, leaning on Mary as they both stand. With Naomi's help, they usher her into the living room and put her on the sofa. Mary walks across the room and dims the lights.

"Go get a cold rag," she tells Naomi.

Janet meets them in the living room, blowing her nose into a tissue. "Get some water," Mary tells her. "And sleeping pills if you have them."

"There are some at my house," Naomi says, handing the rag to Janet and sprinting outside, likely grateful for an excuse to leave. There's a horrible feeling here in the room, with all the grief and hurt surrounding them, but Donna needs them now. She'll lean on all of them in the days to come.

Janet comes over. She places the water on the coffee table and hands the rag to Mary, who places it on Donna's forehead. She rubs her friend's hand until it stops shaking.

"We're here with you," she says, her voice soft like she's cooing her to sleep.

Naomi returns with the medicine. Donna swallows two pills and, after several minutes, drifts to sleep. Only then do Mary's own emotions take over. She begins to sob, quietly, so as not to wake her sleeping friend.

"That's the most tragic thing I've ever seen," Janet says, under her breath.

Naomi rests in a chair across from them, exhausted. "All I can think about is my girls. I want to hold them tight and never let them go."

"I know," Mary says, still rubbing Donna's hand.

Mary can't bear the thought of something happening to Grace. Can't imagine enduring the pain she's just witnessed.

The bloody costume appears in her mind again, and she almost chokes on her own breath. She hopes, more than anything, that it wasn't her daughter that caused all this pain.

TWENTY-TWO

STELLA

The hours after finding Shelby's body have felt like an eternity. Another neighbor heard my screams. An older man who lives in the house closest to the gardens, whose name I don't even know. He intercepted me as I was running away, shouting hysterically, and called the police.

They arrived promptly, instructing me to stay with their emergency vehicles as they inspected the scene. One of the officers wrapped a blanket around my shoulders to help temper the uncontrollable shakes. She said I was likely experiencing symptoms of shock.

Not surprising, seeing as every few seconds my mind revisits the scene, replays the ghastly image of a lifeless body floating in the water.

It took several minutes for the idea to strike me that perhaps I hadn't found Shelby. After all, I hadn't seen a face. But it had to be Shelby. She's the only missing person in our community, even though it's hard to believe she's been so close this whole time without anyone finding her.

More emergency vehicles arrived, as did more curious neighbors. I spotted Naomi and Janet standing behind the yellow caution tape police had ribboned around the scene. We made eye contact briefly, and it was difficult to determine whether they felt concern or morbid fascination at what was unfolding.

The police questioned me, then. They wanted to know everything about the location, if I'd ever been there before, if anything looked disturbed. They especially wanted to know if I'd touched anything at the scene, other than the rake I'd used in the water. I told them I'd searched all around the shed, unable to focus.

They also wanted to know what brought me to the gardens in the first place. That's the first lie I told, or maybe, more of a half-truth. I certainly wasn't going to admit I went there snooping, that I believe my son could have been hiding something there. Likewise, I couldn't deny Hudson works in the gardens part-time. I simply told them I wanted to see what Hudson had been working on, and that's when I found her.

If Hudson was there earlier in the week, I wonder, why was Shelby's body not discovered sooner? She was hidden in the pond, easily overlooked by anyone passing by. And yet, in the short amount of time I was on the grounds, I noticed something amiss. It's the reason I disturbed her watery grave in the first place. If Hudson had worked an entire shift after school, as he claims, wouldn't he have seen what I'd seen? Wouldn't he have done something?

Perhaps I'm not strong enough to face the answers to those questions.

The memories from this morning play throughout my mind on an endless loop, but even those repeated images don't disturb me as much as what I'm about to do next. Something I promised myself I'd never do again.

I'm going to Beau for help.

When he comes to the door, he's wearing his typical detective wear. Crisp shirt and tailored pants, his badge and service weapon attached at his hip. He looks neither surprised nor annoyed when he sees me standing on his front porch. More satisfied, like he was waiting for this to happen.

"Stella." His voice is matter-of-fact.

"We need to talk," I say, walking into his home uninvited. "About Hudson."

His gaze follows me as I walk into the living room, and I cringe at the thought of him taking me in for too long. I focus, instead, on the furniture. A sofa and a big screen and a glass-top table where he can sit his nightly beer, but there's nothing sentimental in the entire space. I think of the time I spent trying to make our old house look like a home. The carefully selected drapes and throw pillows and blankets. The beautiful family portraits. All the details that made us look like a normal, loving family to outsiders, made us feel welcome at the end of a hard day.

But then, the hardest parts of my days only began once he came home.

"What's wrong with Hudson?" Beau asks. I can feel the heat of him as he steps closer. "Where is he?"

"Still at school. He should get out within the hour." I force myself to look at him, then beyond to the front door. "Haven't you noticed what's been going on this morning?"

"I heard a body was found," he says. "That missing teenager, right?"

"Yes." I sit stiffly on the sofa, wrapping my arms around myself. "I was the one who found her."

He comes to me in an instant, placing his hand on my shoulder. "Stella, I had no idea—"

"Don't," I say, jerking slightly.

His hand falls to his side. He opens his mouth like he's about to say something but stops.

"Word around town was that she ran away," he says.

"They thought that, at first. I guess that's why the police

were barely involved," I say. "Her mother and the other women never seemed convinced."

"Looks like they were right," he says, his gaze not quite meeting mine.

"I thought maybe you'd be working the scene."

"I'm in narcotics. Homicide is a whole other team," he says. "I'm sorry you had to see what you saw. It must have been upsetting."

"I'm fine," I say, my voice cold. It may not be true, but I'm not going to open a window for him to comfort me. "Like I said, I'm worried about Hudson. I'm afraid he could get pulled into this."

Beau sits across from me, leaning forward. "What do you mean?"

"We've only been here a few months, but Hudson was apparently dating the girl who went missing," I say. "Shelby."

It strikes me that, from now on, no one else will discuss Shelby in terms of being missing. They'll talk about her being dead. One crime resolved, swapped out for a more tragic one.

"Okay," Beau says. "Did you know the girl?"

"Barely. It wasn't a serious relationship. Even Hudson said as much, but it worries me. If people in the community think they were together, they're going to start asking questions."

"Don't let the police spook you," he says. "It's normal procedure in an investigation like this. They're going to talk to everyone. Family, friends, boyfriends."

"Hudson told me they broke up on Halloween night," I say, dryly. "That's the night she went missing."

Beau remains silent, waiting for me to continue.

"Shelby's body was in the pond by the community gardens," I say. "Hudson has a part-time job there."

Beau massages his forehead with his palms and exhales. "What are you trying to say?"

"You're a detective. It can't be that hard to figure out.

Hudson was dating the girl who went missing. They broke up. Now, her body is found where he works," I say. "This doesn't look good for him."

"She went missing from a neighborhood party. Everyone in the neighborhood was there, and they have access to those same gardens."

"Right now, Hudson has more connections to the crime than anyone. If I'm piecing all that together, it's only a matter of time before everyone else does, too."

"No one is going to accuse a teenager of murder without proof."

"He had a bruise on his face after the party," I say, not sure why I held back this piece of information but feeling it's important for Beau to have the full picture. I'm not being paranoid or overreacting. Our son could very easily get roped into this, and we need to be prepared.

Beau's eyes get big. "Did he say how he got it?"

"He won't tell me anything about that night. I only recently got him to admit they broke up."

Beau is silent for several seconds. He has that look on his face which means he's thinking about a case. I remember it all too well. It always amazed me how easy it was for him to solve everyone else's problems but our own.

"What do you want me to do?" he asks, at last. "Talk to him?"

"No," I say, firmly. There's nothing Hudson will admit to his father that he wouldn't tell me first. I'm sure of that. "You work for the police force. You could call someone. Figure out what's going on with the investigation. There could be a whole other lead they're following we know nothing about. Maybe there's no need to worry."

Beau nods. "I can do that." I sit still, waiting. "You want me to do it now?"

"Please."

When Hudson comes home from school, I'll have to tell him about Shelby, if the flurry of social media and gossip hasn't already reached him by now. I don't think I can face that conversation or anything else until I know more about what's happening.

Beau stands and walks over to the sliding glass door. "I'll give my buddy a call, see what he has to say."

He steps outside, and I wait, taking in more details of Beau's space. Like all the other homes in the neighborhood, it's nice, but Hudson was right. Our place is bigger. I remember him saying his father had a bedroom for him here.

I wander down the narrow hallway, the walls bare and beige. I open the door on the right and find Beau's bedroom. The furniture set is familiar, the same one we had when we were married. I leave quickly, not wanting to see anything else. Across the hall is another room, the one I presume is set up for Hudson.

Of course, I have no intention of letting Hudson stay here. Our agreement awards me primary custody. Even if Beau has bought a house down the street, there's no reason for the two of them to start having sleepovers, legally or otherwise. Still, it's possible Hudson has been here recently. There could be something he hid inside the house he doesn't want me to find.

This room is even more bare. There's a metal double bed in the room's center and a dresser. When I open the drawers, I find no clothes. Only spare sheets and towels. His closet is empty, too. There's a Tennessee Titans poster on the wall, even though Hudson hasn't followed sports in years. I'm not sure he ever liked them, just pretended to in a desperate attempt to earn his father's approval.

I sit on the bed, the wires squeaking as I move. Its presence bothers me. This entire room proves that Beau isn't willing to give up his claim to Hudson easily. Leaving was the hardest part. Once we were out of his hair, I figured Beau's narcissism would take over, and he'd enjoy life on his own terms more than he ever did with us. I thought maybe we'd be able to live in peace.

Now, he's moved to Hickory Hills. Found a new job. Started his entire life over, only a few blocks away. He bought a two-bedroom house and fitted it out with cheap furniture. The reality that I'll have to fight even harder to keep Hudson from him almost overwhelms me. I stand, lifting the thin mattress to see if there's anything underneath; it's the only other hiding spot I can think of in this empty room.

That's when I see it squeezed between the mattress and the metal frame.

A pocketknife.

It's small, barely exceeding the palm of my hand when I pick it up. When I touch it, my stomach twists, as though I'm fending off a jab. Of all things, why does Hudson have a knife? It must be his. Beau would have no reason to hide it. Hudson likely hid it here. He knows better than to bring this into my house; his punishment would be severe.

I slide the blade into my front pocket and return to the living room just as Beau returns from the backyard. Luckily, he didn't catch me snooping around.

"I called my pal in homicide," he says. "This is the same guy that got me on the force."

"And?"

"Sounds like they have no leads whatsoever. The department was still under the impression she was a runaway and would turn up after a few days."

And yet all the women in the neighborhood knew otherwise. Too much time had passed, too much uncertainty in the air. Mothers always know.

"Did he say anything else?"

"It's too early to know much. They'll have to run an autopsy and finish processing the scene. He didn't give me details, but there was trauma to the body. No chance it was an accidental death." He raises his eyes to meet mine. "Did you see—"

"No," I cut him off before he can finish the question. "I got out of there as soon as I could."

"We need to talk to Hudson about this."

"I'll handle him," I say, standing. "But it would be good if you could keep an ear out. Let me know if his name comes up."

"I will, but if they think he's a suspect, they'll quit talking to me," he says. "I told him I was asking for details because the girl lived in my neighborhood. I don't want him to get the idea I'm fishing for information."

"Hopefully it won't come to that."

I'm walking to the door when he asks another question. "Why were you at the gardens this morning?"

"I wanted to make sure Hudson wasn't hiding anything from me, so I went through his room, then I went to his work shed because I thought there might be something there."

Beau squints as though he's in pain. "I need to be clear about this. Are you telling me you're worried other people might think our son did something, or are *you* worried he actually did it?"

"Hudson could never kill someone," I say, harshly, hoping my tone will induce some sense of shame. How could he say those words out loud? But I soon realize the shame sits within myself. I want the words to be true, but I'm not completely sure.

"You're searching through his things," Beau says. "You must think he's hiding something."

"I do think he's hiding something, but that doesn't mean he killed her. I want to stay a step ahead of this in case they do start suspecting Hudson. Everything I told you about that night looks bad for him," I say. "And then there's what happened at his school."

Beau rolls his eyes. "You blew that out of proportion."

"He was expelled."

"The school overreacted, too. Boys will be boys."

"Not everyone can downplay violence as easily as you do."

"What's that supposed to mean?"

We both already know the answer, even if he refuses to admit it. My mind flickers back to the past. The broken door-frame. Beau's weight on my chest, his hands around my neck. My very life flashing before my eyes, thinking one wrong move, or deliberate move, could be the end of me.

I close my eyes, forcing the memories away. I'm stronger now, but that doesn't make his proximity any less intimidating.

"Tell me if you hear anything," I say, opening the door and stepping outside before he can say another word. The afternoon sun is warm on my face, but I still am frozen up inside.

I promised myself I'd never rely on Beau again, not after what he did to me.

But this is about Hudson, and I'm willing to do whatever it takes to keep him safe.

TWENTY-THREE

MARY

It's dark by the time Mary leaves. There are a dozen different things that need to be done, but she couldn't tear herself away from her friend. Donna's pain is so visceral, Mary feels like she is experiencing the grief herself.

And in some ways, she is. Donna has lost her daughter, and Mary's suspicions about her own daughter's involvement put her at risk of losing Grace, too.

Naomi walks beside her, both of them lost in thought. They walk slowly, trying to stretch out the time between leaving the Bledsoe house and entering their own homes with their own families. None of them want to contaminate their lives with all this heartache, and yet, it's too late for that. None of them, not a single person in all of Hickory Hills, will ever be the same.

"Do you think Shelby did run away?" Naomi asks. "Or maybe she sent the message, and then something happened to her."

"It's possible." Mary pauses. "Of course, Donna was never convinced Shelby sent the message. She always thought it was someone trying to interfere with the investigation."

"Who would do that?"

"I suppose the same twisted individual who'd attack a teenage girl." Again, the costume flashes through her mind. She wonders if she'll ever be able to think about Shelby without conjuring that horrible image, the two forever linked in her mind. "At least the police are involved now."

They'd arrived in groups not long after Mary got to the Bledsoe house. The women were still taking turns consoling Donna and each other while they conducted a search of the house. Donna was far too emotional to answer any of their questions, but once she quieted, the police spoke to the rest of them individually. They asked questions about Donna and Shelby, their habits and routines. They mentioned the Halloween party repeatedly, trying to paint a clear picture of everything that happened, everyone who was there.

Considering how rattled she was, Mary handled their questions with ease. She put herself in the mindset of someone else. A person who only existed to assist the officers. Not a worried mother. Not a guilt-ridden friend. Even though she handled the interrogation well, it represented a sick precursor for the questions Grace might have to endure. Now that a body had been found, the police would target everyone who was friends with Shelby, and Mary isn't confident about her daughter's ability to withstand an interrogation. She doesn't have the same thick skin.

"I swear, I'm never letting my girls out of my sight again," Naomi says. "I can't imagine how scary it must be having a daughter the same age as her."

Mary had been so lost in thought she almost forgot Naomi was still there. All of their heads must be clouded with questions and sadness and worry.

"It's horrible. I don't know what I'd do if something happened to Grace."

And she doesn't know what she'll do if Grace did something, either.

"Rick and I don't know what to tell the girls," Naomi goes on. "They're so young, but Shelby is the only babysitter they've ever known. They're bound to have questions."

Mary gasps. "I'd forgotten about that." It's easy to overlook the various connections the residents of Hickory Hills have with one another. Already, she can imagine the details of Shelby Bledsoe's murder haunting children around the campfire for years to come.

"I thought about telling Rick to get the girls out of town for the weekend, but of course I'll stay back. Donna will have to lean on us." She cuts her eyes to the left. "It's not like Janet has been that much help."

"That was ridiculous," Mary says. It didn't strike her until later on that the reason Janet was so emotional was because she'd had too much to drink. It's a vicious cycle, really. Stress makes a person drink. Drinking causes undue stress. Still, if there was ever a time for everyone to hold their wits together, it was now. Janet was such a blubbering mess by the end of her conversation with the police, Mary had ended up calling her husband to come get her.

"At least Donna wasn't aware," Naomi says. "I think she'd fallen asleep by the time Janet had gotten really sloppy."

"Let's hope she can get her act together by tomorrow."

They pause outside the front of Janet's house. The most expensive in the neighborhood, it seems like such a waste. Janet's whole life seems like a waste, really, Mary thinks. Even when her friends need her, she can't be trusted.

The front door opens and Julian walks outside carrying a bag of garbage. They fix their faces, erasing any evidence they've just been gossiping about his wife.

"Ladies," he says, somberly. "How are you two holding up?"

"We're getting there," Naomi says, clearing her throat. "How's Janet?"

He looks over his shoulder, at the dimly lit windows. "She's already asleep. I think today took a lot out of her."

Mary has to fight herself from making a face. Donna's daughter has died, her own daughter might be involved, but let's talk about how difficult life must be for the neighborhood drunk.

"Hey, what's that?" Naomi says, pointing ahead.

The lamppost shines down on Janet's car, revealing a wrecked bumper on the left side.

"Did Janet get in some kind of an accident?" Mary asks.

Julian looks quickly, flashing a nervous smile. "Oh, that. I hit something last week."

"In Janet's car?" Naomi asks.

"Mine was in the shop." He shrugs his shoulders. "Now we're taking hers in."

His tone makes it clear that it feels like a meaningless problem when compared to everything else.

"Anyway, it's been a long day for all you ladies," he says. "You should go home and get some rest. I'll make sure Janet reaches out to you to see what she can do tomorrow."

"That would be great," Mary says, walking away, Naomi close on her heels.

They wait until they're down the block before they say anything.

"Do you think she got in another wreck?" Naomi asks.

"Julian said he did it," Mary says. "I don't know if I believe him. He's always covering for her."

"She should really get some help if her drinking is getting that bad."

"One problem at a time," Mary says. "Right now, all our energy needs to be reserved for Donna."

"You're right. After today, I'd say we could all use some rest," Naomi says, waving as she crosses the street to her house.

Mary watches her leave, the smile on her face quickly

fading. Sure, sleep sounds refreshing, but there's far too much on her to-do list. She can't put off a conversation with Grace any longer. A body has been found. Bloody clothes have been found. Grace must tell her the entire truth about what happened that night, no matter how devastating it might be.

As she approaches the house, she hears sobbing. It sounds as though it is coming from the backyard. Mary approaches her gate, squinting in the darkness to try and see. Grace's old playhouse is still standing, although it has been years since her daughter played in it. They keep it for the memories.

Sure enough, as she approaches in the darkness, she can make out the shape of her daughter. Her grown frame rests on one of the old swings.

"Grace?"

She reaches out to her but stops when she hears another voice.

"Mrs. Holden."

She turns quickly, frightened. From the soft light coming off the house, she can see it is Hudson Moore. Mary's fear and worry hardens as she presses her shoulders back.

"What are you doing here?" she asks, sharply.

"He was talking to me." Grace's voice is scratchy from countless tears. The sound softens Mary's anger, but she still doesn't like the idea of Hudson being this close to her daughter in the dark.

"It's getting late," Mary says to him. "Time to go home."

"Yes, ma'am," the boy replies, offering a final nod in Grace's direction. "Goodnight, Grace."

Mary stands still as a statue, watching as the young man exits their backyard through the same gate she used. When she turns to Grace, her daughter is off the swing, walking toward the house.

"Wait," Mary calls after her, stumbling over garden stones to catch up, but Grace is already inside. Mary chases the sounds of sobs. She follows her up the stairs, where she finds Grace on her bed, crying into her pillow.

The sight is jarring. Mary can't think of another time she ever saw her daughter this upset. She'd hoped to use this time to confront Grace about the costume, about the other secrets that stem from Halloween night. She wants to punish her daughter for being around Hudson Moore. Again! Mary doesn't see how she can do any of it when her daughter is this upset.

She sits on the bed, a nervous hand resting on her daughter's back. "Talk to me. Please."

Grace gasps, turning her head to the side. Her daughter's face is so red it looks sunburned, random hairs sticking to her forehead and cheeks.

"I can't believe she's really dead," she says. "We were together just the other night."

"I know," Mary soothes, but she's not picturing Grace and Shelby together on Halloween. She's seeing a flipbook of memories. Their first day of pre-school in coordinating dresses. Easter egg hunts around the neighborhood. Sleepovers and cheerleading tryouts and volleyball games. Shelby had grown up inside the Holden house just as much as she had her own. For Mary, it felt like having two daughters. For Grace, like having a sister. Now that was gone forever.

"I can't stop thinking about the last thing I said to her." Grace's sobs start up again.

The fight. Mary still doesn't know the subject of their argument, but she can see how heavy the memory weighs on her young daughter. She is tempted to pry for details, to try and siphon out more information.

Instead, all she says is, "Shelby knew you loved her. You were a good friend to her."

Grace shifts closer, resting her head on her mother's lap. Mary can feel her daughter's accelerated heartbeat, tapping into her knee.

There is much Mary doesn't understand, but what's abundantly clear, in this moment, is that Grace is grieving the loss of her friend, and she doesn't know how to handle any of it. The fear, the shame, the regret.

Grace needs a mother, so Mary wraps her arms around her daughter, giving her what she needs.

TWENTY-FOUR

STELLA

When I return home, Hudson still isn't back from school.

I text him immediately, asking where he is, but he doesn't respond. Now that the community gardens have been declared a crime scene, he can't say he's spending time there after school. I'm surprised he didn't reach out earlier. Word of Shelby's discovery must have made the rounds by now, and I thought he might message me, if for no other reason than to confirm the gossip.

I worry about his reaction to learning Shelby is dead and how he'll respond when he learns that I found her.

I'm even more worried about the pocketknife I found hidden beneath the mattress at his father's house.

I pull the blade out of my pocket and place it on the countertop, not wanting it to be against my body any longer. Hudson had promised things would be different here. That we wouldn't have any secrets. And yet, in the past week, that's all there has been between us. He even stooped so low as to use his father's house as a hiding place.

Trying not to panic over his whereabouts, I start tidying the kitchen, a common habit when I'm feeling antsy. Chicken casserole was supposed to be our dinner for the night, but my mind is too wired to focus on cooking, so I reach into the freezer and pull out a lasagna kit. Within ten minutes, the meal is cooking in the oven, and there's still no sign of Hudson.

I walk outside, sitting on the front porch. I'm about to call Hudson again, when I see him walking down the street, coming from the direction of Mary Holden's house.

As he gets closer, I watch every movement, analyzing it. Is he shocked? Sad? Afraid? Regardless of how close he was or wasn't to Shelby, the death of a peer must be traumatizing, and I resent that teenagers, especially boys, are so guarded with their emotions. If he'd let me in, even a little bit, it would dispel so much of the worry inside me.

When he sees me sitting on the porch, he drops his backpack on the ground and sits on the step beside me, hugging his knees to his chest. His hair hangs in front of his eyes, and I wonder if that isn't a deliberate move. If he doesn't want me to see that he's been crying.

"I tried messaging you," I say.

"I know." His face is anchored forward, to the street. "I was walking Grace home."

A preemptive shiver courses through me. The budding closeness between Hudson and Grace in the wake of Shelby's disappearance disturbs me. Or maybe it's the closeness to Mary Holden. There's something about that woman I don't trust.

"She's an absolute mess," Hudson offers without prompting. I assume he's talking about Grace. "Shelby had been her best friend since kindergarten."

"I can't even imagine." My chest pangs for Grace's loss. "I'm guessing you heard about it at school?"

"It's all anyone is talking about. I think we all thought she'd turn up eventually, but this..." His words trail away, his mind lost in thought. "Is it true they found her in the community gardens?"

"Yes." I clear my throat. "I was the one who found her."

He turns his head quickly. "Are you serious?"

"I'm guessing that part got sifted out of the rumor mill."

"I can't believe you found her. Why were you even down there?"

"I went on a walk near the gardens..." I struggle over what to say next. It's not like I can say I went there with the sole purpose of snooping through his things. "She was just there. In the pond. It looked like someone tried to hide the body."

"My goodness, Mom. I'm sorry you had to see that."

I smile tightly, affected by Hudson's compassion in this moment. Then another, smaller part of me wonders, is he only saying that from guilt? That he never meant for me to see what he did?

"At least when people are talking, they're not mentioning my name."

"I think there's enough for them to talk about."

Teenagers are only miniature versions of their adult counterparts. They must be spinning stories around the cafeteria table. Wondering what might have happened, who was involved.

"What are people saying?"

"Most seem to think that one of her mom's old boyfriends was involved." He shakes his head. "But I've heard it all. They're really reaching with this one."

I'm tempted to ask him if *all* means people have accused him, but I don't know how to do that. Instead, I ask, "Are you okay? You must be wondering how to feel about all this?"

"I mean, it's crazy. We've only been here a few months, and now someone from the neighborhood is dead." He looks down at his feet. "I'm more worried about Grace. We've become close, and I know she's struggling."

Part of me takes pride in the fact Hudson is being a good friend, but another part of me worries he's getting too tangled up in this, more than he already is. I don't want him getting reeled even further into the investigation by suddenly befriending the murder victim's best friend.

"It's big of you to be there for her," I say, "but it might be better for Grace to lean on other people right now. Her family. People that knew her and Shelby."

"That's why I feel so sorry for her. Shelby was her best friend, and now she's gone. And she can't really talk to her parents."

"Why not?"

Hudson looks at me, rolling his eyes. "You've met her mom. You know what it's like."

Mary Holden is the type of woman who makes everything look effortless while making those around her feel inferior. I can see why it would be intimidating for Grace to be open about her feelings. Still, that isn't Hudson's problem to solve.

"There's something else I want to talk to you about," I say, trying to find the nerve. "I went to visit your father this afternoon."

"And?"

I figured an impromptu meeting with his father would come as more of a surprise, but Hudson acts as though he was expecting this. His eyes are wide and unblinking, waiting for what I'll say next.

"I found what was hidden under the mattress in your room."

The words come out quicky, limiting the time he'll have to come up with a response. I'm not sure how he'll react. If he'll deny it's his. If he'll say there's a reason he needs it. Whatever he says, he should know there isn't any excuse that will work with me.

"Is there a reason you're snooping through my things?" His voice has an eerie calm.

"There are plenty of reasons," I say, holding eye contact. "I want to know why you have a knife again in the first place."

"It's for protection."

"Must be seeing a lot of action from underneath a mattress in a spare room," I say, unable to rein in my annoyance. "After everything that happened last year, how could you hide a knife from me? What do you need protection from?"

"Last year taught me that I have to be prepared to defend myself," he says, this time staring at the cement steps. "It's not like I bring it to school or take it anywhere else. I just feel safer knowing I have one if I get in trouble."

"If you get in trouble, you should come to me," I say, pointedly. It's difficult for me to control my anger, but I must if I want him to continue being open with me. If this conversation dissolves into yet another argument, I won't get any of the information I need.

"You're not always there, Mom." He stretches out his fingers before clenching them into fists. "I mean, Shelby was murdered. Clearly, there are bad people everywhere."

The image of Shelby Bledsoe floating in the pond returns, and I shiver. I recall what Beau said about the incident. There was obvious trauma to the body. What does that mean? Could she have been stabbed?

"You're sixteen years old. Whatever you're going through, you can come to me, and we'll sort it out. You can't go out of your way to obtain weapons. After what we've been through, you should know better."

"I didn't go out of my way to obtain anything," he says. "Dad was the one who gave it to me."

"What?"

"Look, I don't want it to start anything weird between the two of you. There's just certain things he understands that you don't. A weapon can be a good thing if it's used the right way."

I don't want Beau teaching Hudson life lessons about

anything, especially weapons. I remember how loose he was with his own service pistol, how his hands quickly morphed into a deadly force.

"I took the knife, and I'm not giving it back," I say, trying to keep the focus on what matters. Hudson. I can worry about Beau and the obstacles he represents later.

"Fine." Before I can say anything else, he stands. "I'm starving. What's for dinner?"

"There's a lasagna in the oven," I say.

"Sounds great." He picks up his backpack and moves toward the door. "After I eat, I'm going to call it a night. It's been a long day."

I couldn't agree more. Part of me is surprised he didn't put up more of a fight. After he went out of his way to hide the weapon, I figured he'd be outraged that I took it from him.

Unless, I think with a shudder, there's a reason he doesn't want the knife tied to him anymore.

TWENTY-FIVE

MARY

A little after one in the morning, Grace drifts to sleep.

For several minutes, Mary remains on her daughter's bed, watching her. The darkness of the room and the whirring of the ceiling fan calms her. Grace is so beautiful, she thinks, even with tear-stained strands of hair sticking to her face. Every few seconds, Grace's breathing gasps, aftershocks from the emotional meltdown. It reminds Mary of when her daughter was much younger, woken in the middle of the night by a bad dream, and Mary would have to lull her back to sleep.

This time, however, there is no dream. This nightmare, as awful and tragic as it is, is very real, and Grace is at the center of it. Mary wishes she'd had something more profound to say, but parenting books don't tell you how to navigate the death of your daughter's best friend at such a young age.

And they definitely don't tell you how to react when you have suspicions your daughter might be involved.

Mary never mentioned the bloody costume or asked the countless questions thrumming through her mind. How could she? Grace could hardly breathe, she was crying so hard, struggling to stammer out broken sentences and questions for which

Mary had no answers. There was no reason why any of this was happening, no explanation for why Shelby Bledsoe's life had ended at age sixteen.

Once she's convinced Grace is in a deep sleep, Mary lifts herself off the bed and creeps out of the room, leaving the door open just a crack. Tiredness is burning the backs of her eyes, and she longs to fall into bed in the clothes she's still wearing, to put this horrible day and all its revelations behind her, start tomorrow anew.

The lamp beside her bed is still on, and she's surprised to see Ken sitting up in bed, reading a book. When he sees her, he folds the book closed and stares at her.

"I thought you'd be asleep," she says, her knees sinking into the surface of their downy mattress.

"I wanted to check on you. And hear about Grace," he says. He looks down in shame. "I heard her crying, but I couldn't bear going in there, seeing her like that. It was hard enough when I broke the news at school."

Mary hasn't considered what that moment was like. She'd had her hands full with Donna. Ken, who'd always found young girls tricky, had likely been in a shambles. If Mary was ill-prepared to answer tough questions, Ken was even more so.

"That must have been so hard for you," she says.

"It's like she didn't believe me at first," he says. "Any time I tried to check on her, she yelled at me to go away."

"That's teenagers. It's hard for them to process their emotions," she says. "It's hard for all of us right now."

"I'm happy she talked to you, at least."

"She didn't say much. I think she was in so much shock, all her pain was just pouring out. The hard conversations will come soon enough."

Mary's mind flashes to the bloody Halloween costume, and she flinches.

"Tell me about it," Ken says, continuing the conversation,

unburdened by the discovery Mary made in their daughter's room that afternoon. "We've arranged for grief counselors to be at school next week. I don't think I've ever been more ready for a weekend."

Mary is grateful that her daughter will be home. They've had a good cry, and she knows there will be several more to follow, but at some point, she must ask her daughter about the fight she had with Shelby on Halloween night. She must ask her about the costume.

Part of her wonders if she should tell Ken about it now, before she talks with Grace, but she thinks better of it. They're both desperate for sleep, and Ken already admitted to being clueless on how to comfort their daughter. It's better that Mary uncovers all the facts before involving him with the ugly rest of the story.

"There was something else I wanted to talk to you about," Ken says, sitting up straighter in the bed. "I looked into Hudson Moore like you asked."

At the sound of his name, a spark of adrenaline fires through her. She sits up on her knees, eager to hear what comes next. "Did you find something?"

"It could be nothing," Ken says, in his typical apathetic fashion. "There was an incident at his last school."

Mary swats his leg, irritated. Men are no good when it comes to gossip. "Tell me. It could be important."

"Hudson was expelled from his last school for getting in a fight."

"Okay?" she says, waiting.

"No information was sent over about it in his school file, which is suspicious. Whatever charges there were against him were apparently dropped."

"Charges," Mary repeats. "Is it normal for someone to press charges over a fight at school?"

"No," Ken says. "But this wasn't a typical fight. A knife was involved, and the other student's injuries were so severe he had to be admitted to the hospital overnight. His left eye was damaged so much they thought he might need surgery."

"A knife? Surgery? That sounds far beyond a simple fight." Mary would never have imagined Hudson's past was this dark. She feels like she's been plopped into the middle of some late-night crime drama. Teenagers can't be this casually violent, can they? "Charges shouldn't be dropped over something that serious."

"I'd say it has something to do with fact Hudson's father works for the police department."

Mary considers the information she's just been given. Clearly, Hudson is violent, but because of his father's standing in the community, there is no paper trail to prove it. Still, Mary has never needed evidence when up against a scandal. Word-of-mouth and insinuation work just enough. Personal experience has taught her that, as well as the importance of controlling the narrative. She can use this information to her advantage, use it to deflect any attention that might come Grace's way.

"How were you able to find out?"

"I had a phone call with the principal at his last school. It was a serious situation, bad enough that it led to Hudson's expulsion." He pauses. "However, the principal did say it was out of character. They'd only had minor issues with him in the past. He's not even sure what started the altercation."

It only takes one act of violence to end a person's life, Mary counters in her mind. One argument. One accusation. Teenagers have no means of controlling their feelings, and Hudson's expulsion from his previous school proves that. He could have lashed out at Shelby just as viciously as he did that other student, only this time, instead of going to the hospital, his victim ended up dead.

"It doesn't matter. Even if it was his first time getting into a fight, it shows he's capable of violence. He had a knife! As soon as he moves to the neighborhood, a local girl is murdered. That can't be a coincidence."

Ken sits up straighter. "Mary, you can't start drawing conclusions like that. We have no proof he had anything to do with—"

"Hudson was dating Shelby! What more proof do we need?"

Ken exhales. "Shelby's death is hard on all of us. The school, the entire community. Especially our daughter. I don't think we need to make the situation worse by throwing out accusations."

"Did Grace tell you she got into a fight with Shelby the night she died?" Mary's voice is curt, defensive.

"No," Ken says, uncertainly.

"Whether we like it or not, an investigation is underway, and the police are going to be looking at everyone close to Shelby, which puts a huge target on Grace's back."

Mary pictures the bloody Halloween costume again. She wonders if now would be the time to tell him, and yet, in light of this information about Hudson, the importance of the costume is already waning in her mind. He's the one with anger issues. He's far more likely to commit a murder than her daughter.

Then why was there so much blood?

She shoos away the thought as quickly as it enters her mind.

"We can't have people blaming Grace for something Hudson did."

"No one is blaming Grace!" Ken says, throwing up his hands.

Yet, Mary thinks. It's only a matter of time before the rumor mill begins to turn, and she must control which direction it takes.

"Hudson Moore is dangerous. We know that now."

"Mary, he's only a kid."

"And so was Shelby Bledsoe. Someone murdered her. Why

couldn't it have been him?" Mary falls back onto her pillow, pulling the covers up to her shoulders. For the first night since Halloween, she thinks she might get a restful sleep. "I'm going to do whatever it takes to protect our daughter from him and everything else."

TWENTY-SIX

STELLA

Surprisingly, once I fall asleep, it's heavy and full. I wake in the morning feeling well-rested and optimistic for only a few minutes before I remember the events from yesterday.

Beau. Hudson. Shelby.

I wonder how long it will take me to forget about that morning in the gardens, the horror of finding a missing girl's body. I wonder if I'll ever forget.

Just before I dozed off last night, I received a text message from Naomi. She said that the women were meeting at her house to discuss next steps, that we'd have to take turns being there for Donna in the coming days. Clearly, I'm not close enough to Donna to be included in this, but I suspect the fact that I found the body is what earned my invitation. Knowing the women's penchant for gossip, I'm sure they're expecting all the details they won't find in the morning's paper.

Whatever the reason, it's an opportunity to keep Hudson's name out of the conversation. Making sure my neighbors don't get out their pitchforks is now the priority.

As I'm downstairs making a morning smoothie, I hear a

knock at the door. I suspect it's Naomi or Janet, too antsy to wait any longer.

When I open the front door and see Beau standing there, the breath inside me stalls in my lungs.

"Good. You're up," he says. He's wearing a hoodie and jeans. It must be his day off work.

"What are you doing here?"

"I wanted to check in on Hudson. See if he's doing okay, considering everything."

"I told you, I'd handle talking to him."

"Since it's the weekend, I thought maybe the two of us could hang out together. Maybe play a round of golf."

"Hudson hates golf."

"Okay. How about bowling. He likes that, right?"

"When he was seven."

Beau winces. "Look, I don't care what we do. I just want us to spend the day together. Make sure he's okay."

I poke my head inside the house, checking that Hudson hasn't come downstairs. Knowing him, he's taking advantage of the opportunity to sleep in. I step outside to meet Beau on the porch and shut the door behind me, just to be sure.

"I already told you he's fine. You don't need to check in on him."

"Look, it's the first weekend since I got settled and I don't have to work," Beau says, his tone growing impatient. "I want to spend it with my boy."

"*Our* boy is upstairs resting, and according to our custody agreement, you won't have him until the holidays."

"Are you serious, Stella? You're really going to throw the custody agreement in my face."

"You agreed to it."

"Yeah, because if I didn't you were just going to weasel more money out of me." His voice rises slightly, and I can see him struggling to control himself. "If it had been up to me, I'd have more time with him."

"You're barely contributing to our finances, and you know it. I was never concerned with how much money you did or didn't give us. I wanted to limit your time with him."

"He's my son. You can't do this."

"Yes, I can. Don't think because you moved close to us, I'm going to start bending the rules."

"So, you're telling me I moved all the way here and you're not going to let me see him until Christmas?" He's not even trying to lower his voice now.

"I have no say over where you decided to live," I say. "But I do have control over how much time you spend with Hudson."

He clenches his jaw and waits until he can't hold back anymore. "You bitch."

I close my eyes, trying not to let the words affect me. I remember how quickly things would spiral. His words turning to threats turning to shoves.

Don't you think I'm smart enough to leave bruises where no one will see?

"I'm going to need you to leave."

"That's not happening. He's my son, if I want to see—"

"Is everything okay over there?" The voice comes from across the street. Annette Friss stands at her mailbox, her full attention on us.

Beau appears aggravated that someone overheard us. He's used to only talking to me in that way, in that tone, behind closed doors.

I clear my throat before shouting out a response. "All fine here." I look at Beau, warning him with my eyes. "He was just leaving."

Beau turns on that winning smile and waves at Annette. When he looks back at me, his eyes are pure cold. "We'll talk about this again later."

He goes back to his car and pulls out of the driveway. Once he's gone, my body relaxes, a totally different vessel when away from his presence. As soon as I look up and see Annette still watching, my cheeks blush with shame. It wasn't supposed to be like this here. I wonder how many more moments of tension and embarrassment are to come now that Beau is so close.

I wave quickly, and head in the direction of Naomi's house. Hopefully, the next time Annette and I have a friendly conversation, she won't bring up Beau's visit.

For a lazy Saturday morning, the neighborhood is buzzing with activity. People raking leaves in the yard, washing cars, and some even starting to hang Christmas lights along their rooftops. I don't remember my neighbors ever being this busy on a weekend, and I wonder if everyone isn't trying to get a better glimpse of the Bledsoe house, which already has a few police cruisers parked out front.

When I reach Naomi's front door, I can see the neighborhood clique is just as busy, arming forces for whatever is ahead. From the large bay windows offering a glimpse inside Naomi's house, I can see she's already sitting around the kitchen table with Mary and Janet. They must be in the middle of a heated conversation, their mouths moving quickly and hands gesticulating as though in competition.

I notice that when I knock on the front door, their frenzied activity suddenly stops. Several seconds pass, and I still don't hear anyone coming to the door. I wonder if I should just walk in, but that seems too informal. Even though I've been invited, we're barely friends, and I don't want to seem forward. I knock again, and when there's still silence, I step around the corner so that I'm standing in front of the window.

All the women are still sitting at the table, staring out the window as though waiting for me to appear. When I see them, I wave, but they all seem frozen in place, as though I'm staring at a lifeless portrait.

Finally, Naomi reacts. She stands and smiles, although the expression seems strange. She points at the front door, instructing me to meet her there. When she does open the door, instead of welcoming me in, she steps outside, closing the door behind her.

"We weren't sure if you were coming," she says, that same strained smile on her face.

"I got your message," I say. "I went to bed soon after. I was completely wiped."

"I'd say." She nods vigorously, her hands cupping each other in front of her body. Something about her is different, nothing like the woman who was galloping around the neighborhood putting up flyers and gossiping only days ago.

"So, have the other women decided what we need to do about Donna?" I say, stepping closer to the house. "I can't imagine what the past twenty-four hours have been like for her."

Naomi moves to the left, blocking me from going further. "I don't know if that's a good idea."

"If what's a good idea?"

"It's just, you know..." She's floundering. Without the other two by her side, it appears harder for her to speak her opinion. "The rest of us have known Donna for so long. I just think it's best we handle it from here."

"I don't understand," I say. "You invited me over."

"I know, but the thing is..." She looks from her left to her right, to see if any other neighbors are out. "After I texted you last night, I came across some information. About Hudson."

It feels like an arrow has struck me in the chest. "What about Hudson?"

"I didn't realize he had such a violent past."

"What are you talking about?" The words come from a place of shock and denial, and I regret them the moment they leave my mouth; now all I've done is provide her permission to voice what she clearly knows.

"It's been spreading through the neighborhood that he was expelled from his last school." She waits, monitoring my reaction closely. "The rumor is he attacked a student with a knife." She pauses again, this time more menacingly. "Is that true?"

"That's not exactly what happened." Except it is true. I can't deny that. I only object to the way she brings it up, making it sound worse than it is. That's not the full story.

She steps closer, her volume an octave lower, creating a fake sense of intimacy. "You should know that's what people are saying, and if it's not true, you need to make that known."

"How?" My voice breaks, and I loathe myself for how desperate I must sound. "I mean, who is spreading these rumors?"

"It doesn't matter," she says, resting her hand over mine. I'm too stunned to pull it away. "But you understand how it looks, right? Everyone is talking about Hudson's past, and then he was dating Shelby when she went missing."

"They weren't dating." Because they broke up that night, I think. Right before she died. "Hudson didn't do anything to hurt Shelby."

"And then you found the body," Naomi continues, rattling off reasons to be suspicious of my son, not even listening to what I have to say. "I just think it would be best for you to focus on your family right now. Don't worry about Donna. We can handle her."

Just like that, she turns and goes back inside the house, closing the door behind her. I've been dismissed. My eyes flick to the left, and I can see Mary and Janet watching me from the window. They were probably there during the entire exchange, practically salivating.

I turn quickly, marching down the street back in the direction of my house. The tears come fast and hard. This is the one thing I didn't want to happen. I don't want people in the neighborhood to use his past against him.

I don't want them blaming him for something he didn't do.

Even if it appears to everyone, including me, at times, that he did it.

TWENTY-SEVEN

NAOMI

Halloween Night

Naomi couldn't stop staring at her phone.

The party was winding down. Most of the adults in the neighborhood were drunk, herself included. Her mother had called an hour before to say the kids were fast asleep. She should have been able to enjoy a few hours alone, and yet she couldn't.

She'd been waiting for her husband to call all night. It was always nerve-wracking when he traveled for work, particularly because he was staying at a hotel only two hours away. He could have come home for the Halloween party and returned to the convention in the morning, but he didn't. Hopefully, he hadn't taken the opportunity to hit up the bars in the city, which she was sure his work colleagues would pressure him to do.

What if he met a woman at the convention? They might have had drinks at the hotel bar. Perhaps they were as drunk as she is now, and they'd already gone up to his room—

"Would you get off that thing?" Donna's words slurred as she playfully slapped the phone out of Naomi's hand.

"Checking on the kids," she lied, sliding the phone into the pocket of her dress. Little Red Riding Hood. Her husband was supposed to be a wolf, before he got called out of town at the last minute. Now she just felt stupid. A grown woman dressed like a character from a child's story.

"Is Shelby with them?" Donna asked, slurring her words.

"No. She wanted to come to the party, remember?" Naomi looked the street up and down. She'd seen Shelby just a second ago, hadn't she? "My mom is with them."

"I should have made Shelby babysit for you." Donna was drunk, but there was an unmistakable meanness in her words. "Babysitting is the best birth control for teenagers."

Naomi laughed. "Tell me about it. It's fine, really. I don't blame her for wanting the night off. You're only young once."

"If you say so," she said, spreading her arms like a bird. "I'd like to think I'm forever young."

She started to walk backwards, and bumped into Mary, who said, "Careful, Donna. There are still kids around."

"Where? What kids? Don't they have parents to look out for them?" She began to shout. "Last call for candy, kids. Time to call it a night!"

"She's on another level," Mary said, a conspiratorial smile on her face. "Speaking of, have you seen Grace?"

"No," Naomi said, looking around the street. "No telling where the kids took off."

"That can't be good," she said. "Maybe I should send Ken and some of the other dads to look for them."

"Let them have fun, Mary," Donna interrupted. "Better yet, let us have fun."

"I think you're having enough fun for all of us."

The man Donna had been flirting with half the night returned, the monster mask still pulled over his face. He wrapped his arms around her waist, and she started grinding into him. It made Naomi uncomfortable to watch.

"Should we intervene?" Naomi whispered to Mary.

"It wouldn't do any good," she said, watching the drunken couple closely. "Donna's too far gone. And what about Janet? Have you seen—"

"I'm here!" Janet stumbled toward them from the direction of her house. Her hot pink dress looked more disheveled than the last time Naomi remembered seeing her.

"Where have you been?" Naomi asked.

"I had to run back to the house really quick." She stretched on her toes to look over at the bar booth. "I see the party is still going."

"You've definitely had enough," Mary said, sounding more like a mother than a friend.

"Oh hush." Janet swatted her arm as she went to the bar. "My husband's still up drinking. I can, too."

Mary opened her mouth, as though she was going to say something else, but a phone began to ring. Naomi's phone. She almost squealed when she saw her husband calling.

"I have to take this," she said, hurrying away from the crowd of people around the bar to find a quiet place on the sidewalk.

"How's the party?" her husband asked when she answered.

"Just as fun as last year." Naomi tried to sound like she was having fun. She wanted to convey the image of a confident wife; someone her husband could miss. "I wish you were here."

"I hate I had to miss it," he said. "I wanted to call before it got too late."

You *didn't* have to miss it, she thought, but she didn't say it. The last thing she wanted to do was start a fight when they were apart. She'd only hoped he'd be as keen to spend time with her as she was with him.

"The party is still raging here," she said instead. "What about you? Calling it a night?"

"Maybe." He paused. "Some of the guys might head to this bar across the street."

Naomi's throat felt raw, her stomach rotating like she might be sick. She should have told him not to go. She should have told him that just the thought of it would keep her up all night worrying. That she'd revisit the memories of what happened last time, when his betrayal humiliated her in front of everyone.

Instead, she said, weakly, "Have fun."

"Love you, babe," he said. "We'll celebrate when I get back."

She listened to the dead air after the phone hung up, and cursed herself. Why didn't she say something? Their therapist had been encouraging her to be more vocal, to tell her husband when he behaved in ways that triggered her, but she was afraid her honesty would push him away, into the arms of another woman.

It was so disastrous last time. Reading the text messages she found on the phone. Finding the expensive gifts he'd bought his mistress, never her. All this after the woman had confronted Naomi herself. Turns out it was an open secret in the community. Even her friends—Mary and Janet and Donna—knew but never told her. She must have looked like the biggest idiot in the world, and she still felt that way at times.

Naomi made a big deal about kicking him out of the house, with the support of her friends. All he had to do was beg her to come back, and she took him. It wasn't just her husband she was forgiving. Rather, she was making a choice to keep their family together. She never wanted her girls to grow up in a broken home. And if he was willing to come back, and she refused, wouldn't that mean she was the one who was breaking it?

It had been over two years ago, and yet the wound was still tender every time she thought about it. Every time he went out of town. *Some of the guys might head to the bar*. And now a string of possibilities would run through her head for the rest of the night.

Looking back at the bar booth, Naomi watched her friends. The same women who didn't tell her when her husband was having an affair, and yet comforted her after she found out. Mary and Ken stood tall, the King and Queen of the neighborhood, delighting at the clowns around them. Janet was getting loud, her husband trying to quieten her, and she could already predict a fight would brew between them later in the night. Across the street, she spied Stella, the new neighbor. She seemed nice, like maybe she could be a genuine friend. This very minute, she was helping Annette Friss pack up her table from the baked goods booth.

To the left, she heard rustling in the trees. The man wearing the monster mask stepped out of the darkness, waving for Donna to come join him. She skipped over, lifting the man's mask so that it rested on his forehead. The two kissed each other hungrily. The man's hands ran up and down Donna's body, the raw sexuality on display making Naomi uncomfortable again.

She tried not to think about her husband with another woman. She tried, instead, to focus on how far they'd come. Hadn't they?

Naomi marched in the direction of the group when another person ran past, clipping her shoulder.

"Grace!" She took a step back. "I'm so sorry."

"It's okay, Ms. Davis," she said, out of breath.

Naomi looked her up and down, staring at her dress. "Oh, Grace. Your mother will kill you."

"What?"

"Is that red wine down the front of your dress?"

Grace looked down at herself, her hands trying to cover the crimson stains on her chest. She looked from left to right before locking eyes with Naomi. "Please don't tell her. You know how she can be."

Naomi did know. Mary was a useful person to have as a friend, but she could only imagine how domineering she must be as a mother.

"She's already looking for you," she warned.

"I'm going right now," she said. "To change. Please don't say anything?"

Naomi sighed. We were all young once. "Fine. Your secret is safe with me."

A desperate smile spread across Grace's face.

Naomi watched as Grace ran in the direction of the Bledsoe house, before typing out a message on her phone, asking her husband what he decided to do.

TWENTY-EIGHT

MARY

The women in Hickory Hills have started looking after Donna in shifts. It's too painful otherwise, all of them sitting in that musty living room, stripped of light and life, watching one of their closest friends fall apart.

Janet is taking this hour's shift, which provides Mary and Naomi some time to enjoy the afternoon sun as they walk about the neighborhood. It's deceptively warm now, reminding Mary of a spring day instead of approaching winter.

"And that's when the therapist suggested we start coming twice a week," Naomi says. For the past ten minutes, she'd been talking about her rocky marriage, which speaks to their shared desperation to talk about anything other than Shelby and police officers and death.

"How did Rick react?" Mary asks, trying to keep her thoughts from drifting.

"You know, he was hesitant to even do counseling, but he seems committed to fixing the marriage."

"As he should, seeing as he's the one who messed it up." The words slip out before Mary can stop them, and she pauses.

She always carefully selects her words, rarely speaks her mind. "I'm sorry, Naomi. That was insensitive."

"You're right," she says, sliding her hands into her jacket pockets. "I feel the same way. I mean, I can't be the only one sacrificing to make this work. I didn't do anything wrong in the first place."

"You're absolutely right," Mary says, grateful the conversation is moving along. If a passerby were to overhear them, she wonders what they would think, if they'd deem the women callous for talking about their own problems during a situation like this, but even amid chaos, life doesn't stop. Dishes still need to be washed, dinner still needs to be prepared and marriages still need to be fixed.

"Have you and Ken ever tried counseling?" Naomi asks.

The question is innocent enough, but Mary is offended. Why would Naomi even suggest something like that? Their marriage hasn't always been perfect, but it's nowhere near as dysfunctional as Naomi's.

"No, Ken is easy."

"He is," Naomi agrees. "Sometimes I wish I'd gone with easy instead of my heart."

Poor, dumb Naomi. Can she not stop putting her foot in her mouth? Ken might be easy, but that doesn't mean Mary didn't marry him for love. In fact, love was the driving force behind their relationship. She'd never experienced any other sensation like it.

"Your kids are still young," Mary says. "That can put a lot of stress on a marriage."

"You're right." Naomi's eyes scan the area, hoping no one is around to overhear. "Sometimes I wonder if we'd stopped at one, if things wouldn't be better between us. Isn't that awful?"

One of those dark, desperate thoughts all mothers have, but should never voice aloud. Especially, Mary thinks, because Naomi is right. Rick's affair started when Naomi was postpartum, and while that's clearly no excuse, it's a precipitating factor. If they'd not gone through a second round of pregnancy and breastfeeding and sleepless nights, maybe Rick wouldn't have cheated, and maybe Naomi wouldn't obsessively work out the way she does now to hold onto him.

Mary doesn't tell her friend any of this, though. Sometimes the truth is not what we need to hear.

Just then, Mary looks over her shoulder, back at the Bledsoe house. Two cop cars, and three media vans are parked outside. About six people are standing in the yard, and from this distance, she can't tell if they're detectives or reporters. The death of a young girl in such a small town has caused a frenzy unlike anything they've ever seen.

"You're right about that," Mary says. "Let's go inside for a drink. One of us will have to relieve Janet soon enough."

And, Mary thinks but won't say, Naomi is the only neighbor with whom Mary can drink anymore. She certainly isn't going to crack open a bottle with Janet.

They walk the short distance to Mary's house and enter. The familiar smells of home relax her. She's dreaming about that cold glass of wine when she hears footsteps pounding on the stairwell.

"Mom!" Grace's voice is a terrifying teenage squawk. "Mom! We need to talk."

Naomi and Mary share a quick look before Grace appears in the kitchen. She's clearly agitated. Red cheeks, unbrushed hair, and her demeanor doesn't soften at the presence of company.

"Did you really tell the whole neighborhood that Hudson murdered Shelby?"

Mary and Naomi exchange another glance, as the latter takes a step backward. "I'm going to relieve Janet," she says.

"Grace, you need to calm down," Mary says, once Naomi has left.

"Answer me!" Grace shouts, her voice somehow louder than it was before.

The room goes silent. Mary waits for the sound of Naomi closing the front door before she speaks. "You cannot talk to me like that. Especially in front of other adults."

"I don't care," Grace says, raising her hands and letting them drop at her sides. "I'm not like you. I don't care what people think of me."

"That's good, considering you just came off as a disrespectful brat."

"Stop stalling," Grace says, taking a step closer to her mother. "Hudson just called me. He said you figured out he got into a fight at his old school. That you're telling everyone in the neighborhood about it, using it against him as though that's a reason for him to kill Shelby."

"As if a teenage boy knows what I talk about with my adult friends." Mary turns quickly, opening the fridge to grab that bottle of wine. She needs it even more now.

"One of your friends must have said something to his mother about it," Grace says. "You know none of them can keep their mouths shut. You knew exactly what you were doing."

"I didn't say anything that wasn't true," Mary says, reaching into the cupboard for a glass. "Your father talked to the principal at his last school. The fight was so intense it led to the other student being admitted to the hospital. He's clearly dangerous, Grace."

"No, he's not! That fight wasn't even his fault."

Mary turns quickly. "You already knew about it?"

"He told me what got him kicked out of his last school," she says. "As soon as you heard about it, you couldn't wait to tell other people. You know exactly what you're doing."

Mary's tempted to drink straight from the bottle, but, because she's civilized, she waits, watching as the pale liquid fills her glass. Mary hates it when Grace does this. Overreacts.

She shouldn't have to explain her reasoning to a teenager. They're not equals.

"Say something!" Grace shouts, still agitated.

"Why are you even still talking to him?" Mary asks. "I told you to stay away from him."

"He's my friend, Mom. And you're painting him out to be this bad person. It's not fair."

"No, you're refusing to see what's right in front of you. Hudson's violence got him kicked out of his last school. He was dating Shelby at the time of her death. Her body was found in the gardens where he works. You really don't think there is any connection?"

"He wouldn't hurt her."

"You've only known him a few months. That's nothing. People have a way of hiding the darkest parts of themselves. I'm starting to wonder if he's showing you all this attention in the wake of Shelby's death to take the heat off him. He's using you as a shield."

"He's not using me," Grace says, but she stumbles over her words, as though Mary nicked an insecurity that was already there. "You're doing what you always do. Turning people against each other for your own entertainment."

"Is that what you think being an adult is?"

"I think that's what being Mary Holden is," Grace says defiantly. "My best friend was murdered, and now you're targeting my other friend for no reason at all."

There is a reason, Mary thinks. Hudson has to be at fault, otherwise people will start looking at Grace. They'll start asking questions.

Why did you get in an argument with Shelby at the Halloween party?

Why weren't you worried when she was reported missing?

Why was your costume covered in blood?

"I'm trying to protect you," she says. It's all she can say

without diving into everything else. Mary has been wanting to confront Grace about the dress, but now the moment has presented itself, she no longer has it in her. If her daughter was involved in Shelby's death, Mary's not sure she can handle the truth. Besides, if the blame shifts to Hudson Moore, everything in their lives can go back to normal. Doesn't Grace see that?

"Hudson didn't kill Shelby," Grace says, the certainty in her voice sending a fresh chill down Mary's spine.

"You don't know that."

"Yes, I do." Her eyes narrow, darkening. She takes a step closer to her mother. "You don't know the half of what happened that night."

Sudden fear slices through Mary. She stares into her daughter's eyes, searching. There must be something in them, a glimpse of the innocent girl she'd always believed her to be, and yet Mary can't see past the anger.

"Grace, did you—"

Before Mary can finish her question, there's a knock at the front door. Grace uses it as an opportunity to end the conversation, turning on her heels and entering the foyer.

"Get back here," Mary says, chasing after her, the full wineglass in her hand.

Grace ignores her, grabbing her purse off the bureau. She swings open the front door.

Janet is standing on the front porch. "Did I come at a bad time?"

"No," Grace says, shooting one more look back at her mother. "I was just leaving."

"You are not," Mary says, following her. "We are going to finish this conversation."

But Grace is already gone, cutting through the grass to the sidewalk. Mary can't stop her without chasing after her, and with everything else going on, the last thing she wants to do is cause a spectacle.

Janet watches Grace storm off, her eyes wide with questions and confusion. She looks back at the wineglass in Mary's hand and nods.

"Thank God you have wine," she says. "I could really use a drink."

TWENTY-NINE

STELLA

When I return home, the first thing I do is tell Hudson what the other women said.

As much as I want to shield him from such hurt, I can't risk him being blindsided the way I was. He's been dreading the possibility people would find out about his past as much as I have. Even though he's made it clear several times he didn't want to move here, I think the one silver lining was that he could start over.

That's no longer the case, not if the entire neighborhood is whispering about the fight at his last school. Hudson was prone to trouble from time to time, but never anything drastic. He always maintained good grades, and most of his teachers made positive remarks about him during classroom conferences.

The fight with the other student took things to a different level. When the school called to tell me what happened, my body felt afire with anger and embarrassment, but when they told me a knife was involved, that the other student might need surgery to recover, I was distraught. I couldn't wrap my head around the idea that my child was responsible for inflicting such pain. And yet, Hudson sat beside me, a swollen eye and bloodied knuckles as proof. Unfortunately, there were also several students who captured the altercation on video.

Thankfully, the other student only remained in the hospital for two days, and surgery wasn't required. The knife actually belonged to the other student; he'd whipped out the blade during the argument, but Hudson overpowered him and swiped at him in self-defense. Still, because of the presence of a weapon, both students were expelled. I enrolled him into a state-approved homeschool curriculum until we made the move to Hickory Hills.

For weeks, Hudson refused to talk to me about the fight, and no amount of threatening could get him to open up. He was completely content without his phone and his television and his computer, if that meant he didn't have to tell me what happened.

Eventually, his resolve weakened. He told me the student had been hounding him for months, bullying him. His former teachers and administrators said as much when they spoke to me after the fight, but the extreme damage was too much for anyone to overlook. Even though the other student had the weapon, Hudson was labeled a monster for inflicting the more severe injuries.

"I just snapped," Hudson told me. "The moment I saw the knife, I lost control. I was afraid he'd hurt me. I didn't know what happened until a teacher was pulling me off him."

There was so much I regretted about the entire incident. That Hudson had endured bullying for so long and never told me. If I'd known, I could have spoken to his teachers before it escalated to such an extreme level. And I felt a certain amount of guilt, too, imagining how afraid he must have felt. What Hudson did was wrong, but I know my son. He wouldn't have taken the fight to such extremes if someone hadn't threatened him first.

At least, that's what I wanted to believe. Always, in the back of my mind, was that connection to Beau. My constant worry was that Hudson had inherited his father's violence. It was clear the other student was a bully, some might even argue he had it coming, but no child deserves to end up in the hospital. For months, I grappled with the fact my son had put him there.

And yet, the fight at his school was also the event that broke my marriage with Beau. I'd endured his abuse for years, learning to live in silence. After Hudson was expelled, that niggling fear that Beau's behavior might influence our son became impossible to ignore. I decided the only way I could make sure Hudson was headed down the right path was to leave, put as much distance between him and his father as possible.

Reliving what happened then is just as difficult for Hudson as it is for me.

When I tell him that the other women are talking about it, he runs out of the house in anger. I chase after him, but it's no use. By the time I make it outside, he's already halfway down the street, and when I call his name, he doesn't respond.

I sit on the porch, in the very spot where we sat last night and talked about the discovery of Shelby's body and put my head in my hands. It feels like everything in my life is spiraling out of my control. All the horrible aspects of our previous life have followed us here.

Beau.

Hudson's past.

It's all merging together in the worst way possible, painting Hudson guilty of a crime he didn't commit.

For a crime I hope he didn't commit.

"Are you okay?" says a voice.

When I raise my head, the sun is directly in my eyes, making it difficult to see. I move my head to see Annette Friss standing beside me. I hadn't heard her walk up.

"Not really."

"I wasn't trying to pry," she says, gently. "I saw the way Hudson stormed out just now. It didn't look like a pleasant conversation."

"That's an understatement," I say, embarrassment again washing over me. What must people think when they look at me? What kind of mother do they think I am?

As though reading my mind, Annette says, "Don't fret too much. Shelby Bledsoe's death has this whole neighborhood upside down. The adults don't even know how to react. I can only imagine what the kids must be feeling."

She's right, and I'm immediately comforted by the fact Annette categorizes Hudson as a kid. Not a threat. Not a monster.

"I've never even asked," I say to her, eager to change the subject. "Do you have children?"

"No. Never did," she says with a laugh that isn't entirely believable. "Only a husband many years ago, and that was enough for me." She pauses. "That man who was here this morning. I'm guessing he's your ex?"

An exhausted breath leaves my lips. "Yes. We divorced last year. Moving here was supposed to be a fresh start. Then he decided to move down the street."

"I know we're only neighbors, but when I saw the way he was talking to you this morning, it reminded me of my own marriage. Too much." She pauses, raising her face to the sun. "My husband was quite the gem, too. I stayed longer than I should, but things were different then. Divorce happened, but it was still frowned upon. For years, I worried what everyone would think. Not about him, which should have been my concern. I worried about what they'd think of me. Worried they'd consider me weak for staying, or dramatic for leaving. Even worse, that they wouldn't believe me at all. Once I finally found the courage to go, that's when my life really started. For the first time in my life, I felt in control. The most important thing a woman can have is choice when it comes to her own life. I didn't have that with him. I had so little."

"I worried about the same thing when I was leaving Beau," I say. "He's so likable, and I knew when it came time to choose sides, everyone would choose him. And I was right. Instead of people seeing the truth about our relationship, he twisted everything to make it look like I was the bad guy."

"It doesn't matter what truth he twists. It's the lies he tells himself that will ruin him in the end."

Somehow, maybe because of her own experience, Annette can see Beau's core, an ugly sight I believed was only reserved for me. I've never admitted the abuse to anyone before, for fear no one would believe me. Beau is a police officer, a pillar of the community. He's the guy people remember storming the football field and who, one time, told a really funny joke at a party. No one wants to believe a man like that is capable of unspeakable malice behind closed doors.

"No one else ever seems to see him for what he is," I say, defeated. Even if Annette believes me, that's two people against the entire world.

"It's the subtleties that give it away. The harshness in his voice. The way he was chasing after you at that party."

I raise my head in surprise. "Beau was at the Halloween party?"

"He was," Annette says. "Didn't you know?"

"No."

I didn't even know he was living here at the time. Part of the reason I was so at ease at the party was that it signified the beginning of a new chapter. Building friendships, making memories. Beau and our horrible past had been the furthest thing from my mind.

"Of course, he had on that monster mask half the night. No wonder you couldn't tell," she says. "It caught my attention right away, and I noticed he was always a few steps behind. I didn't know he was watching you at the time. I just assumed he was ogling all the women."

"I had no idea," I say, still struggling to place Beau in this life I've built for myself. Now, even the happy memories I've made feel tainted, somehow. Nothing can ever really be mine when he's so close.

"He caught my attention when he took off his mask to play tongue hockey with Donna Bledsoe."

Tiny glimpses from the night flash through my mind. I recall all the women crowding around the bar, their husbands and some of the other single men not far behind. Donna became louder and drunker as the night carried on, I remember. She fell into the arms of one man in particular, but every time I saw him, the monster mask covered his face. I shiver at the thought of Beau behind that mask; he watched me the entire night, and I never knew it.

"He was with Donna?"

Annette nods. "I guess he gave up on chasing you and moved onto her. I'm not sure if the other women have mentioned it, but she can get quite friendly with the other men in town."

"They told me," I say, with a groan.

Donna's promiscuity doesn't faze me, but Beau being inserted into the picture changes everything. If Beau was around Donna that night, he could have easily been around Shelby. And if he was drunk, there's no telling what could happen. For him, alcohol and violence go hand in hand. I run my hands across my neck, taming the memories into place.

When we were passing out flyers, the other women had theorized one of Donna's many lovers could have attacked Shelby. Of course, they only threw out names and descriptions, nothing concrete. I know my ex-husband is dangerous, a loose cannon. Maybe they were right all along, and Donna's interaction with Beau set a dangerous play into motion.

"Between this drama with your ex and this terrible tragedy with Shelby, I think you have too much on your plate," Annette says, forcing me out of my head. "As hard as it is, try not to focus on him. Right now, you need to worry about your son and his reputation."

"You heard about it too?" The alarm surrounding Beau is quickly replaced by my defensiveness for Hudson. The thought of more people gossiping about him makes my entire body tense.

"I went to my weekly tennis session at the club this morning. Everyone was talking about it."

"How? I mean, I haven't even met half the people in this town. How could word spread so quickly."

Annette looks in the direction of Mary Holden's house. "Those women. They spin stories faster than a grocery aisle tabloid."

"But how do they know? Why do they care?" I stare at the pavement, defeated. "It doesn't matter."

"I wasn't going to say anything. I saw you flitting about with them at the party, and that's fine. You're all around the same age. Most of you have kids. I'd hoped they were being genuine. But those women are no good."

"I should have known, seeing how they talk about Donna. They claim to be friends, and they've all taken turns by her side since Shelby went missing, but the way they were gossiping about her earlier in the week... no wonder they turned on me so quickly."

"Listen, every one of them has their own problems. Janet is a drunk. Rick had an affair that nearly drove Naomi round the bend. And Mary, well, I'll be honest, I don't know what Mary Holden's secret is, but there's something there." She pauses. "No one gets off on gossiping about other people like that unless they're trying to make up for something else."

It bothers me I ever thought I could be friends with these

women, seeing how easily they tear each other apart. All the secrecy and deflection. It's a dynamic I thought we would have outgrown by now, between the years of getting married and starting careers and having children. And yet, Annette's perception is right. They seem to get some sick pleasure from breaking others down, as though it somehow makes their own troubles appear smaller.

"You probably think I'm no better, telling you all this," Annette continues, "but unlike them, I don't enjoy revealing my neighbors' secrets. I'm telling you because I don't want them to tear you down. Every one of them has problems, whether they want to face them or not. This is an entire neighborhood of glass houses."

My throat feels raw from trying not to cry. This conversation with Annette has made me confront more truths than I was prepared for.

"Hudson is a good kid. Not perfect, but the way they're twisting his past to connect him to Shelby's murder is just wrong."

"I believe you," Annette says.

Across the way, I see movement on the front porch of the Holden house. In the time I spoke with Hudson, they must have changed locations. Janet and Mary now sit in wicker chairs, enjoying the sunshine, a bottle of wine between them.

I stand, turning my head to look at Annette. "Thank you for telling me the truth."

I appreciate her kindness, but I'm no longer in need of comfort. I crave something darker. Confrontation. Revenge. Before I know it, I'm marching in the direction of Mary Holden's house.

Mary is raising the wineglass to her lips when I mount the porch.

"We need to talk," I say, my tone conveying this conversation isn't optional.

"Good afternoon, Stella," Mary says, calmly, a small smile on her lips. "Long time, no see."

Beside her, Janet smirks. They're no doubt thinking about how Naomi banished me from her home this morning, the two of them watching from the window like nosy schoolgirls.

"I know you're the one spreading rumors about Hudson."

Mary's posture straightens as she puts the wineglass on the table beside her. "I can assure you I'm not saying anything inaccurate."

"You're telling everyone Hudson is violent. That he's not to be trusted."

"That's not a rumor, is it? He was expelled from his previous school."

I'm briefly distracted by Naomi, who walks up behind me. She must have sniffed out the drama from across the street.

"Ladies, what's going on?" she asks.

"The other student pulled a knife on him. He was only defending himself," I say, ignoring her and keeping the focus on Mary. "Hudson's only a kid. He doesn't need adults gossiping about a situation they know nothing about."

"See, I have a different perspective. One of our own has just been murdered. I don't think it's a coincidence that it happened right after your son moves to the neighborhood, given he's already put one teenager in the hospital." She pauses. "I'm only trying to make people aware."

"You're turning this into a witch hunt! Hudson doesn't deserve to have his past used against him. He didn't do anything to Shelby."

"None of us know if that's true," she says. "After all, he was her boyfriend—"

"Would you just stop!" I shout, loud enough to make Janet sit back in her seat. "Ever since Shelby went missing, you keep going on and on about them dating. I've seen him with Grace more times than I ever did with Shelby."

At the mention of her daughter's name, Mary's expression hardens. She stands. "That's precisely why I'm telling everyone about him. I want them to guard their children, just as I'm trying to protect my daughter."

"Protect her from what?" I shout, letting the question linger. Mary's expression seems to tense even more. "I can promise you Hudson isn't a threat to her. Or anyone else."

"I think we should probably let the police decide that," Mary says.

"Aren't you ashamed of yourself?" I say, shaking my head. I might as well be speaking another language. Nothing I say is getting through to her. "You're going after a young boy for no reason at all. The way you're inserting his name into everything makes me think *you* have something to hide."

"I've already told you," she says, her voice filled with snark. "I'm only trying to do what's best for my daughter."

"Maybe try being a better example? It can't be easy for Grace to have a mother like you. A mother who has never progressed beyond being a teenage mean girl."

That comment does it. Mary's eyes narrow, her cheeks an uncomfortable crimson.

"I don't think I'll be taking life advice from you," she says, struggling to control her reaction.

"Tell me, Mary, what's the real reason you're doing this?" I've hit a nerve and it's exhilarating. I take a step closer, recalling what Annette had said about her only minutes ago. "What's your secret?"

Her jaw clenches as she raises her chin. "Hudson isn't the only person whose name is making the rounds. We all know the real reason you moved here."

I take a step back, almost falling off the porch. She can't know about what happened with Beau. Why I needed to escape.

"Your ex has been busy telling his new neighbors all about

you," she says. "How you broke your family apart. Left town in the middle of the night, son in tow. I guess I'm not the only one with secrets."

I inhale sharply, unsure of which emotion takes precedence: disgust that Beau has already tried his best to tarnish my reputation in a new community, or relief that she doesn't know the real horror, the truth I've kept from everyone.

"I didn't break my family apart," I say.

"Well, if I've got it all wrong, you shouldn't be this upset," she says, glancing between Janet and Naomi, who are watching our exchange with wild-eyed merriment. "Unless, of course, there's even more you're hiding."

My hands are clenched into fists, and I struggle to keep them at my sides. Through gritted teeth, I warn her, "Leave my son's name out of your mouth. He doesn't deserve this."

It takes every ounce of my being not to tear into Mary Holden, right there in the middle of the street. I want to attack her, rip her apart, shred to shred, as she's doing to my son's reputation.

Before I can react, I turn, not able to stand the sight of her.

As I walk away, I think that maybe Hudson isn't the only one to inherit his father's demons. Maybe Beau's violence and cruelty and ruthlessness has also rubbed off on me.

THIRTY

MARY

Mary, Naomi and Janet watch as Stella Moore storms off in the direction of her bungalow. Mary watches her, skin prickling with annoyance, and dare she say it, shame.

"She's totally losing it," Janet says, shaking her head softly. "That was just sad."

"The whole neighborhood knows her kid is a psycho," Naomi adds, crossing her arms in front of her chest. "What do you expect?"

A small smile creeps across Janet's face. "At least she knows not to come for Mary again."

Mary slaps her arms against her sides.

"Can the both of you just shut up?!"

She turns on her heels without waiting for a response and marches back into her house, slamming the door behind her, leaving her two closest friends with dropped jaws.

Mary doesn't have the time for it anymore. All the petty neighborhood drama. Who is sleeping with who and who is drinking too much and who said something snarky at the last PTA meeting. It all seems meaningless now compared to what she's facing.

A young girl's murder. Her daughter's involvement. Hudson's involvement. Stella Moore's rightful anger.

Ken tried to warn her about going after the boy in a court of public opinion, but in the early hours of the morning, with little sleep and too many uncertainties muddying her thoughts, it seemed the best plan of action. Or perhaps she's just making excuses. She can't blame her indictment of Hudson Moore on anyone other than herself. This is exactly what Mary does when her back is up against a wall. She lashes out at others. A wounded animal casting one more strike for the sake of battle.

When Stella Moore confronted her, there was a sadness in her eyes Mary isn't used to recognizing in the faces of her opponents. Desperation. Fearfulness. She only caught a flash of it, whatever it was, but it was enough to make Mary regret her decision to tell the other women about Hudson. She was overcome with the very rare feeling that she was in the wrong. There was almost something in Stella's stare that reminded her of herself. Stella must have recognized it, too. It's the reason she asked about Mary's own secrets; she'd never been more rattled.

Mary heads to the kitchen, grabs another bottle of wine from the fridge and pours a glass. She downs the entire glass in only two gulps, and greedily pours another.

The front door opens, the interruption tempting Mary to scream, until she realizes it's only Ken. He's wearing his Saturday afternoon running gear, a V-shaped ring of sweat around his collar. He smiles quickly, panting as he makes his way to the refrigerator for a cold glass of water. As soon as he's taken a sip, he looks back at Mary.

"The neighborhood is busy this morning."

"It's the first weekend since the body was found." She sips her wine. "Everyone's out for blood."

"What's wrong?" Ken asks, nodding at the wine bottle.

"Stressful morning."

"Did you and Grace get into it again?"

Mary is taken aback by his question. Normally, she and her daughter don't fight, only the odd squabble here and there. Since Shelby's disappearance, they've had multiple disagreements. She wonders what Ken thinks of that.

"Yes, actually," Mary says, placing her wine on the counter. "And I got into it with Stella Moore. And just before you arrived, I told Janet and Naomi to take off."

"Janet and Naomi?" He seems stunned. "You always get along with them."

"Sure, we get along, but do we actually like each other? Naomi gossips about Janet's drinking. Janet whispers about Naomi's marriage. There's no telling what they say about me when I'm not around."

"They practically worship you."

"Yeah, well, I'm sick of that, too." She takes another drink. "I'm starting to think I'm not worthy."

Ken pauses, then, "You said you got into it with Stella Moore."

"I made sure to tell every neighbor I could see about Hudson's violent past," she says. "The news got back to her, and she confronted me about it."

"Mary..."

"I know." She raises her hand, stopping him. "You were right. I shouldn't have gotten involved."

"You can't inspire the neighborhood to start grabbing pitchforks," he says. "We don't know anything about Hudson."

"I said you were right." Her voice is sharp, on the verge of pushing attitude. "I regret that now."

Ken inhales deeply before looking away in shame. His expression wounds Mary. Normally, all she cares about is making him happy, organizing a life in which they can both be proud. She hates to disappoint him.

She thinks again of the broken woman that was Stella Moore. How she'd retaliated by bringing up the rumors Beau had started. More unfounded accusations piled up against the poor woman, and she barely seemed able to defend herself. Mary didn't feel good. About any of it.

"Like I said, the neighborhood is busy," Ken says, making his way for the stairs. "I'm sure Hudson isn't the only thing people are talking about."

"Let's hope," Mary says, but she doesn't feel hopeful.

"I'm hopping in the shower," he calls down, long after he's disappeared to the second floor, leaving Mary alone in the kitchen with her thoughts and her shame.

Long ago, she'd found her power was directing the course of a conversation, and she deliberately decided to vilify Hudson Moore. Why? Because he was an outsider and the details fit?

No, a voice inside whispers. You did it to protect Grace.

Now she's recalling the fight they had had this morning before her daughter went storming out of the house. If Stella Moore's stare was filled with sadness, Grace's was overcome with rage. It was terrifying to witness. She didn't know her daughter was capable of such anger, and it makes her wonder how else Grace might act.

Mary lifts the wine bottle, surprised to find it empty.

She has consumed an entire bottle of wine while standing in her kitchen. This isn't like her, and yet Mary finds herself grasping for items she normally wouldn't need just to cope. The revelation about Hudson Moore's past was supposed to be reassuring, but it had proved to be the opposite, and now she's left with just as many unanswered questions.

What else can she do?

Clearly, her daughter isn't going to talk to her, and she can't force answers out of her without admitting the horrible thoughts inside her. That Grace might be involved. That she might have hurt Shelby. Mary is still too afraid to share these thoughts with Ken; she can't imagine confiding in anyone else.

She decides she needs to find Grace, wherever she went,

and get to the root of what's bothering her. Ask her about the costume and what really happened that night between her and Shelby.

Mary heads to the front door, stopping by the coat rack to grab her jacket. That's when she sees Grace's gym bag. She's already searched every inch of her daughter's room and, because Grace doesn't yet have a car, there are very few places she can hide things. The drunken part of her brain tells her to ignore it, but another part, the intuitive part, stares at the bag as though it might hold the secrets she's been searching for.

Back in the kitchen, Mary unzips the duffel bag and empties the contents onto the kitchen counter. Old uniforms that smell of must and sweat. Loose hairpins and misshaped scrunchies. And beneath that mess, something else. A Ziploc bag.

Mary lifts the bag, and when she sees what's inside, she almost falls over.

It's a pregnancy test. Two pink lines, bold and unmistakable, on full display.

For several seconds, Mary stares at her discovery, then she drops it and rushes to the kitchen sink. The wine she's consumed exits her mouth in the form of hot bile. She turns on the garbage disposal and runs the faucet, splashing water into her face.

A pregnancy test. Her daughter is only sixteen!

Mary can't handle the scandal of it all. Ken Holden, principal of Hickory Hills High School and his delinquent daughter. Mary Holden, lead soprano in the First Baptist Choir, who can't even control her own household.

Beneath all those initial, superficial reactions, is something worse. Poor Grace. She isn't ready for this, can barely handle being a teenage girl and all the turmoil that comes with that. How is she supposed to handle being an adult? A mother?

A memory flashes in Mary's mind. The day Ken proposed.

She was only nineteen at the time. They'd been together long enough that she felt confident about their love, and yet, part of her wondered if it was too much. If she was ready for this next step.

Of course, those were all internal thoughts. She'd taken the ring immediately, flashing it proudly to anyone who glanced at her hand. She busied herself with planning a wedding and buying a dress and perfecting the reception décor, but none of those distractions quieted the voice in her head.

She was a young girl playing dress up. Acting the part of an adult, a wife.

If she'd ever voiced her concerns with Ken, he would have been heartbroken, so she remained silent.

Over the years, she convinced herself those quiet feelings were wrong. Experiencing the same cold feet every woman feels when they're making such a commitment. Her situation with Ken worked out, but how many people her age could say that? Far more people take on too much too soon, and they spend the rest of their lives paying for it. Mary doesn't want that for her daughter, but if Grace is already pregnant, she doesn't know how to stop it.

And yet, this explains her daughter's deception in recent days. The wall between them. Hudson's voice on the phone, urging Grace to talk with her mother. Is it possible Grace felt more comfortable disclosing her pregnancy to a boy she'd just met over her own parents?

Or worse, maybe the only reason Hudson knows is because he's the father. Maybe the fight between Grace and Shelby on Halloween night was because Shelby's boyfriend is the father of Grace's baby. The thought of it makes Mary want to retch again, but she holds it together.

Worse than the shame and embarrassment, Mary fears this brings everything back full circle, overrides what she'd been trying to do by ruining Hudson's reputation:

A teenage pregnancy provides motive.

Just when she thought she'd done enough to protect Grace, Mary fears nothing will be able to erase suspicion, because whatever happened is already set in stone.

Grace found out she was pregnant. She told Hudson and Shelby about it. An argument ensued. What followed remains a mystery, but the result was a bloody costume in her daughter's closet and Shelby's dead body discarded in the community pond.

Overwhelmed with emotion, Mary realizes she can't hold back her suspicions from Grace any longer. The time has come for total transparency. It's the only way she can reclaim control of this situation, which continues to spiral into more chaotic territory. She must find her daughter and uncover the truth.

THIRTY-ONE

STELLA

I'm still fuming from my confrontation with Mary Holden when my phone rings. Beau's name appears on the screen, and I immediately reject the call.

Sitting on the sofa in the living room, the fan swirling overhead, I'm trying to calm down, and yet I can still feel the blood boiling beneath my skin. I can't figure out how everything has fallen apart so quickly in the days following the Halloween party. Everything I'd tried to accomplish by moving here has been destroyed.

And every time I think of that pious look on Mary Holden's face, I want to hit something.

Beau calls a second time, and this time, I'm so irritated, I pick up immediately.

"I'm not in the mood for—"

"I have Hudson," he says, plainly, before I can finish. "We're at the police station."

"The police station?"

"An officer picked him up for vandalism and brought him in," he says. "Thankfully, they gave me a call."

I place a flat palm against my forehead, trying to keep up.

Vandalism? What on earth could Hudson have been doing to get himself arrested? And why is Beau acting as though his being called is some type of answered prayer? He might have connections on the force, but that doesn't erase the history between us.

"There's something else you need to know," he says, his voice muffled, as though he's covering the receiver. "When they got him down here, they started asking questions about Shelby Bledsoe."

My heart starts racing, climbing up through my chest and into my throat. "What?"

"Don't worry, I shut it down," he says, the second time he's been a savior in this phone conversation. "I told them we wouldn't answer any questions without a lawyer present, but it's not a good look. You were right about what you said earlier."

I close my eyes hard. Of course I was right. I predicted all of this, almost as if I believed it into existence.

"I found out more about the case, too," Beau says, forcing my attention back to him. "We have an official cause of death for Shelby Bledsoe."

"What is it?" I ask, hanging on his every word.

"Strangulation. Looks like there was a struggle before she died."

"There wasn't a knife involved?" The words fall out of my mouth before I can stop them; I have to be sure.

"No." Beau's words are clipped. I wonder if he shared the same fear, or if he's judging me for my skepticism.

My chest deflates in relief, then immediately tenses in shame. A teenage girl has been attacked and murdered, but at least there wasn't a knife involved. That's one less connection to Hudson, and considering the day we've had, I'll take what I can get.

"Keep him at the station," I say, reaching for my car keys. "I'll be there as soon as I can."

"No need. He'll be released within the hour and I'll bring him home to you."

Before I can object, or say anything else, Beau ends the call. I hurl my phone across the room and scream inside the empty house. Just one more thing I have no control over.

I call Hudson's phone repeatedly, but he doesn't answer.

Beau said they'd be home within the hour, but it's starting to turn dark outside, and they've still not arrived.

I hate having to share my son with him. On the surface, it's a selfish statement. As he corrects me time and time again, he's our son, not mine. Beau just uses Hudson now as a pawn in this twisted game I'm never able to quit. He doesn't have the paternal connection a father should have with his son. He never did.

When I told Beau I was pregnant, he wasn't happy. Truthfully, at first, I wasn't either. After years of his increasingly controlling behavior, I'd come to the conclusion that Beau wasn't going to change. I'd just come around to the idea that I needed to leave, when I took an at-home pregnancy test, and saw those two pink lines come into existence.

My first thought was: now I'll never be able to leave.

But that thought was quickly followed by the possibilities to come. I imagined chubby arms and legs pressed against my skin. Tiny fingers wrapped tightly around my own. Giggles and smiles and coos. And then I thought beyond that, what type of life I wanted to provide for my child. What interests he or she might have. What sports he or she might play. I thought about names: Sarah for a girl, Hudson for a boy, both names I'd pulled from my family tree.

All this went through my mind in a matter of seconds, erasing the hardship of knowing I was now in a marriage I couldn't leave.

By the time I emerged from that bathroom, I was in love with my child yet to come. I have been ever since.

When I told Beau, he didn't feel the same way. We'd always talked about children in a hypothetical sense, yet he insisted now wasn't the right time. He wasn't at a good point in his career. He wanted to wait until we were older, and had more money saved away.

It's not that his hesitancy was completely irrational. If we were planning a pregnancy, taking those things into consideration would have been key. But I was already pregnant, and I knew with every fiber of my being I wanted to keep it. I wanted to be a mother.

Beau was just as adamant with his stance.

He started sending me information about clinics in the area that could terminate the pregnancy, articles from women talking about how it had been the right decision for them. And maybe it had been, for them, but this was my pregnancy, and I was determined to go through with it, even if it meant having a child with a man who wasn't ready, even if it meant staying with a man I was convinced didn't love me.

When sending me articles didn't work, he started to pressure me verbally. Day in and day out, he'd provide reasons for why we weren't ready, never once considering that I was.

Despite his threats, I didn't listen, and eventually, enough time passed. As soon as I edged out of the first trimester, I made a social media post about it. Once our family and friends knew, Beau understood he couldn't pressure me to terminate anymore. What would his loved ones think if they knew how strongly he felt about not being a father? So, he fell into a new role, that of the doting father-to-be, and played the part with compelling accuracy. It's a role he's still playing.

For the first time in my marriage, I put my foot down, and there was no shifting it. Sometimes I wonder if that wasn't the beginning of the end.

When someone knocks on the door, I stand quickly, wiping the tears away from my face. I hadn't even realized I was crying.

Right now, I can't focus on the past. I must pour all my thoughts onto Hudson and his future, that little baby I'd so wanted and loved, now an almost-adult, and yet not mature enough to navigate the situation at hand.

When I swing open the front door, Hudson and Beau are on the porch. Hudson's hands are in his jacket pockets, and he's staring at the ground.

"Where have you been?"

"I already told you," Beau says. "We were at the police—"

"I'm talking to my son," I warn him, looking back to Hudson. "Tell me what you did. I want to know everything."

"I'm going to bed," Hudson says, not once making eye contact. His shoulder knocks mine as he walks through the doorway, putting me off-balance.

"No, we need to talk. You already stormed away from me once today," I say. "And then you got yourself picked up by the police. I want to know what you did!"

Hudson ignores me, stomping up the stairs, unfazed by my yelling.

When I turn around, Beau's standing inside the foyer, and I startle. His presence always makes me anxious, but it's worse now that I know he was at the Halloween party. He could have a connection to Shelby's death, too.

"He got caught spray-painting a trash can behind a gas station," Beau says.

"What?" I swallow my unease, focusing again on Hudson. "He's never done anything like that before."

"That we know of," he says. "Maybe this was just the first time he's been caught."

My first reaction is to defend Hudson, but given his behavior tonight, I'm not sure I can. Clearly, I don't know what's going on with my own son. "Where did he even get the spray paint?"

"That's my fault," Beau says. "He must have come by the house while I was at work. My garage door was open, and he took it from there. We should be thankful he was only using it for graffiti and not huffing it."

I'm irritated by the entire situation, and more so because it appears Hudson's first stop after storming out of my house was to see his father. I didn't know he depended on him like that. I'd hoped, selfishly, he was only close with me.

I'm about to mount the stairs when Beau stops me.

"Let him rest," he says. "It's been a hard day. You'll get more out of him tomorrow."

I jerk my hand away from him. "You said you'd be here hours ago. Where have you been?"

"I wanted to talk to him on my own," he says. "And I spent some time talking to his lawyer."

"His lawyer?" I say. "I should have been there for that."

"It's a guy I know through the department. Trust me, there couldn't be a better person in Hudson's corner."

"I don't trust you," I say. "You're not taking the lead on this, even if you do have buddies on the force."

"Do you want to know what they were asking, or not?"

"Tell me."

"Someone dropped a tip to the police department about Hudson's fight at the old school."

"I know the women in the neighborhood have been talking about it."

"That coupled with the fact Shelby's body was found where he works, they wanted to talk to him. I shut it down immediately. Even if it's a friendly conversation, given the topic, he should have a lawyer present."

"Give me his contact information," I say. "I'll make sure to go straight to him if we hear anything else from the police."

"I want you to keep me in the loop."

"That's not going to happen. You moving here has done nothing but cause problems for us, especially him." I pause, trying to control the anger pouring out of me. "I found a knife in his bedroom at your house. He told me you gave it to him."

"Why were you snooping around his room at my—"

"That's not the point and you know it!" I shout, raising my hand. "What were you thinking giving him a knife? After his fight last year, that's the last thing he needs."

"He needs to be able to protect himself," he says. "I'm trying to teach him how to be a man. I'm not going to let you turn my boy into some pansy because you want to coddle him."

My jaw drops in disbelief. How could Beau—or anyone— think I'm the negative influence on our son?

"We need distance from you. Now," I say, defiantly. "The police called you because you're his father, but I can handle this on my own, just like I do everything else."

"You're choosing to handle all this on your own."

"I know."

The most important thing a woman can have is choice, Annette's voice comes back to me.

"Now that I'm here, you don't have to do that anymore."

"I never asked you to be here. I moved away for a reason. Is that a gun?"

He glances at his holster. "It's my service weapon."

"I don't care! You should know better than to bring a gun into my house."

"Please, Stella. Don't be so dramatic."

Within seconds I'm back at our old house.

I'd put Hudson to bed, and was in my room reading. Beau had been out drinking, and it was late when he returned. He was drunk and upset about something, although I had no idea what. Next thing I knew, he was in our bedroom, accusing me of stealing money.

I had no idea what he was talking about. He'd had ten thousand dollars cash, he said, and he couldn't find it. I'd never even seen that amount of money, let alone inside my own house.

I tried explaining all this to him, but he was too drunk to speak rationally.

I took my book and my pillow and went down the hall to the spare bedroom, hoping to avoid another fight.

A few minutes later, I looked up to see Beau standing in the doorway. He had his service weapon in his hand. "Tell me where you put the money," he ordered.

Being married to a cop, I'd been around guns countless times, but I'd never had one pointed at me. It was like my entire vision narrowed to that one point, the weapon he was holding unsteadily in his hands.

"Beau, I don't know what you're talking about," I said. "Please stop this."

"I know you're lying, bitch."

The way he stumbled for balance terrified me. He could barely stand up straight. How easy would it be for him to pull the trigger, either intentionally or by accident?

"You're scaring me," I said. "Please, this is dangerous."

"What, are you scared?"

The gun still pointed at me, he started to laugh, then shook the gun like it was a toy.

I screamed, holding a pillow in front of me, as though fabric and feathers were any match for a bullet. I started to cry, feeling like every second could be my last.

"Stop being so dramatic," he says. "The safety is on. See?"

He pushed a button on the side of the gun, then laughed harder. "Oops. Now it is."

His response sent a chill through me. The thought of how easily he could have shot me. How easy it would be for him to still shoot me. And I still had no idea what he was talking about.

When he finally left the room, he passed out on the sofa downstairs.

I ran down the hallway to Hudson's room, and exhaled a sigh of relief when I saw he was still sleeping. The last thing I wanted was for him to overhear the drama between us. I stayed awake the rest of the night, afraid of what might happen if I shut my eyes.

I never knew what money he was talking about, and I didn't care.

When I think back to the night now, I'm ashamed I stayed. I should have left then.

Staring at that same gun, all the memories come rushing back.

But I'm no longer on my knees pleading.

I'm in a house that doesn't belong to him. He has no ownership over me or this new chapter of my life.

"Get out of my house."

"Stella, we're only talking—"

"Leave or I will call the police."

"What? You're going to call the cops on a cop?"

It's a threat he's used against me before. One I've never taken him up on, even when I should have. But times are changing. I have changed.

"This is the last time I'm going to tell you," I say again, my voice strong.

Already at the front door, it only takes a few steps for him to be outside.

"Fine. But you can't keep me away forever. He's my son, and he needs both of his parents right now."

"That's what you don't get, Beau. He doesn't need you," I say, pushing his chest to create more distance between us. "If you bring another weapon into my home, you'll never see him again. Do you hear me?"

Beau begins shouting a response, but I ignore him. I don't say anything else before slamming the door shut and clicking the lock.

THIRTY-TWO

MARY

On Sunday morning, Mary wakes up with a massive headache. The pulsing starts before she even opens her eyes, and once she does, the sharp bursts of light coming in from the bedroom window make the pain intensify.

"Is it morning?" she asks, trying to remember details from the day before. She remembers multiple fights. Lots of wine. What else?

"It's almost ten o'clock." Ken is in bed beside her, and it only takes one look for her to see he slept more soundly than she did.

"I don't even remember going to sleep." She tries to sit up, and the world around her spins violently. "I must have drunk more than I realized."

"Don't worry," Ken says. "I already called the choir and told them we wouldn't make it to today's service. Considering everything going on, they were understanding."

Mary wasn't worried about that. Normally, she would be. She was anxious about Grace, about the conversation they needed to have. She'd been so nervous she'd downed another bottle of wine in an attempt to soothe her concerns and passed out.

"Did Grace come home?"

"She came back in time for dinner, but you were already asleep," Ken says. "She's in her room."

Mary struggles to get out of the bed, hurrying for their bedroom door.

Ken touches her hand, keeping her in place.

"Mary, what's going on with you?" he asks. "You need to tell me."

"I will," she says. Mary is torn. She wants nothing more than to soothe her husband's concerns, but she can't do that without confronting their daughter. One more tough conversation, and everything will go back to the way it was. "But I need to talk to Grace first."

Before she knocks on her daughter's door, she takes five minutes to pull herself together. She brushes her teeth and splashes water on her face and pulls back her hair into a claw clip. When she looks in the mirror, despite the hangover, she looks like a woman capable of having a difficult discussion with her teenage daughter, even though her every action leading up to this moment has proved otherwise. Even though the conversation she's about to have is so much more difficult than the normal mother/daughter spat.

Pregnancy.

Murder.

She's let these secrets exist in her own house for too long, and it's time she confronted them.

She raps gently against her daughter's bedroom door. Without waiting for a response, she pushes it open. Grace is sitting on her bed, criss-cross applesauce, a Chromebook in her lap. She raises her head only for a second.

"We need to talk," Mary says, calmly.

"I'm not in the mood," Grace tells her, making a point to not look at her mother.

"I don't care." Mary sits on the bed across from her daughter, demanding her attention. "We can't put this off any longer."

Grace lets out a heavy exhale and closes the computer. She stares at her mother, disinterested.

"What?"

"Well, let's start with you." Mary pauses. "How have you been feeling about all of this?"

The question catches Grace off guard. She had arsenals of teenage angst ready to explode, but her mother's benign question has left her with nowhere to unload it. She shrugs.

"I'm heartbroken about Shelby," she answers honestly, "and I'm angry with you for what you did to Hudson."

Mary looks at the floor. "You feel like I betrayed you."

"I feel like you betrayed him," she says. "You did what you always do. Throw other people under the bus to make yourself look better."

"Is that what you think of me?"

The two lock eyes, and it's clear each is afraid to look away first. As hurtful as Grace's assessment is, Mary knows part of what she says is true, and she's in awe of her daughter's astuteness.

"Sometimes," Grace says, weakly. "I know you don't know enough about Hudson to be spreading rumors about him. It isn't fair."

Hudson. Why is a boy even at the center of this? Out of all the revelations the past week has brought, surely he isn't Grace's biggest concern. Mary takes a deep breath.

"Grace, I need to talk to you about a few things. They're going to be very difficult."

"Okay." Grace hugs her knees to her chest, looking up at her mother with childlike eyes.

Mary reaches into her robe and pulls out the Ziploc bag, placing it between them on the bed.

"Let's start with this," she says.

Grace stares at the pregnancy test, eyes wide, cheeks beginning to blush. "You've been going through my things?"

"Yes, and we're not going to argue about that. Not right now." She looks down at the test. "I'm your mother, and while I've made mistakes, it's my job to protect you. I've had this feeling like something is wrong with you since Shelby went missing, and clearly, I was right."

"I don't know what to say," Grace says, hugging her knees tighter.

"We need to come up with a plan. Discuss next steps—"

"Mom, do you think that's mine?"

Mary blinks several times. "I found it hidden in your gym bag."

"I'm not pregnant," Grace says, scooting closer to the headboard. "How could you even think that?"

Mary looks between the test and her daughter and repeats, "You were hiding it in your bag."

"I was hiding it because I was trying to avoid a conversation like this." She exhales heavily. "For your information, I'm still a virgin. There's no way I can be pregnant. That test belonged to Shelby."

"Shelby was pregnant?" She'd been so disturbed by her discovery she'd never considered this possibility.

"I found it the night of the Halloween party," Grace says. "I went over to her house and found it in the bathroom trash."

"She didn't tell you?"

"No." Grace looks wounded.

"Is that what you were fighting about that night?"

Grace's eyes dart to the right, looking out her bedroom window, searching for escape. "That was only part of it."

Mary moves closer to her daughter, grabbing her hand. "Grace, I know this is hard, but you must tell me everything. It's important."

"When I found the pregnancy test, I confronted her. I'd

assumed the father was Hudson, seeing as he was her boyfriend and all..."

Mary closes her eyes, bracing for the rest. This is what she'd feared. A love triangle that ended in violence.

"...that's when she told me she'd been cheating on Hudson," Grace continues. "With a married man."

"What?"

"I mean, the fact she cheated on Hudson wasn't that shocking. They'd only been dating a few months, and she'd cheated on boyfriends before. It was admitting that her boyfriend was a grown man that bothered me."

"Did she say who it was?"

"She didn't have to." Grace sighs. "Shelby has been Naomi's babysitter for years. She always used to talk about having a crush on her husband, I just never thought she'd act on it."

"Shelby was sleeping with Rick?"

"The way she talked about it," she says, a shiver running through her, "it's like she was proud of what she was doing. She was going on and on about how they were in love and they would raise the baby together. She didn't care that what she was doing was wrong.

"I told her it was disgusting. She was only sixteen, how was she going to raise a child? Especially with a man who'd run out on his own children to be with her. I called her a slut and a homewrecker. It's the first real argument we've ever had, and she didn't even seem to care."

"Rick knew about the baby?"

"She made it sound like he did. She said they had plans to run away together." Grace pauses. "That's why I wasn't worried when she was reported missing. I figured she'd just made good on her plan. I knew Rick was out of town on business; I figured he'd sent a car for her or something. Even when he came back, I figured it was only a matter of time before he left again to join her."

That explains Grace's reaction. She didn't seem to care that her friend had been reported missing, but she was devastated after Shelby's body had been found. Until then, she'd thought Shelby was in control.

"I really didn't think anything had happened to her. The whole town was worried about where she'd gone, but I didn't want to get involved with the affair and the baby. I figured the truth would come out eventually when Rick finally ended things with Naomi, but I was wrong." Grace pauses again. "My best friend is dead. And all I keep thinking about is the last thing I ever said to her."

"You couldn't have known what would happen," Mary says, trying to comfort Grace and herself at the same time. "There's something else I need to ask you about that night."

"What?" Grace says, wiping away tears.

"Before I found the pregnancy test, I went searching in your room. I found your costume," she says. "It was covered in blood." She waits again, forcing the question out of her mouth. "How serious was the fight between you and Shelby?"

"It wasn't physical," Grace answers. "The blood on the costume wasn't from Shelby. It was from Hudson."

THIRTY-THREE

STELLA

It is a restless night with very little sleep.

My day starts before the sun rises, the darkness outside my bedroom window mirroring the gloom that lives within these walls. I go to the kitchen, brewing a strong cup of coffee, the rich aroma awakening my senses, preparing me for what needs to happen.

I must talk to Hudson today. It can't be put off any longer.

I suspect his sleep was as fitful as mine. I can hear him moving around, though he doesn't leave his room. We're avoiding each other, it seems, both dreading what comes next.

When the sun rises, it rings an alarm inside me. I knock on his bedroom door. When I enter, his hair is tousled with bed head, but his eyes are wide awake, mirroring the exhaustion and despair in my own.

"We have to talk," I say, sitting at the foot of his bed, much like I used to do when he was a toddler, and it was time to start our day.

"I don't want to—"

"I know. I don't want to either." I pause, trying to make sure he hears me this time, that he doesn't reject the conversation as he has before. "The reality is, our neighbor was murdered. The police are starting to ask questions. I need you to tell me everything before they come to you for answers."

"I don't know what you want me to say." He faces his bedroom window, the rising sun cutting through the blinds.

"The truth." Such a simple request. "That's all I want, no matter how hard it is."

He looks at me, his eyes wide and cautious. "I didn't hurt Shelby."

"Okay." I so badly want to believe him. "The two of you were dating, right?"

"I guess. I mean, I thought we were. I never had, like, a real girlfriend before, so I didn't know what to expect. Girls never seemed interested at my old school, but we'd always known each other. We moved here, and I was the new kid. I think Shelby liked that."

Watching his face light up softens something inside me. Oh, to feel that rush of young love again. I want all those feelings for him, but am crushed to know how it all ends.

"Did it start right after we moved?" I ask.

"Pretty much. Shelby and Grace were always together, and I started to tag along. I thought we were all just friends at first. Then Shelby started to act like she liked me. I never thought a girl that pretty would give me the time of day. I mean, she never came out and said she was my girlfriend, but whenever we were together, we were all over each other. She was holding my hand and kissing me."

"And you were still dating the night of the Halloween party?"

"Yeah. She was really excited about the party. She talked about it for weeks. I thought we'd wear one of those couple costumes, but she decided to partner with Grace instead."

Grace. Her name keeps coming up, and I'm trying to figure out how she fits into all this. Did she put a wedge in their relationship? Did she resent Hudson for intruding on her friendship? Did she develop feelings and want him all for herself?

"Is that why you got into a fight that night?" I ask. "Because she wanted to match Grace instead of you?"

He laughs. "No. It was nothing like that. The night started off great. It was like the first big event since we moved here. They were introducing me to all their friends. It's like I really belonged, you know?"

I do know, because I felt the same way. Decades apart, and our desires were so simple.

"As it got later, one of the older kids brought out some booze," he continues, watching me to gauge whether or not he'll get in trouble. "We went down to the community gardens to pass around the alcohol. Some of the others took off and left me alone with Shelby." He pauses again. "I thought we might kiss and stuff. I wanted to be romantic, so I told her how special the last few months had been to me. How much I liked her."

I remain neutral. Underage drinking and fooling around with his girlfriend are the least of our problems, and I want him to continue talking.

"Before I even finished, she started laughing at me," he says, his face as tender as an open wound. "She made it clear she didn't feel the same way. She told me I wasn't really her type. I asked her why I was her boyfriend then and she said I wasn't. I didn't understand. All those times we'd been together, all the things she told me, and then she was acting like I was some kid with a crush."

"That must have been hurtful," I say, unsure how much I should interject.

"That's why I denied dating her when you asked me about it," he says. "I didn't realize everything was one-sided. It's just embarrassing."

"You shouldn't feel embarrassed," I say, squeezing his hand.

"She said she was seeing someone else. That she was only

spending time with me to make the other guy jealous." His expression hardens. "I was so angry when she told me that."

"What did you do?"

"I yelled. Called her names. Then I just stormed off. That's the last I saw of her."

He looks up at me with the innocent, questioning eyes I know so well. I so badly want to believe him, to believe that their interaction ended that moment, just as he said. And yet, I know that can't be true. There's more to the story he's leaving out.

"That can't be everything," I say. "You still haven't explained how you got the bruises on your face."

Hudson shifts, putting distance between us. "I don't want to talk about that."

"You have to." I'm pleading. "No matter how difficult it is. Whatever happened, I'll try my best to understand. I promise."

For a moment, he stares at me, trying to decide how long he can wait this out, stall this conversation as he has so many times before. His face crumbles as he begins to cry.

My insides seize with fear.

This is it.

He's about to tell me the truth.

THIRTY-FOUR

HUDSON

Halloween Night

Hudson could feel pressure building behind his eyes.

He couldn't understand why he felt so upset. It wasn't like he even liked Shelby Bledsoe that much. Sure, she was beautiful, but she wasn't very nice. When they were hanging out, he spent most of his time talking to Grace. The two of them had a lot more in common.

It was the way she had laughed at him that bothered him. The way she had acted like dating him was somehow beneath her, even if it was. She was the first girl to seem like she liked him, and she just as swiftly took that flattery away. It was cruel.

"Have you seen Shelby?"

Hudson was walking back from the community gardens when he passed Grace on the walkway. At first, he was caught off guard by what she was wearing. Her white dress, bright against the backdrop of the night. The furry wings at her back and halo atop her head. He'd almost forgotten it was Halloween. Everyone was pretending to be someone they were not.

"She's at the gardens still," he said, his gaze back on the pavement. "She broke up with me."

"What?" Part of him had been worried Grace already knew what was going to happen, that the two of them were laughing at him behind his back. Based on the tone of her voice, he believed she was as shocked as him.

"According to her, we were never together in the first place," he said. "She said she has another boyfriend already."

Grace laughed in disbelief. "That can't be true. I'd know about it."

"Maybe that's just the excuse she gave me," he said. "But she seemed pretty believable. She was even bragging about how the guy bought her some fancy necklace. Said I couldn't do something like that." He paused, fresh hurt setting in. "And she's right."

"Maybe she's had too much to drink," Grace said, pulling out her phone. "I'm going to call her. None of this makes any sense."

She stepped off the pathway, phone to her ear, but Hudson didn't want to wait around. He continued walking in the direction of the party, ready for this awful, embarrassing night to end.

"There you are!"

Another voice came out of the shadows, but this time it wasn't Grace. He turned around, the voice familiar, yet unnerving in the woods at night. A tall man stepped out of the bushes. He had a monster mask pulled over his face. Hudson's first reaction was to run away, then he remembered, again what night it was. Recognized the familiar voice.

The person took off the mask, revealing himself.

"Dad?" Hudson asked, stepping closer.

"I was hoping I'd run into you here."

Even though his father had told him about the move last week, Hudson hadn't fully processed it. He was still adjusting to his own move, wondering how he'd break the news to his mother that his father had followed them here.

"I figured you'd have to work," Hudson said.

"I thought I'd have to, too. Good thing I got off in time for the party." His father held a bottle of beer in his left hand. He lifted it to his mouth and drank. "Where's your mom?"

Hudson felt himself tense. He didn't like getting in the middle of whatever was going on between them. "She's hanging out with her friends."

"She has friends already?" Beau tried to make the question casual, but it came out more menacing. "What about a boyfriend?"

"I don't know, Dad."

Hudson turned around, walking away from him.

"Hold on." Beau reached out and grabbed his son's shoulder. "Where are you going?"

"I'm going home. It's been a rough night."

Beau tried to turn Hudson around, but when he did, he lost his balance, almost stumbling off the sidewalk and into the shrubbery. Hudson realized his father had had a lot more to drink than a single bottle of beer.

"Are you drunk?"

"It's a party, isn't it?" Beau replied.

"The party is over for me." Again, he tried to leave.

"The night is young. Let's head back together. We can find your mom and surprise her."

"I don't think that's a good idea."

"Why?"

"Because you're drunk," Hudson said, his tone accusatory. "And Mom is having fun. Let her enjoy her night."

"And you don't think she'll enjoy it if I'm around?"

"Dad, you know she won't."

"She's getting into your head," he said. "That's it, isn't it? You can't believe anything that bitch says."

The slur had taken it too far. Hudson turned around, angry. "Don't call her that!"

"It's true, son. Your mother can't be trusted."

"I said stop." Something came over Hudson then, a rage he'd only felt one other time in his life, at that dreadful fight at school when the bully took it too far. He lurched forward, pushing his father hard in the chest with both hands. He didn't care that his father was taller, stronger.

Beau pulled back his arm, then swung it forward, his fist connecting hard with his son's face. The pain was sharp and blinding, sending Hudson to the ground.

A scream.

Hudson heard the sound but struggled to make sense of it. His senses were still disoriented from the punch. When he looked up, he saw Grace standing on the sidewalk, her phone on the ground. Up ahead, he could see his father running back toward the party.

"Who was that?" Grace asked. She was beside him, reaching for his face. Blood spilled over his fingers, his blood, he realized.

"My father," he said.

"Why would he do that?"

Hudson couldn't answer. There was no reason. This was who his father was, he'd learned. Not all fathers were dependable and strong. Some could only exert their strength by feeding off the weakness of others.

"We have to clean this up," Grace said. "I'll be right back."

She ran off in the same direction his father had just gone. When she returned, she looked more stunned than she did before. Hudson realized just how bizarre this situation was, how broken his family was. She bent down beside him.

"Grace. You ruined your dress."

"I don't care," she said, moving quickly.

"I'm sorry you had to see that," he told her, as she put a wet paper towel over his right eye.

"Don't apologize. You didn't do anything wrong."

They didn't say anything else to one another. Grace simply sat with him, waiting for his nerves to settle, waiting for the bleeding to stop.

THIRTY-FIVE

STELLA

Warm tears roll down my cheeks and fall into my mouth. I'm not sure which is more heartbreaking: picturing Hudson being abused at the hands of his father, or knowing he felt he had to keep that secret for so many days.

"Your dad gave you that bruise?" I ask.

He nods. "He'd been drinking, and he didn't like what I said to him."

"That's not an excuse," I say, wiping away my tears. His hand is soft and pale in my own. Not long ago, it was smaller and pudgy, sticky with juice or dusted with crumbs. He's still a child. How could his own father do that to him? "Hudson, you should have told me right away."

"I just wanted to forget about it," he says. "Pretend it never happened. Hope it would never happen again."

For years, I followed that same reasoning, hoping each act of aggression would be his last, ignoring the pattern of how his violence grew worse over time. All the while, I worried about what behaviors Hudson would inherit from his father. I never considered how my own patterns would rub off on him, too. His quietness and complacency... he got all that from me.

"Hudson, your father is not a good man," I say, the most forward I've ever been.

"I know," he says plainly. Painfully. "But I wanted him to be."

Yet another attitude he inherited from me. Hoping Beau would change even when confronted with evidence of the opposite. I've kept Beau's secrets so long, and yet here I am, about to reveal my truth for the first time, to our son.

"Your father has told you his reasons for why we divorced," I say, "but the truth is he was abusive. That's why I had to leave."

"I know." His response stuns me. For years, I thought I'd hidden it from him. "I'm sure I don't know everything, but I would overhear the fighting. The way he'd talk to you."

"I never wanted you to know."

"That's why you stayed," he says, speaking wisdom beyond his years. "You didn't want me to grow up in a broken home. You couldn't see that it was already broken. You stayed for me, and you left for me."

I cry harder now, trying to muffle the sounds by covering my mouth. "I never wanted you to go through any of this."

"I'm sorry I gave you such a hard time about moving here. The change was overwhelming, but I know it was the right move for both of us," he says. "If I didn't understand before, I definitely know after Halloween."

"Did you talk to your father about what happened?"

"I didn't see him the rest of the night. Grace ran to Shelby's house to get some paper towels and bandages. You should have seen her. She had blood all over her dress."

I'm upset that another child witnessed Beau's behavior, but I'm immediately grateful Hudson didn't have to go through that experience alone.

"The next day, he was blowing up my phone with apologies. He wanted me to stop by his house after school," he says. "That's why I was late that day."

He wasn't avoiding me or trying to hide any evidence about Shelby's disappearance; he was at the mercy of his father, listening to the same apologies I heard time and time again. He was never at the gardens at all. Relief, warm and welcoming, spreads through me as I realize all the horrible scenarios I've conjured in the past week are of my own creation. Hudson was never involved.

As though reading my mind, he asks, "Mom, did you really think I did something to Shelby?"

"I thought you were hiding something from me. You acted so different since the party. And those bruises."

"Mom, I could never hurt someone like that," he says. "What happened at my last school was different. The other kid came at me with a knife, and I was defending myself. But I'd never hurt a girl, not after seeing the way Dad treated you."

I cry again, but this time the sobs come from a place of relief. I wish Hudson had never had to go through any of this, but at least living under the same roof as his father taught him what not to do. He's still a child, so he's tried to make sense of this dynamic as best he can, build a separate relationship with his father, but his instincts are strong, and his nature is good. As his mother, that's all I ever wanted.

"So, now you know the truth about what happened that night," he says. "That still doesn't tell us anything about Shelby."

As I process this information, I'm not sure that's true.

In an instant, I'm back in the past, reliving the most traumatic night of our marriage.

It was about six months after the gun incident. Nothing major had happened since then, mainly because that night had rattled us both so much.

Hudson was out of town on a school trip, and I was grateful

to have some time to myself. I was downstairs reading when Beau came home. It was late, and I could tell by the loud noises he was making as he lumbered up the stairs from the garage that he was drunk. A fight ensued; over what, I don't even remember. Too tired to engage with him, I went upstairs, locking the bedroom door behind me.

Beau didn't want the night to end that easily. He started pounding on the door. When he realized it was locked, his fists banged harder.

"You're not going to lock me out of my own house," he roared.

Everything that happened next was so fast, and yet the memories are excruciatingly slow as they play back in my mind. Beau pushed the door open, the door frame breaking off in splinters.

Within seconds he was on top of me on the bed. First, he rammed his fists into my stomach, blasting one side, and then the other. I couldn't even feel the pain. All I was aware of was the breath rushing into my lungs.

Then he moved his hands upward, wrapped them around my neck.

I could feel my eyes growing wide as that sweet, fresh air I'd inhaled only moments ago left my body, and it was impossible to get more.

Above me, Beau's face was a mask of anger and rage and glee. Red cheeks, a wicked smile. He shouted the same phrase repeatedly.

"You are nothing!" His voice played like a skipped record, over and over, a horrifying soundtrack to the scene unfolding. "You are nothing!"

My thoughts slowed, taking in the situation around me. Just like the night with the gun, I thought about how easily he could kill me. Between his rage and drunkenness, he could snap my neck without realizing. Or worse, maybe Beau knew exactly what he was doing. Maybe this was the way it all would end.

In an instant, he let go of my neck, and precious air was mine again.

Still kneeling over me, he spat in my face, punctuating the ordeal by letting me know just how little I meant to him. *You are nothing.*

Then he calmly walked away, leaving me alone in the room, knowing my life would never be the same. I still didn't find the strength to leave him that night. That came later, when Hudson's fight at school opened my eyes to how easily he could end up like his father if I didn't intervene. It was always easier to defend Hudson than it ever was to stand up for myself.

My memories of the past meld with what I know about the present.

Beau was at the Halloween party that night. He spent most of the night with Donna Bledsoe, which may have put him in a closer proximity to Shelby than I realized. He was drinking at the party, to the point he became violent with his own son. Could he have encountered Shelby after that? Her cause of death was strangulation. Could he have wrapped those mighty hands around her neck just as easily as he did mine?

I clear my throat before I speak. "We need to go to the police about what happened that night."

"No," he says, immediately. "I just want to forget it."

"You won't forget it. Ever," I say. "Trust me. I didn't confront his abuse for years and look what happened. He's taken his anger out on you."

And maybe, I think with a shudder, Shelby Bledsoe.

Hudson is quiet for several minutes, thinking. I can almost picture the mental back and forth going on inside his head as he tries to decide what to do.

"Will you come with me?"

"Every step of the way."

I wrap my arms around my child, each of us replacing the love that was taken from the other.

THIRTY-SIX

MARY

"You saw Beau Moore hit his son?"

"Yes. It was terrifying. I've never seen a grown man do something like that. I've never seen a father hurt his own child." She waits. "That's why I was so angry about you throwing Hudson under the bus. You don't know anything about his life. About what he has to put up with."

"And the blood got on your costume because you were trying to help him."

"That's why I ran to the Bledsoe house. I went for towels and bandages," she says. "And that's when I found the pregnancy test."

Mary raises her head to the ceiling and lets out a sigh. Finally, everything lines up. There's an explanation for all of it, and the fears she's housed about her daughter can be put to rest. "I wish you'd told me all this sooner. It would have saved me so much grief."

"Mom, did you actually think I hurt Shelby?"

In this moment, peering into her daughter's bright eyes, it doesn't seem possible. It was the combination of discoveries that made her think otherwise. The argument and the costume and the rage in Grace's eyes after her friend's death.

"When things like this happen, there are too many unanswered questions floating around," she says. "That's why we need to tell the police what we know."

"No. I don't want to get involved. It's like I'm betraying her by sharing her secrets."

"If it helps find her killer, then it's not a betrayal. It might be the only way she can get justice." Mary looks at the test again. "Besides, the police probably already know Shelby was pregnant. An autopsy would reveal it, even if they haven't announced it yet."

"If they know, then why do we have to tell them anything?"

"They're likely trying to track down who the father could be. We need to tell them about Rick," she says. "And about Hudson."

"I already told you, Hudson had nothing to do—"

"Grace, if Shelby was pregnant, that leaves two possible suspects. Rick wasn't even at the Halloween party. That only leaves Hudson. Were you with him after your fight with Shelby?"

"No. I went home for the rest of the night."

"So, it's still possible he hurt Shelby. They could have had their own confrontation after you left, and things went south."

"We don't know that."

"We don't. But we can at least give the information to the police and leave it to them to sort out what happened."

"I'll always regret my last conversation with Shelby," she says. "The last thing I want to do is betray another friend."

"Even if it means finding Shelby's killer?"

Grace looks out the window again, her gaze filled with melancholy. Mary wonders what she's thinking about. If she's returning to that night in her mind, returning to her conversations with Hudson earlier in the week. Or maybe, she's going farther back, wondering where they all went wrong to end up here in the first place.

"Fine," Grace says at last, leaning against her headboard. "If you think it will help the investigation."

"I really do," Mary says.

She squeezes her daughter's hand. There's a newfound lightness in her chest. After days of uncertainty and paranoia and denial, Mary finally feels in control again, and, more importantly, she believes her daughter is safe.

Mary rushes down the hallway, her thoughts spurring her forward.

Her sense of gratitude is overwhelming. Grace isn't pregnant. Grace didn't hurt Shelby. The blood on the damned costume belonged to Hudson, the aftermath of the wounds inflicted by his father.

At the same time, she's guilt-ridden that she'd ever considered other possibilities, that she had thought Grace might be involved even for a second. She was only being a good mother, she tells herself. People assume following their children blindly is the best method, but that's not always the case. You must be equally prepared for your child's shortcomings, be ready to pounce should your child ever need you to come to their defense.

All of Mary's paranoia and suffering has resolved her end goal—to make sure Grace was safe. Even better than that, she thinks with pride, Grace was being a good friend to Shelby, trying to steer her in the right direction. She accepted Shelby's pregnancy revelation with support and open ears, but also voiced her concern that her friend was in over her head. Sleeping with a married man. Planning to run away with him. It was a dangerous situation, and Grace was trying to protect her friend from it, even if she ultimately failed.

Grace tried to be a good friend to Hudson, too. Mary is disturbed that her daughter had to witness such violence between a father and son. The more vicious part of her wishes she could get her own hands on Beau Moore, teach him a lesson about harming children.

And yet, the incident between Hudson and his father that night could have very well have been the precipitating factor that led to Shelby's murder. Grace admitted she didn't know where Hudson went after he left her. If he met up with Shelby after the argument, and she shared with him her ridiculous plans of running off with another man, he could have lashed out because of jealousy.

Or maybe Shelby didn't tell him about the other man at all. Maybe she simply told him about the pregnancy, and Hudson assumed he was the father. After an altercation with his own father, that could have pushed him over the edge, might have inspired him to prevent Shelby from further complicating his life. Hudson's expulsion from his last school coupled with his fight with his father on Halloween night paint a clear portrait of violence.

And now there are two possible motives for why he would have wanted Shelby Bledsoe dead.

Mary bursts into her bedroom, nearly running into Ken as he exits their en-suite bathroom.

"Has something happened?" he asks, sensing the alarm in the air.

"I talked to Grace," Mary says. She takes the pregnancy test in the Ziploc bag and places it inside her purse, then turns to the closet. "She finally told me everything."

Ken, struggling to keep up, sits on the bed. "Told you everything about what?"

"She told me what the argument was about on Halloween night. Shelby was sleeping with Rick Davis."

"What?"

"I know. Cheating pig. It's bad enough what he put her

through with his affair, but the babysitter? Naomi will be devastated."

"My goodness. I can't believe it." He pauses, thinking. "Are you going to tell Naomi?"

"Eventually. I mean, she deserves to know, but I don't think Rick killed Shelby. I still think it's Hudson."

"Why?"

"Rick wasn't in town the night of the party, remember? He was on that business retreat. Apparently, Shelby had plans to run off and join him there. That's why Grace and Shelby got into a fight, and why Grace didn't react when she first heard Shelby had gone missing."

Ken raises his hand to his forehead. "I can hardly keep up. Why do you still think Hudson Moore was involved?"

"Because Shelby was cheating on him with Rick Davis," Mary says. "She must have told Hudson about it at the Halloween party, and he lashed out. And now there's proof."

"What do you mean?"

"That wasn't the only secret Shelby was keeping," Mary says. "She was pregnant."

"Pregnant?" It almost sounds like he's choking on the word.

"Yes. Either Rick is the father, and he couldn't control his jealousy, or Hudson's the father and he didn't want the burden of a baby. This is it," Mary says, fumbling to pull a jacket from its hanger. "Now we know why Hudson killed Shelby. The police have to know about it."

"You're going to the police?"

"Of course. They'll find out she was pregnant soon enough, if they haven't already. Between this and everything else we've uncovered, it should be enough to arrest him. Shelby deserves justice."

Finally, the jacket yanks free from the hanger. Mary pulls it on, zipping it up to her chin. It's nearing winter so she needs to dress warm, despite the fact her insides are bursting with tropical heat. She can barely put one foot in front of the other, she's so thrilled with excitement and vindication. For Grace. For Donna. For Shelby. Mary was the first to figure out what happened, and she's going to share that fact with the rest of the world.

She's so distracted, she hardly realizes her husband has fallen silent, until his strangled voice recaptures her attention, "Oh, Mary."

The strangeness of his voice alarms her. She turns around suddenly, sees him sitting on the foot of the bed. His neck and face are red, almost look bruised, and there are tears in his eyes.

"Hudson isn't the father of Shelby's baby."

Mary squints in confusion. "How could you know that?"

He stands now, placing his hand over hers, gently. "Don't go to the police. We need to talk."

"Talk about what?" she spits, jerking her hand away as though it's been burned.

"There's something I need to tell you," he says. "About Shelby."

In a flash, that same heat inside her turns to ice. She feels frozen in place, heavy with dread. She stares ahead, part of her already aware of what her husband will say next. Ken sits on the bed again, lets out a deep exhale.

"It's me, Mary. I was sleeping with Shelby."

"What?" Mary heard him clearly, and yet she'll have to hear it over and over again for the weight of his words to sink in.

"Shelby and I were sleeping together. If she's pregnant, the baby is mine."

Mary's chest feels as though it's coming apart, each bone being ripped from her rib cage, one by one. She leans forward, steadying herself by reaching out for the closest dresser.

"You were sleeping with our daughter's best friend?" she asks. "You were sleeping with a teenage girl?"

"I'm so sorry, Mary. I never meant for any of this to happen."

"How long?" she asks, breathless.

"It doesn't matter—"

"Everything matters!" Mary shouts, a rage she never even knew existed escaping from her lungs. "You're the vice principal at the high school. Shelby Bledsoe has been murdered. And you're telling me you were sleeping with her?"

"I didn't kill her, Mary," he says, pleading. "But I have to be honest now. If what Grace says is true, it's only a matter of time before the police try to discover the paternity of her child. We can't let them get back to me. We have to figure out what we're going to do."

Suddenly, the room is spinning, Mary's past and present thoughts colliding with one another at a sickening pace. All of it is too much, insurmountable. Shelby is dead, and the baby inside her will prove her husband was her lover. It will prove that her husband was having sex with an underage girl. The pure thought of it sickens her.

And yet, Mary realizes she should have known better.

Because Ken did it to her first.

THIRTY-SEVEN

GRACE

Halloween Night

The gardens had always been a special place for Grace Holden and Shelby Bledsoe, ever since they were girls. It was the setting of elaborate pretend games, an enchanted fairyland, a haunted wilderness. When they got older, it was where they'd go to dodge their parents, listen to music and gossip about people at school.

The music and banter from the Halloween party grew quieter as Grace walked downhill, eyes searching for her friend. At night, the gardens were all navy and gray, black trees hovering in the distance. She found Shelby sitting by the water. A series of solar powered lanterns decorated the bridge stretching across the pond, the only light in sight.

"We need to talk," Grace said, feeling for the Ziploc bag in her jacket pocket. What she'd just experienced with Hudson had been a shock, but it hadn't dulled the most outrageous discovery; her best friend was pregnant and hadn't told her.

Shelby stood quickly, her head twisting from side to side, as though she was searching for someone else.

"What are you doing here?" she asked, her gaze focusing on Grace's dress. "And what happened to your costume?"

Grace looked down, wincing as she saw the bloodstains. Her ruined dress wasn't important, though. "Hudson got into a fight."

"What?" Shelby came alive with the drama. "Why?"

"Not that you care," Grace said. "You just broke up with him."

Shelby sat back down, lazily. "You're welcome."

"Excuse me?"

"It's no secret you've been pining after him for weeks. Now that I'm done with him, he's all yours."

The way Shelby talked about Hudson, like he was some discarded toy, bothered Grace, but she refused to get flustered. There were far bigger matters that needed to be confronted. She held up the bag, high enough that the moonlight would catch it.

"I ran to your house for some paper towels to help him," she says, "and I found this in your bathroom."

Shelby's face went still. It was too dark to see, but Grace imagined her friend was blushing. Embarrassed, perhaps.

"It's my mom's," Shelby said quickly.

"It can't be. Your mom had a full hysterectomy last year," Grace said. "Shelby, are you pregnant?"

The girl exhaled, pulling her hand through the water below, avoiding her friend.

"This is serious, Shelby," she said. "You have to tell me."

"Yes," she said, at last. "I found out a few days ago."

"And you didn't tell me?"

"I didn't know how to feel about it," she said. "It was a big shock."

"That's an understatement." Grace sat beside her friend. They were too young to have this type of conversation. She didn't even know what to say to her friend, what advice to give.

Still, Grace was determined to be there for her, as she always had been before. "We can figure out what to do together. I'll help you, whatever you decide to do."

Shelby put her hand over Grace's and squeezed. "Thanks."

"I don't understand though," Shelby said. "Why break up with Hudson now? You're going to have to tell him."

Shelby laughed. "He's not the father."

Grace didn't know for sure if the couple had even had sex. Shelby had told her about every guy she'd slept with since she lost her virginity last summer, but Grace certainly hadn't known she was sleeping with someone else. It was hard to keep up with the revelations.

"If Hudson's not the father, who is?"

"I can't say."

"I'm your best friend," she said. "You have to tell me."

"It's complicated."

"I don't understand. You've been cheating on Hudson this whole time?"

"Hudson and I were never really dating. I knew he liked me, and I played along to help keep my cover." She paused. "My real boyfriend is married."

"Your real boyfriend is *married*." Grace could feel her cheeks filling with heat. "Who is it?"

Shelby remained silent, her hand still playing in the water.

"It's Rick Davis, isn't it? You've watched their kids for years. Always talked about your little crush."

Shelby laughed again, refusing to reveal anything else.

"This isn't some kind of joke. You're sleeping with a married man, and now you're pregnant. Do you have any idea how many lives this could ruin?"

"We're in love, okay? I didn't mean for any of it to happen, but I couldn't stop myself. And now we're going to have a child. We're going to build a life together."

"You sound ridiculous," Grace said. "Rick Davis isn't going

to leave his wife for you. He already has kids. You're living in some type of fantasy."

"You don't know anything."

"I know you're a bad friend. A bad person," she said, her anger growing. "I can't believe you'd do this to Ms. Davis. To their kids."

"This stupid town with all its stupid people doesn't matter anymore, okay? We're going to run away together, start over."

"You sound so foolish," she said. "You're about to be a mother. You have to grow up."

"You're just jealous. You've always been jealous of me."

"Well, you're a homewrecker. A slut," Grace said. "Just like your mom."

It was a ruthless remark, and Grace could see the hurt register on her friend's face, but she didn't care. Someone needed to call Shelby out for her behavior. Someone should have called her out years ago, and maybe they wouldn't be in this situation.

"That's a cheap shot, talking about my mother," Shelby scoffed. "I can't wait to see the look on Mary Holden's face when she hears the news. All these boring housewives who think they've got their lives figured out. I'm going to prove them all wrong."

Grace couldn't understand what that meant. She was done with this conversation, done with this friendship. If Shelby couldn't admit what she'd done was wrong, the relationship was unsalvageable.

"I hope your life is everything you want it to be," Grace said, turning away and walking up the hill, leaving her friend alone in the dark gardens. "Good luck with Rick."

Shelby shouted after her one last time, "You don't know what you're talking about!" Grace was so far ahead, she barely heard her.

THIRTY-EIGHT

MARY

The most convincing lies are born from truth.

Mary and Ken met at school. That's the story she's told people, time and time again, quickly followed by the explanation that while she was earning her bachelor's degree at a small university near her hometown, Ken was finishing his master's degree.

What Mary didn't tell people was that the college she and Ken attended was not where they met. They'd begun dating when Mary was still in high school, and Ken was the newly hired history teacher.

Their age difference wasn't completely alarming. She was seventeen, and Ken was twenty-eight. Eleven years. Mary knew husbands and wives with far bigger age gaps; some couples were decades apart, and no one ever seemed to bat an eyelid, as long as one half of the couple was incredibly attractive and the other half extremely wealthy.

Eleven years was nothing, but because of their circumstances, Mary had to be careful how she explained their relationship, make sure she didn't let anything slip that would raise eyebrows.

When she met Ken, she was immediately struck by his good looks, as were all the girls in her grade. She sat in the back row of her American history class, nervous around her teacher in the same way she was when near an attractive boy her own age. Over time, Ken's looks became secondary. Mary was attracted to his mind, the way he would dissect and explain the most complicated events. All her other teachers were boring, counting the days until summer break, and retirement beyond that.

Not Ken. His youth gave a vibrancy to his lessons. Mary, who'd never been big into reading and writing, suddenly found herself looking forward to class, looking forward to school in general, because it gave her time around him.

An entire semester passed, and it became clear that the respect and admiration she had for her teacher was mutual. Ken —she called him Mr. Holden back then, of course—always seemed to value her analytical comments and input. There were some days Mary would forget they were in a room surrounded by her peers, they were that connected.

By the spring semester, Mr. Holden had taken over the yearbook committee, and Mary was happy to join him. It wasn't only her, of course. A dozen other students from the school joined, and yet, just like in class, Mary imagined it was only the two of them in the room whenever the committee met after school. The more they worked together, the more Mary picked up on signs that he was equally happy to be around her. His stare would linger on her just a second longer than his other students, and there were times when he was walking around the room, and she suddenly became overwhelmed with the closeness between them. The heat coming off his body, his heavy breaths when he bent down to look at her notebook.

Still, the more immature part of Mary's mind believed this was nothing more than an innocent crush. At home, she'd think about him as she was drifting to sleep. She'd imagine Mr.

Holden confessing his love for her, taking her into his arms and kissing her. She'd imagine what it would be like when she turned eighteen, the two of them taking off together, going on safaris and adventures. She'd always wanted these things for herself but imagining Mr. Holden by her side made the dream even more thrilling.

And yet, none of it felt real. A fantasy never does. When a child hosts a tea party with his or her closest animal friends, a part of them knows their stuffed animals aren't real, that it's only them pushing the conversation, pouring the imaginary beverages. That was all her fantasies about Mr. Holden were. Fanciful visions rooted in real desire, but nothing would ever come of it, and she was okay with that.

Then one day, after everyone had left, and it was only the two of them alone in the classroom, he bent down and kissed her on the lips. She stood still, like a statue, trying to decide what to make of the interaction. It was frightening and exhilarating all at once.

It was like she'd called upon a shooting star, and her wish had come true. Now, her feelings were real, and his were, too. The kiss was real. The warmth of his hand on her lower back was real. Everything that followed was real, too. And before she knew it, Mary was in the very first relationship of her life with a man in his twenties.

Being in love was unlike any sensation she'd ever felt before. Mary had watched couples on television, but none of them seemed to have the spark she had with Ken. They were addicted to each other, couldn't keep their hands to themselves, but eventually their obvious affection for one another would become their downfall. They'd never been caught outright, but whispers were starting to spread around the school. Mr. Holden was dating a student. It was the type of rumor with not enough evidence to do anything about it, but just enough scandal to keep it in rotation.

By the time Mary turned eighteen, just before the end of her senior year, an entire plan was in place. Ken and the school had amicably decided to part ways, to spare the latter from any undue investigation that might cause humiliation. He'd decided to go for a graduate degree, at the same university Mary would attend.

Just like that, their dream was a reality, though slightly less glamorous than the one she'd had in her head. Instead of traveling the world, the couple explored the college campus, Ken sharing stories from his own undergraduate years. Instead of safaris and jungles, they had a small one-bedroom apartment, far removed from the people and gossip in her hometown.

Mary was happy in those early years, but beneath that happiness was something else. She felt indebted to Ken. For all he'd given up. For all he'd risked. He'd chosen her, and it only felt right that she chose him in return. As their relationship matured and they racked up years together, Mary started to forget the scandalous circumstances of their beginning.

And for years, that was what she told herself. It didn't matter how their relationship started. Look at how much they'd built together. An entire life. A marriage and a home and Grace. Sweet, beautiful Grace. How could what happened between them have been bad when so much beauty had come from it? For years, this was the truth that got Mary through. She clung to it, whenever memories from the past beckoned her to a different place, and she started to believe it.

Until now. Until her husband admitted to sleeping with another teenage girl.

"Mary, please say something," Ken says, his voice broken. He's still sitting on the bed, his elbows on his knees. "We have to figure out what we're going to do about this."

"I don't know what to do," she says, her voice a whisper.

Mary stares at her husband, for the first time, seeing him for what he is. A weak man. She'd told herself the opposite for years. That he was mature and intelligent and strong. He chose her, out of all the women in the world. Now, she sees that choice for what it was. Mary had been a consolation prize because Ken was too undeveloped to have an adult life, to pursue adult women.

"She was pregnant," he says, as though he can only half-believe it himself.

For a flashing moment, Mary is grateful the girl is dead. Then, in the same instant, she hates herself for ever thinking such a thing. That self-hatred remains with her, heavy in her chest. She realizes she has hated herself for a long time. Mary hates the person she has become. It's so far removed from the girl she'd once been.

She closes her eyes and remembers. She was like Grace once. No, she was more like Shelby. Headstrong and passionate and confident. What had happened to the girl she once was? With a shudder, she has her answer.

Him. Ken. He ruined her, just like he ruined Shelby once he realized his child was growing in her stomach.

All these years, Mary had been trying to deny what their relationship was, how it originated. She told herself it was her choice, her life. But she was too young to make such decisions, just as Shelby was too young to take on the burdens of motherhood.

And far too young to be ripped from the world altogether.

"You murdered her," Mary says, her voice solid, strong.

Ken stands. "I didn't. You've got it wrong. Yes, we had plans to meet at the gardens after the Halloween party wrapped up, but when I arrived, she wasn't there. I came home, and that's the truth."

"Shelby told Grace you were going to run away together."

Ken exhales heavily, shaking his head. "It's something we'd talk about, sure. But it was a stupid, stupid plan. I could never walk away from the life we've made together."

"Did she tell you she was pregnant at the party?" Mary goes on, certain her theory is correct. "It started a fight, and you killed her."

"Mary, you must believe me. That's not what happened."

"I can't believe anything you say anymore!"

Whatever chain has been between them is breaking, and they both stare ahead dumbfounded. It might have appeared like Mary Holden was the one in control, but she was only playing a part, the role she'd agreed to play when she was seventeen years old and decided to start an affair with her teacher. A choice she was always too young to make, the consequences of which were always too intense for her to understand.

"I love you, Mary. You have to believe that."

"Then why were you sleeping with a teenage girl? Our daughter's friend!" She takes a step back toward the hallway. "Why did you sleep with me?"

"Mary, you know why."

Love. What a silly, worthless excuse. She sees now it wasn't her that he loved, but her age. It's an attraction he can't control, a part of herself she can never be again, which is why he had to seek it in someone else.

"You need to leave this house," she says.

She rushes down the stairs, her phone in her hands, and calls the police.

THIRTY-NINE

STELLA

Hudson sits beside me in the passenger seat, silent.

"Are you okay?" I ask.

He nods, reaching out his hand to squeeze my own.

We're on our way back from the local police department. Reporting Beau to the cops, some of whom are his very own colleagues, wasn't easy, but it was long overdue. Staring at my teenage son, I can't find the right words to express just how proud of him I am. He's already braver than I ever was. If only I could have had his strength more than a decade ago, when the abuse first started.

As we turn into the neighborhood, bursts of red and blue color the surroundings. However, they're not parked in front of Donna Bledsoe's house, as they have been throughout the week. The vehicles are in front of the Holden house, blocking the driveway.

"Mom, that's Grace's house," Hudson says, his eyes fixed ahead. "What's going on?"

"I don't know," I say, looking up and down the street. I see Annette Friss standing by her mailbox, like us, unable to pull away. Stunned by the scene unfolding, we park in our driveway and hurry across the street to her.

"Any idea why the police are at Mary's house?" I ask Annette.

She shakes her head. "Not a clue."

I can see Mary on her front porch. She's seated in one of the oversized rocking chairs, two police officers talking to her. I'm a bit astonished by how collected she seems. Across from her house, I see Janet and Naomi on Naomi's porch, watching.

"Hudson, stay with Ms. Friss. I'll be right back."

I jog across the street, mounting Naomi's porch. The way the women have treated me over the past few days is an afterthought.

"What's going on?"

"They're arresting Ken Holden for Shelby's murder," Naomi says.

"What?"

The names and faces won't connect in my mind. Ken Holden. The vice-principal. Husband to the Queen Bee of the neighborhood. My stomach twists in an unsettling way.

"Apparently, he was having an affair with Shelby," Janet says, her words slurred. "They must have gotten into some type of fight on Halloween night, and he killed her."

The shock of this news overcomes me. I sit in the open chair beside Janet to stop from falling.

"The vice principal of the high school was having an affair with a student?" I ask. "His daughter's best friend?"

"It's awful," Naomi says.

"Think about Donna!" Janet blurts. "Her best friend's husband murdered her daughter. I can't believe it."

Even as they deliver more information, it's hard to process. The entire neighborhood has been spreading rumors and pointing fingers all week. Ken Holden's name was never mentioned once. Mary was spinning most of the drama; I can't believe her husband was the culprit the entire time.

"How did everyone find out?" I ask, still watching the police across the street.

"Mary must have found out somehow and called the cops," Naomi says.

"She turned in her own husband?"

"What choice did she have?" Janet says. "I can't imagine what she's going through. How she's going to explain all this to their daughter. None of them will ever be the same."

The flashing emergency lights and lampposts overhead illuminate the darkness enough for me to see Hudson still standing beside Annette Friss. I wonder what thoughts are going through his mind. He's already suffered one trauma tonight, having to report his father's abuse to the police. Now, after days of gossip and finger-pointing, Shelby's killer has been found, and I'll have to figure out a way to tell him.

I stand, not even giving Naomi and Janet a second look. They've known the Holdens far longer than I have and have undoubtedly had better experiences with them. There's a lot they'll have to process, but right now all I care about is my son, making sure he's okay.

When I join him across the street, his hand feels clammy in my own.

"What happened?" he asks me.

"We'll talk about it when we get home," I say, gently pulling him in the direction of our bungalow.

"Is Grace—"

"Grace is fine," I tell him, and this single piece of information seems to be enough to settle him.

His shoulders relax as he exhales. "I didn't know how much more I could handle."

"You've been through a lot. We both have," I say, unlocking

the front door, holding it open so he can walk inside. "Maybe you just need some rest. We can talk more in the morning."

He nods, appears relieved he doesn't have to process any more distressing information. Even though tonight was necessary, it was equally exhausting. What we both need, more than anything, is rest. All our questions about Shelby's murder and the Holdens' involvement can wait until tomorrow.

"I'm going to hop in the shower," Hudson says, mounting the stairs.

I watch him, still in awe at how much he's been able to handle in the past week, how he's not willing to let complicated emotions interfere with what he knows is right. After tonight, I'm convinced that my influence as a parent is good, and it counteracts whatever negative behaviors Beau exposed him to.

Beyond the kitchen lights, the rest of the house is dark. I drop my belongings on the table, and walk into the living room, flicking the lamp to my right.

Beau is sitting in the armchair directly across from me. His presence startles me, and I jump. Before I can open my mouth to say anything else, he raises a hand.

He's holding his service weapon.

The sight of it stuns me into silence. It feels as though an icy hand grabs at my heart.

"Don't you dare scream," he says, his voice low and calm. Terrifying.

I nod in understanding, my eyes flicking in the direction of the stairs, where Hudson just went. I hear running water in the upstairs bathroom. Having my son this close to an enraged Beau is frightening, but at least he can't hear what's coming next. I know from past experiences it won't be good.

"Beau, what are you doing here?" I ask quietly, my voice already beginning to break.

"I'm a cop, Stella," he says, crossing one leg over the other, his weapon still pointing at me. "Did you really think I wouldn't find out what you did?"

The police station. It would be too soon for them to question him about the assault, particularly with all the drama going on in the neighborhood, but he has friends, connections. Isn't that what he always warned me? That I could never do anything to him without him having the upper hand? That he'd kill me if I ever stood in his way?

I stare at the weapon in horror, realizing every threat he's ever aimed at me is coming true in this very moment.

FORTY

MARY

Mary shuts the door and closes her eyes.

She can imagine the madness taking place on the other side of the wall. The police officers. Their cars. Her nosy neighbors with all their questions.

It's overwhelming, and she doesn't know how she can manage any of it. For decades, she's depended on the idea that her life must be perfect. If she could keep up the image, the façade, she wouldn't lose the life she's worked so hard to build.

Now, she realizes the foundation was never solid. The cracks were there from the very beginning.

It felt like, in many ways, Mary had stifled the truth about her marriage, reworked the narrative so it made sense in her mind. Now, memories she'd buried long ago crawl to the surface. The impropriety of their relationship from the very beginning. All the secrets she had to keep, the stories she had to spin, to cover for the fact that the way they met wasn't okay.

She'd thought she was doing this to protect herself, but now, she realizes she was, instead, protecting Ken, protecting the predator she could never admit he was, and the guilt is over-whelming. Not only did she convince herself that his behavior was acceptable, but she allowed him to believe that, too. And what had that led to? Another affair with a teenage girl, and this time, the victim ended up dead.

It didn't matter how many times Ken pleaded his innocence; she wouldn't believe him. He'd never been innocent. What he did to her was self-serving and manipulative and dirty, and what he did to Shelby was even worse.

The quiet in the house is unsettling. Maybe it's because she can still hear the commotion from outside. People walking around and asking questions. Maybe it's because just days ago, she spent hours making this house look impeccable, as she always did. The tree stands in the living room, large ornaments precisely placed, glimmering thanks to the string of lights behind them. Anyone looking at Mary's living room at this very moment would think exactly what she wants them to think: that her life is flawless.

Looking at the same room now, it feels like a heavy rock is sinking inside of her. Nothing will ever be the same. Not her family, not her life, not her friendships. But maybe, just maybe, Mary can do what she's always done, take the mess she's helped create and turn it into something sparkling, and this time, it will be better. Of course, it will be hard starting over without Ken. His sickness and betrayal now cast a dark shadow over their twenty years together. Still, she'll grieve the happy times, grieve the life she so desperately wanted to believe was real.

Of course, it's not just about Mary. She must make sure Grace is okay, too.

During Mary's argument with Ken, Grace mostly stayed in her room.

Mary had run to Grace's bedroom first, ordering her to lock the door and not come out until she told her otherwise. Grace obeyed without asking questions. Mary would like to think it was because of the newfound closeness between them, but it very well could have been fear. She could barely imagine what her daughter was thinking. She'd never heard her parents fight. Rarely had they even said a cross word to one another.

After the police arrived, Mary had no choice but to tell her daughter what was happening. With the assistance of another officer, they'd told Grace that her father had admitted to having an affair with Shelby. That he was, in fact, the father of Shelby's child.

Grace had broken down completely, falling to her knees in the middle of the living room. Mary had held her daughter's shaking hands, trying to tell her everything would be okay, even though it seemed that would never, could never, be true.

Within the course of an hour, Grace had had to confront the fact her father was sleeping with her best friend, that he'd impregnated her, and murdered her. Mary didn't even get into the true nature of her own relationship. That would be a conversation for another day; in that moment, Grace had had all she could take.

One of the police officers helped Mary escort Grace upstairs, back to her bedroom, and sat with her until she went to sleep, while another officer asked Mary more questions.

Now, it's just the two of them alone in the house. Mary peers into her daughter's bedroom, relieved to see that she is still asleep. Grace needs rest like never before, and Mary needs time to decide what she will say to her daughter when tomorrow comes.

It's not the only conversation she'll have to have.

She'll have to explain to everyone, in one way or another, what happened. Janet and Naomi and all the other neighbors. Donna! How will she ever mend all this with her friend? Admit that her husband was the person who killed her daughter? Mary can't expect her friend's forgiveness; she only hopes she'll one day understand how sorry Mary is, and that she'll carry this with her for the rest of her life.

There's only one person Mary feels she needs to talk to

right now: Stella Moore. She deserves an apology, as does her son. Mary was so determined to cast him as a suspect, she didn't realize she was once again protecting Ken, the true predator.

Mary glances out of the kitchen window. Some of the police cruisers have pulled away, but there's still a ton of commotion outside. The last thing she wants to do is walk out of her front door and be confronted by the entire neighborhood, so she sneaks out the back. She cuts through her neighbors' backyards until she reaches Stella Moore's home.

She plans on slinking around to the front of the house to knock on the front door, but another voice interferes with her thoughts. Someone is yelling, and someone else, it sounds like, is crying. Fear grips her, as she looks around the backyard, fully aware of how alone she is. Then, she realizes the voices are drifting out from inside Stella Moore's house.

Mary approaches the back of the house, her position still concealed.

She leans her head close to the sliding glass door, and listens.

FORTY-ONE

STELLA

Beau appears eerily calm as he sits in the armchair across from me, his gun still pointed in my direction.

Details in the room stick out to me, providing clues on how to act. I notice there's a near-empty glass on the table beside him. He's likely drunk. Alcohol always brought the violence out of him. My eyes shoot to the sliding glass door, then back to the front. It would be so easy to dart in either direction, but I can't do that. Not with Hudson upstairs.

"Sit," he orders, reaching for the last sip of his drink.

"Beau, we can talk—"

"I said SIT!" he screams, my body jumping at the vibrating anger in his tone.

Even though the last thing I want to do is obey him, the weapon frightens me into submission. It doesn't matter how much time has passed, how much has changed, how much I've changed, Beau will always be in control of my thoughts and actions, because he's willing to go to whatever lengths necessary.

I sit on the sofa across from him, my posture stiff and poised, as though I can morph this threatening confrontation into a civil conversation.

"I'd be more comfortable if you put the gun away."

"All I've ever cared about is making you comfortable, Stella," he says, sarcasm spewing, the gun staying in the exact same place. "Problem is, it's impossible to meet your standards. Everything I've given you over the years, and how do you thank me? You leave. And take my son with you."

"Our relationship wasn't working, Beau." I must choose every word carefully. Make sure not to come off too judgmental or accusatory. "It hadn't been working for years."

"Whose fault is that? You take a few little incidents and blow them out of proportion."

Is that truly what he believes in his warped mind? That somehow, I brought on his abusive behaviors. That I should condone being pushed and shoved and threatened and choked. That I should tolerate him spitting in my face. That I should allow him to point a gun at me. For the first time, I look at Beau and see how truly broken he is. He'd treat anyone this way if given the chance. Anyone who dared to step in his way.

"And now you're teaching our son to do the same thing," he says.

"You hit him," I say, slowly. For years, I've overlooked his behavior toward me, but I can't minimize what he did to our son. Even with his gun pointed at me, I refuse to let him think his actions are okay. "He's a child, and you gave him a black eye."

"He came at me first!"

"It doesn't matter! You're his father. He looks up to you. It's your job to teach him right from wrong, and you've done nothing but squander the opportunity!" I shout, rising out of my chair. "That's why I had to leave. I couldn't let him end up like you!"

Beau stands now, the weapon at his side. He leads with his

chest and his anger as he takes a step closer. "There's nothing wrong with me."

"Do you really believe that?" I'm fueled by anger and fear, but beyond that, pity. Beau truly doesn't see. "This isn't how you treat people you love. People who love you! You can't scare them into submission. You can't act however you want and expect them to stand beside you."

He grabs my arm, twisting my wrist so hard it begins to burn. "Stop talking."

"Please, Beau. Just stop this. Let us move on with our lives."

"And what about my life?" He jerks my arm as he speaks, each tug sending a new shot of pain throughout my body. "I don't have a wife. My son is gone. And now I could lose my job. All because the two of you reported me. Everything I've ever cared about is gone, because of you."

It sinks in, finally, that this confrontation is worse than all the others before. Beau has always had the upper hand. The better reputation, the respected job, the charming personality. Now all these descriptors are collapsing in on one another, and he's hopeless.

And there's nothing more dangerous than a desperate man.

"Leave now, Beau," I plead. "I won't tell anyone you came here."

"I'm not going to give you the chance," he says, pulling me toward the front door. "I'm going to do what I should have done a year ago, when you first tried to leave."

He drops my arm for only a second, but it's long enough for me to dart away from him. Like every threatened woman in a B-movie, I dart up the stairs. Exiting the house seems an impossibility, and I'm still keenly aware that Hudson is nearby. The water has prevented him from hearing any of this, and I must warn him.

It could very well be too late for me, this time, but not him. I can still save him.

I rush up the stairs, Beau only a few steps behind me.

Memories fly, as though our life together is flashing before my eyes.

Racing away from him. The scattered laundry and the shattered glass and the broken doorframe.

You are nothing.

All I've ever done is run away from him, it seems, and it's never been enough. My body braces, waiting for him to jerk my hair and pull me back, waiting for his fingers to reclaim their place around my throat. Then—

A cry rings out, and to my disbelief, it isn't me screaming.

It's Beau.

FORTY-TWO

MARY

Mary listens, each passing second proving more horrific.

Rarely has she ever heard a man speak like that to a woman. Even hours ago, when she accused Ken of murder, he was calm, docile, in denial. There's a dangerous tone in Beau Moore's voice that keeps Mary still, afraid to move.

She's even more worried for Stella Moore.

The calm in the other woman's voice suggests this type of behavior isn't new. The threats and the yelling. Did she say he had a gun?

Mary hunches down closer to the patio, trying to get a better look, but then Beau stands, and her vision is blocked again. Is he grabbing Stella's arm? Twisting it?

Despite the many revelations on this shocking day, Mary finds herself going back even further in time, to when she was only a child, and she used to listen to her parents fight. It was the same dynamic she's witnessing now. An enraged father, a compliant mother. She thinks about Hudson, and wonders if he's close enough to hear the commotion taking place between his parents.

She thinks about herself, that young girl hiding under the

covers. She thinks about her younger brother, how he'd never remembered a time when their parents weren't at war, and how quickly it all came to an end when their mother died, and then it was just Mary, defending her brother against their father.

Until she met Ken, that is, and she left her younger brother to fend for himself. A searing anger spreads through her chest when she thinks about all the mistakes she's made, about all the victims that have been left in her wake. She knows that the cycle must end with her.

She's not even conscious about it. Her body reacts before her mind can concoct a plan. The sliding glass door glides soundlessly, and she's inside the house, following Stella and Beau Moore to the stairs.

Stella is several steps ahead, still trying to make it to the top of the stairs. Beau is right behind her, his long legs taking the steps two at a time, and in his hand, just as she feared, there's a gun. Before fear and defensiveness can speak logic, she's grabbing the heaviest thing she can find—a decorative statue in the living room—and bringing it down hard on the side of Beau's head.

The man yelps in pain, his free hand rising to his head. Before he can turn and see her, Mary hits him again, this time on the shoulder, trying to disarm him.

It works. The weapon falls from his hand, clunking against each step. Instinctually, Mary jumps back. She's never liked being around guns. Isn't sure how easy it is for one of them to go off. Only now does the clear disadvantage she's at sink in. Beau is an experienced police officer who knows how to handle a weapon. And what is she? A housewife. A—

Before she can finish her thought, Beau comes tumbling down the staircase, almost collapsing on top of her. Stella is standing behind him, her arms outstretched.

"Grab the gun!" she shouts.

Mary's eyes dart to the right, jumping forward for the

weapon before an injured Beau can make it to his feet. She holds the weapon in her hands, the weight of it sending nervous pinpricks across her arms.

"Mom?" Hudson calls from somewhere upstairs, unseen. "What's going on?"

"Lock the bathroom door," Stella shouts behind her, never once turning, never once taking her eyes off Beau hunched over at the foot of the stairs.

Unsteadily, she leaps over him, her hands reaching out toward Mary for balance. The two women cling to each other, staring at the large man beneath them. Mary continues to hold the weapon out in front of her shakily.

"Are the police still outside?" Stella says, her eyes wide.

"They were just a moment ago," Mary says, her own gaze tightening around Beau. With each passing second, her anxiety falls away. She's becoming less afraid, more in tune with this new role she must play.

She's a protector. Defending her neighbor, a child, herself.

Stella dashes to the front door and pushes it open. "Help! We need help!" she shouts.

Mary walks backwards in that same direction, but keeps her arms out ahead, her full attention on the target.

By the time Beau Moore makes it to his feet, two police officers are inside the house, their own weapons drawn. Mary raises her hands then, making sure they can see the gun in her hands.

"He was threatening her with the gun," Mary says, immediately. "I watched the whole thing."

One of the officers removes the weapon from her hands and pushes her back. Beau puts up a small fight, but quickly calculates that it's only making the situation worse. He glares at Mary as they get the cuffs on him, and brushes her shoulder as they escort him outside.

The second officer instructs them to stay inside, that they'll return to retrieve their statements. Mary sees Stella leaning against the doorframe, watching her ex-husband being escorted outside, like she can't quite believe it's real.

Stella looks up and locks eyes with Mary, and says, "Thank you."

Mary struggles for a response. She is horrible at being vulnerable, and yet, Mary sees more of herself in Stella Moore in this moment than she ever has before. Even with so few details, she knows both of them have confronted their darkest monsters today, and they've both made it out on the other side.

"Mom?"

Mary turns around and sees Hudson standing at the head of the stairs, confusion written all over his face.

Stella springs off the wall, rushing past Mary and up to the second floor. She wraps her arms around Hudson. It makes Mary long for her own daughter.

Her darling Grace, who is fast asleep, only a few doors down the way.

FORTY-THREE

STELLA

The events from yesterday don't seem real.

I wake up on Monday in disbelief about everything that's happened. Ken Holden was outed for having an affair with Shelby Bledsoe, and subsequently arrested for her murder. Hudson found the courage to report his father for the abuse that took place on Halloween night. In retaliation, Beau attacked me, and, of all people, Mary Holden came to my rescue. I watched as Beau was hauled away in handcuffs, a sight I never believed I'd live to see.

Hudson spent the night in my room, sleeping at the foot of my bed like he did when he was a small child. He's much bigger now, of course, and I figured he'd wake up sore from the cramped position. Instead, he appears refreshed, stretching his arms wide when he stands, staring out my bedroom window as sunlight invades the room.

"Should we make breakfast?" he asks.

"Sure," I say, my own movements much more rigid in the morning.

Hudson slices strawberries and bananas as I whisk batter

for the waffle maker. He talks the entire time, telling me about his classes at school and funny videos he's seen online. It's obvious he's trying to avoid the neighborhood tragedy, prevent memories of last night's altercation with his father, but I don't mind. Despite everything we've been through, it finally feels like the burdens weighing us down have been lifted. Beau won't be able to worm his way back into our lives as easily as he did before.

We continue chatting as we eat our meal, and I hope we'll have more mornings like this. Just the two of us. Hudson's finished his last bite when his phone pings. He looks at the screen, and frowns.

"It's Grace," he says, his eyes still staring at the device, as though he doesn't know where to look.

"What's she saying?"

"Her mother has to go to the police station to answer more questions," he says. "She doesn't want to be alone."

Normally, I wouldn't encourage my teenage son to be alone with a girl his age, but then I recall the circumstances. Hudson and Grace had a burgeoning friendship before the events of this past week. Now, they'll lean on each other even more. They've both had to face painful realities about their fathers. It's a complicated situation few people their age will ever understand.

"Come on," I say, grabbing both our plates. "I'll walk you over there."

"Are you sure?" Hudson appears confused. "I know Mrs. Holden doesn't like us being together."

"I think she'll be thankful to anyone who shows her daughter kindness," I say.

The Mary who appeared in my living room last night is far different from the woman I've come to know in recent months. That woman was calculated, domineering, only willing to act when it would benefit herself in some way.

When Beau was attacking me, Mary threw herself into the middle of the situation, risking her own safety to protect me. There are still several conversations to be had between us, but I believe she'd want me to show compassion to her child in the wake of what's happened.

There are still police cars scattered around the neighborhood. I imagine they're conducting interviews with other people around the block, trying to build a strong case against Ken Holden. As we approach the Holden house, I see Grace sitting in one of the cushioned chairs on the front porch. She stands when she sees Hudson, and waves. I can't imagine how lonely that child must feel, knowing her father was abusing her friend. Knowing her father murdered her friend.

I stand beside the picket fence, arms crossed over my body, as Hudson joins her on the porch. They sit beside each other and begin talking. Although I can't hear what they're saying, I know they now share a unique bond.

As I turn to walk home, I spot Naomi and Janet across the street on Naomi's front porch. I'm tempted to walk right by them but stop when I hear Janet shouting my name.

"Stella," she calls. "We'd like to talk to you."

"I'm okay," I say, raising a hand.

I understand what these women are about now. They want to get more details about what happened with Beau. They want to gossip about Mary and Ken's marriage. After what I went through last night, I want no part in it.

"Please, Stella," Naomi says. "We want to apologize."

I turn around slowly and see that both women are frozen in place. As I walk closer, I can tell they've both been crying.

"We feel awful about everything that's happened in the past week," Janet begins.

"We never should have spread those rumors about Hudson," Naomi adds. "You tried telling me I didn't have the whole story, but I didn't want to listen."

"It was wrong of us," Janet says, her sobs beginning again. "We were convinced an outsider must have killed Shelby. We could never have imagined it was one of our own."

I nod in understanding. No one wants to admit the severity of the problem right in front of them. It's why I stayed married to Beau for as long as I did.

"We don't expect you to forgive us," Naomi says. "We want you to know we truly feel horrible about how we treated you."

Janet shakes her head vehemently. "We had no idea what you were going through behind closed doors."

The familiar flush of shame fills my cheeks. "The past week has been hard on all of us."

"We should have picked up on what was happening sooner," Janet says.

"I know what you mean," Naomi says. "I think of all the times Shelby looked after my children. Not once did I pick up on the fact she was being abused."

"You'd both been friends with the Holdens for a long time," I say. "It's natural you'd only see the best in them."

"The night of the Halloween party, I was so wasted I ran over Annette Friss' mailbox. Again," Janet admits. She is sitting in a wicker chair, hunched over like she might be sick. Naomi stands beside her rubbing her back. "I doubt it would have made a difference, but I'll always wonder how that night might have unfolded differently if I'd been a little more aware."

"I feel the same way," Naomi says. "I was glued to my phone. More worried about what Rick was doing than enjoying the moment."

I remain silent, recalling how I was also distracted that night, so desperate for these women to like me.

"It's all so overwhelming." Janet stands suddenly, her balance teetering. "I think I'm going to be sick."

Sure enough, she hurries to the railing off Naomi's front

porch and retches into the bushes. Naomi and I rush over to her, the ripe smell of rot and alcohol making me gag.

"I'll stay with her," Naomi says, still rubbing her back. "Grab some towels from the bathroom."

Quickly, I run into the house, searching for the downstairs bathroom. I've never even been in her house. The one time I was invited, my invitation was rescinded. To think of how everyone has acted this past week, how we've all treated each other, and Ken Holden was at fault the entire time.

Past the kitchen, I find a small half-bath. I bend down, opening the bathroom cabinets and pulling out towels. I place them under the faucet, dampening the fabric. I'm rushing out of the small room, when something from inside one of the towels falls to the ground.

I bend down to pick it up. It's a necklace, the center pendant adorned with rubies and diamonds.

I hold the jewelry in my hands, reading the name on the pendant. Shelby.

Why would Naomi have Shelby's necklace inside her downstairs bathroom? Could it have been left ages ago, at one of the gatherings the wives take turns hosting? Or when she was babysitting? And yet, the jewels sparkle under the overhead light like they're brand new.

My conversation with Hudson yesterday springs back into my head. He said Shelby's other boyfriend had given her an expensive necklace as a gift. Did Ken Holden give this to her? If he did, why is it in Naomi's house?

"Did you find the towels?" Naomi comes around the corner faster than I can stand up. When she sees what I'm holding, she says, "Where did you get that?"

"It was under the sink," I say, numb and confused.

"Oh." She holds out her hand. "Give it here."

I clutch onto the jewelry tighter, moving my hand to give

her a better view of the pendant. "Look. This necklace belonged to Shelby. What is it doing here?"

Naomi stares at the pendant, then me. "I have no idea."

"Hudson told me Shelby was wearing an expensive necklace at the Halloween party," I say. "We should turn this over to the police."

Naomi moves closer to me. "No, don't do that."

The tone of her voice and the expression on her face is startling.

"Naomi, what's going on?"

She's breathing faster, her eyes cutting from left to right, but it's only the two of us in the house.

"The night of the party, I heard Grace and Shelby get into a fight. Shelby said she was sleeping with a married man, and..." She stops, unsure whether she should keep going. "I thought it might be Rick."

I look at the necklace again, the sequence of events becoming horribly clear in my mind.

"She said she was pregnant," she says. "I couldn't stand the thought of him cheating on me again, especially with someone so young. And she was having a baby."

She stops again, crying into her hands. I imagine how she's had to swallow down the truth for the past week. When we were passing out flyers in the community. When we were comforting Donna.

"If I'd known she was sleeping with Ken, none of it would have happened, but I just assumed—"

"Naomi, did you do something to Shelby?"

"I didn't mean to," she says, "but it all happened so fast. I was on top of her, and then I couldn't let go. I took the necklace to confront Rick. I wanted to know if he'd bought it for her. If I'd only known the truth!"

I realize, again, we're the only two people inside the house, and I'm holding direct evidence of her crimes in my hands.

Even the parade of police vehicles outside doesn't comfort me. It feels like the walls of the bathroom are closing in, and all I want is to be outside, away from Naomi.

"I can't imagine what that must have been like for you," I say, stepping forward to gauge whether she'll let me pass. She doesn't move. "You weren't in your right mind."

"I really wasn't," she says, clinging to that comment like it's a life raft. "And after it was over, there was no bringing her back. I took a rope and bricks from the shed and used it to weigh her down. I left her in the pond because I didn't know what else to do."

"It's going to be okay—"

She interrupts me, finding it impossible to stop talking now that the truth has come out. "I had her phone, too. It wasn't hard to unlock, and I was hoping to find out the truth about what happened with Rick, but she didn't have messages from any men. Not even Ken.

"After talking to that cop at Donna's house, I got spooked about them being able to track her phone. I drove across town to ditch it. I sent that message to buy myself some time until I figured out a plan, but it was too late. Her body floated to the surface and—"

"It's going to be okay," I tell her, trying to step around her. "None of this is your fault. It's all one big misunderstanding."

"Exactly! It's not like I wanted it to happen."

"Of course you didn't," I say, relieved to only be a few steps away from the door, close enough that someone could hear me scream. "You did what you had to do."

"I really did. I love Rick. I was only trying to protect my family."

Naomi stares at me, her expression manic. Her words fall into each other, rushing to get out. She's desperate for me to understand her. Like Beau, she's a person living in an alternate reality, unable to see how their own behavior causes endless pain for those around them. And yet, I do sympathize with her motives, even if I don't condone her actions. If the past week has taught me anything, it's that I'd do whatever it takes to protect the ones I love.

"I understand, Naomi," I say, swinging open the front door, the necklace clutched tight in my hand. "I really do."

FORTY-FOUR

SHELBY

Halloween Night

Shelby Bledsoe's eyes burned as the tears began to build.

Grace Holden was her best friend in the entire world, the person she thought she could go to about anything. Why would she treat her like that? Say the things she said?

Sure, Shelby hadn't always been the friend Grace deserved. Shelby liked having the spotlight, having all the attention on her. Over the years, she'd assumed Grace had gotten used to it. The second fiddle still made a tune, didn't it? Life could be worse.

Grace had her panties in a wad not because Shelby was sleeping with a married man, but because she secretly had feelings for Hudson. If anything, Grace should be happy with how things had unfolded. Now she could have Hudson all to herself.

Of course, if she was this angry now, Shelby could only imagine how Grace would react when she found out the truth. That the baby inside her belonged to her father. Her affair with Mr. Holden wasn't something she'd planned, but it had happened, just as it was meant to, and there was no means of stopping it now.

The tears that had been brewing now trailed down her cheek, but Shelby wiped them away quickly.

She was a woman now. A mother. There was no time to worry about what other people thought of her. All that mattered now was the life that she and Mr. Holden would build together.

"Is it true?"

The voice came from the darkness, startling Shelby. She jumped back so fast, she nearly tripped over an exposed root on the ground. When she looked up and saw Naomi, she raised her hand to her chest.

"Ms. Davis, you scared me," Shelby said.

"I heard you talking with Grace. Is. It. True?" the woman repeated, this time with a finality in her voice that startled Shelby to her core. What had she heard? Did she know everything?

"It was just a little argument," Shelby said. "It was nothing."

"It didn't sound like nothing," Naomi said, taking a step closer. "She said you're sleeping with a married man."

It was as though all the blood in her body went rushing to her cheeks. Shelby felt like she was going to be sick. Not the morning sickness that had plagued her the last week. No, this sickness was different. More brutal.

"You have to understand—"

"I let you around my children," Naomi said. Her voice was low but heavy with accusation and rage. She took another step forward. "How could you? After everything you know we went through."

"Ms. Davis, I haven't done anything to you."

"You're sleeping with my husband! Trying to tear apart my family!" Her voice was louder now, but not enough to draw anyone's attention. "Do you have any idea how hard it is trying to keep a family together? Trying to keep your husband satisfied? Your kids happy? Give everyone around you what they need, at the expense of your own self-worth?"

Shelby didn't understand. She could barely follow what Naomi was saying. Venting, more than anything. The anger on display was nothing Shelby had ever witnessed before, and she didn't know how to handle it. All she could do was try and tell her the truth.

"You've got this all wrong," she said. "I'm not sleeping with Rick."

"Don't you say his name!"

Something dark flew out of Naomi's hand, striking Shelby on the side of the head. She immediately fell to her knees. What had that been? Some kind of rock? She put two fingers to her forehead, and when she pulled them away, she saw they were stained with blood.

She looked up, confused and stunned. Naomi moved quickly, pouncing on her like an attacking animal. Shelby could barely catch her breath before her back was flat against the ground, her hair rustling against the dried leaves and wet earth.

Naomi's hands found their way to Shelby's chest and ripped away the necklace. Her fingers wrapped around her throat and began to squeeze. Shelby could hardly get the words out, "Please. Stop." Her every action was costing her more precious air. She tried staring into the eyes of Naomi, this woman whose children she'd watched, whose laundry she'd folded, whose husband she'd never touched.

Those eyes were almost completely black, filled with a rage that, until that moment, Shelby had never known existed. She kept trying to plead with her, although no sounds came out, tried to claw at her hands, but the force being used against her was too strong.

Shelby's gaze drifted, away from the mad woman crushing her chest and lungs, and up to the stars overhead in the night sky. She thought about her life, short and tumultuous as it had been. She thought about her mother, how her desperation to be out from underneath her had caused her to make so many horrible decisions. She thought about Grace, how she'd never deserved such a good friend. And she thought about the child growing in her stomach, withering away with each gasping breath Shelby pushed out.

She didn't think about Mr. Holden or Hudson or any of the other boys who'd run through her life, but she did think about love. How wonderful a feeling it must be when it's felt. The closest she'd ever come to it was what she had with her own unborn child, and she wondered if her other attachments, any of them, were real at all...

In her final seconds, her eyes flickered back to Naomi, taking in the ugly sight of a woman scorned. As her thoughts drifted off into the ether, Shelby realized love could be just as ugly as it was beautiful.

FORTY-FIVE

STELLA

Two Months Later

Hudson drinks the rest of his orange juice. He reaches into the bowl on the kitchen island to retrieve the car keys.

"I'm working at the gardens after school," he says. "You want me to pick up dinner?"

"I'm always happy with pizza," I say, my fingers still typing on the laptop in front of me.

"Pizza it is," he says, giving me a hug before he heads out the door.

Ever since he got his driver's license, he's been fully playing into the role of man of the house. He offers to grab dinner, run errands. Sure, some of that comes with the new freedom of being able to drive without supervision, but I think, given everything we've been through together in the past few months, he likes stepping up for other reasons.

I finish sending the last of my work emails. Business has been steadily growing, and I'm on track to make more than I thought I would. I usually start working in the afternoons and don't finish until Hudson comes home at the end of the day. My mornings I've set aside for me.

Most days, I sit alone on the front porch, watching the neighborhood come alive. People heading to work and to school drop-off. On Mondays and Wednesdays, Annette Friss and I walk the neighborhood, trying to get our steps in before my afternoon work shift begins.

"Chilly this morning, isn't it?" Annette says when she walks across the street. She's bundled up in a heavy coat and scarf.

"I'm ready for spring," I say, pulling my hat down to cover my ears.

"Oh, the gardens are so beautiful that time of year," she says. "I can't wait for you to see!"

It's only after she says this comment she remembers. The beautiful gardens that she has devoted so much time to over the years now represent something different for the entire community. Especially me. It's the place where Shelby Bledsoe died. I'm not sure I'll ever feel comfortable going back there, regardless of how beautiful the scenery is.

We brave the cold, following the familiar trail that leads to the front of the neighborhood and back. Along the way, we take in our neighbors' houses, and silently wonder about all the changes that have come.

Donna Bledsoe was the first to leave the neighborhood, not that anyone could blame her. I can't fathom juggling happy memories of my child with the sickening reality that her killer lived so close. I think about her often. No one stays in touch with her, aside from Janet, but I hope one day the woman will be able to find peace.

Rick Davis still lives in the same house, raising his daughters alone. There has been so much chaos since Naomi's arrest, I don't think he's had time to process what happens next for any of them.

A little further up the road, we make it to Beau's house. My chest fills with warmth when I spot the For Sale sign in his front yard. Naomi Davis isn't the only person who left in handcuffs; Beau did, too, and surprisingly, not for the reason you'd think.

Beau was arrested for his assaults against Hudson and me, but his list of crimes was much longer than any of us knew. It wasn't long before more charges were brought against him. As it turned out, he'd been a dirty cop for years, redistributing narcotics he'd confiscated for personal gain. Looking back, I wonder if the time he confronted me over the missing cash was linked to his criminal misdeeds. They'd opened an investigation against him in our former hometown, the main motivator for why he left to follow us to Hickory Hills.

Internal Affairs had already collected evidence against him, and they approached him to turn on the others in the operation. His cooperation earned him a shorter prison sentence but ruined his reputation amid the community and amongst criminals. Most importantly, it ensures he'll remain incarcerated until after Hudson graduates, keeping him out of our lives.

After everything he put me through, it's rewarding to know his true colors eventually revealed themselves to everyone, and a bit amusing how quickly the tough guys fall when they're cornered.

Along our walk back, we pass the Holden house. A moving truck is parked outside. Crew members in crisp blue shirts carry cardboard boxes from the house to the vehicle. For a moment, we stop and stare. I think about what this family has gone through and what they'll continue to go through in the years to come. I think about Grace, the kind and quick connection she formed with Hudson when he was still new and unsure of himself. And I think of Mary, how the potential destruction she tried to pour over us hit her family tenfold.

Just then, Mary walks out the front door. She stops when she finds Annette and I watching. I'll never call Mary Holden a friend, but I can't deny the connection between us. Despite all her transgressions against me and my son, we were two mothers desperate to protect our children. Beyond that, we were two women whose lives had been defined for far too long by their abusers. And I'll forever be grateful for her willingness to defend me against Beau. I shudder to think of how that night might have ended if she hadn't got involved.

For several seconds, we continue to stare, then she slowly raises her hand, and waves goodbye.

FORTY-SIX

MARY

Two Months Later

Mary turns quickly, still struggling with shame.

She doesn't feel humiliation over what Ken did, although it sickens her. Sleeping with Shelby Bledsoe was his mistake alone, and now he's paying for it. Of course, without a living victim, he won't receive a full sentence, but he will spend some time behind bars, and when he's eventually released, he'll have to register as a sex offender. Never again will he have the opportunity to work alongside impressionable young girls.

Mary realizes, now, that's what she was when they first got together. It wasn't a torrid love affair driven by passion and romance. She was taken advantage of by an adult who should have known better. Even if she did eventually develop genuine love for him and the life they'd built together, it didn't change the fact he'd lured her when she was still too young to make such choices, and, clearly, his predatory ways continued with Shelby Bledsoe.

But Mary does feel shame over her own behavior. She regrets the way she treated people over the years. Grace's, and everyone else's, assessment of her was correct. She was often cruel and cunning, all to conceal the truth about her own past. She succumbed to the belief that if she made others feel inferior, they wouldn't pry too much into her own life.

Mary doesn't want to be that type of person anymore, and she wants to set a better example for her daughter. She doesn't think it's possible for them to do that in Hickory Hills. She believes it's best for both of them to start somewhere new, figure out a way to rebuild together.

The sale of the Hickory Hills house will provide a nice cushion. She's already put a down payment on a seaside condo in Florida. It's much smaller than what they're accustomed to, but there's a view of the ocean and an excellent school district. Mary has even found work at a local interior design firm. It's a bit late for her to enter the workforce, but she feels more than capable for the tasks ahead. Most importantly, Mary's brother lives less than an hour away.

After Ken's arrest, she reached out to him. It's something she's considered doing over the years, but never did. Her estrangement from her family was yet another casualty of her marriage; it was easy to feed a false narrative about their relationship to everyone else, but not them.

Surprisingly, Mary's brother received her with open arms. Grace is looking forward to the opportunity to live near her cousins, even if it means taking her away from Hudson Moore. In this day and age, teens can stay in contact across state lines thanks to social media. Mary actually encourages her friendship with Hudson; they've both endured so much hurt in recent months, and she's thankful they can lean on each other.

The combination of modern technology and social media will keep them connected, despite the move, but Mary has ensured her daughter has other resources, too. They're both attending ongoing family and individual therapy. Grace has a lot of big revelations to process, and Mary is determined to help her in any way she can. Out of all the missions she's taken on in her life, this is the most important.

"Would you like to drive?" Mary asks Grace, holding out the keys.

"Are you serious?"

Grace stands in front of the passenger side door. She slides her phone into her back pocket and holds out her hands eagerly.

"Just for the first leg of the trip," Mary says. "I'll take over after lunch."

Grace takes the keys giddily, slipping into the driver's seat.

Before Mary enters the car, she takes one more look at her beautiful house. It sold well over market value, a testament to Mary's abilities as a homemaker. Even the scandalous backstory couldn't deter people from the manicured lawn, the pristine floors, the well-executed color combinations. Mary is sad to leave this place behind. She hopes whatever family takes her place in Hickory Hills will be far happier than she ever pretended to be.

Grace honks the horn and Mary jumps. "Are you coming?"

Grace's excitement to drive outweighs whatever sadness she feels about leaving. As Mary bends down to smile at her daughter, she feels the same way. All the positive attributes of her former life she still carries with her. Her intellect, her strength of spirit. Her daughter.

Finally, Mary and Grace can start over together, and Mary can decide what type of woman she wants to be.

A LETTER FROM MIRANDA

Dear Reader,

Thank you for taking the time to read *Loving Mothers*. If you liked it and want information about upcoming releases, sign up with the following link. Your email address will never be shared and you can unsubscribe at any time.

www.bookouture.com/miranda-smith

This book was a true labor of love. From the beginning, I was intrigued by Mary and Stella. While on the surface they appear different, their complicated pasts unite them in ways you wouldn't expect. I feel we're often guilty of judging someone's behavior without considering how their experiences might have shaped them. There's something powerful about reexamining the past through a more mature lens, which both women are able to do, and they're both stronger for it. And, of course, at the center of this story is the unconditional love both women have for their children and their determination to break generational patterns moving forward.

If you'd like to discuss any of my books, I'd love to connect! You can find me on Facebook, TikTok and Instagram, or my website. If you enjoyed *Loving Mothers*, I'd appreciate it if you left a review on Amazon. It only takes a few minutes and does wonders in helping readers discover my books for the first time.

Thank you again for your support!

Sincerely,

Miranda Smith

facebook.com/MirandaSmithAuthor

x.com/msmithbooks

instagram.com/mirandasmithbooks

ACKNOWLEDGMENTS

There are countless people who come together to make every book the absolute best it can be. To my editor, Ruth Tross, thanks for your endless encouragement and creativity. I'm fortunate to be in such great hands, and I look forward to working on many more projects together.

To the rest of the Bookouture team, especially Kim Nash, Sarah Hardy, Jane Eastgate and Liz Hurst, thank you for everything you do at each stage of the publishing process.

To my friends, community and extended family, thank you for your enthusiasm and support. To my parents and sisters, thank you for being such an important part of my life. To Chris, Harrison, Lucy and Christopher, I love you all very much.

Most importantly, thank you to the readers, whether you've been following my career since the beginning or if you took a chance on one of my books for the first time. It's because of you I get to do what I love. I'm forever grateful.

PUBLISHING TEAM

Turning a manuscript into a book requires the efforts of many people. The publishing team at Bookouture would like to acknowledge everyone who contributed to this publication.

Audio
Alba Proko
Melissa Tran
Sinead O'Connor

Commercial
Lauren Morrissette
Hannah Richmond
Imogen Allport

Cover design
Lisa Horton

Data and analysis
Mark Alder
Mohamed Bussuri

Editorial
Ruth Tross
Imogen Allport